The Fairy Thorn

a novel by

Dorothy M. Keddington

This is a work of fiction. All characters are fictional and any resemblance to persons living or dead is purely coincidental.

Published and Distributed by:
Stonehaven Publishing

Page Layout and Design by Myrna Varga
Cover Design by: Steve Gray
Cover Art by: Cliff Vestergaard

ISBN: 978-1-59936-049-2
Library of Congress Control Number: 2009939641

Printed in the United States of America

First Printing, December 2009
1 3 5 7 9 10 8 6 4 2

Acknowledgments

Many hearts and hands have helped make this book possible and I am infinitely grateful to the following:

Nancy Hopkins, the one and only 'fairy godmother of the Northwest' and forever friend

My dear stepmother Gloria McDonald, for introducing me to Mazatlan, Mexico

My brilliant and beautiful editor/daughter Laura, much love & thanks

The fabulous 'Fortnightly Group' Carol Warburton, Ka Hancock & Charlene Raddon—your critiquing, encouragement & friendship are beyond price

LouAnn Anderson, a true friend and great reader of books—for memorable research trips to Whidbey & San Francisco, & happy years of friendship

Sylvia Butterfield, a wonderful friend and 'brain-storming' whiz—thank you for your endless enthusiasm and encouragement to finish this book

Doris S. Platt, brilliant writer & friend, thank you for years of caring and sharing

Shanda Cottam, LDS Women's Book Review —I'm so grateful you enjoy my writing

My wonderful supportive family … I love you all!

For my dear friends . . .
thank you for years of support
and encouragement

Journal Entry

His featureless face haunts my dreams and his presence walks beside me during my waking hours, this man I was meant to love and whom I have yet to meet. There are those who try to convince me that such dreams are foolish—that this love of mine does not exist—but I know better. The heart has a wisdom of its own and mine tells me he is there . . . somewhere.

I don't know how or when we will meet. It may be as simple and unexpected as finding an agate on the beach—looking down and suddenly seeing the translucent shine of something wonderful lying amidst the ordinary. Our coming together might be as natural as the phases of the moon, when our thin inner selves gradually wax into rounded fullness. Or it may be as powerful as the changing tide, when all that was rushing out suddenly shifts and surges to meet the rush of waves coming in.

The rest of the world will go on, unaware of this powerful

change—this cataclysmic meeting which has taken place—but the sea and the land are subtly and inexorably altered. As will my life and his be sublimely changed.

I am restless tonight, longing for this changing of the tide and eager to hold the precious stone of our meeting in my hand. Hurry love, hurry. . . .

Bronwyn McBride

CHAPTER ONE

The Calendar of Sameness

I stood at the edge of the drive with poems by Wordsworth and E. E. Cummings running through my mind and a bittersweet yearning inside. It was "just spring" and there were "daffodils fluttering and dancing in the breeze," and the world really was "puddle luscious" because it had rained softly during the night, and birds were singing their hearts out in the old hawthorn tree behind the house. And here I was, feeling the soft air and the fragrance and all the stirrings of spring, standing on the edge of things the way I always did.

Uncle Milt and his friend Charlie Roberts were busy wrestling with the logistics of stuffing six suitcases in a car trunk designed to hold four, while I wrestled with unnamed longings and tried to convince myself that it didn't matter if I weren't going anywhere. One thing was certain. I didn't want to go on the cruise with my aunt and uncle and their friends to Mexico and the Caribbean. This was their time and goodness knows they had earned it. Besides, the idea of being a tag-along on a two-week cruise with four senior citizens wasn't exactly my idea of high adventure. But if only I could go somewhere, do something out of the ordinary.

"Milton, did you get the sun block?" Aunt Ivy was asking. "I think I left it on the counter in the bathroom."

My uncle gave the suitcases a shove and answered without glancing up. "I put it in my shaving kit."

Seeing my aunt's doubtful expression, I offered, "Would you like me to run in the house and check?"

"No thank you, Lucy," she said, giving me one of her soft smiles.

My aunt is all softness and roundness, handling life and its many complexities the way she handles the dough for one of her famous pies—mixing ingredients with a deft, knowing touch, then rolling the shapeless mass into a lovely smooth circle. Going on a cruise was a huge step outside that smooth circle for Aunt Ivy. She thrives on domestic order and routine and has never entertained the least desire to extend her world beyond the narrow confines of her home on Washington State's Whidbey Island. Indeed, Ivy Willoughby's world is her home. She and my uncle rarely travel farther from Whidbey than Seattle to the south or Bellingham to the north, where their married sons live.

Uncle Milt is as angular as my aunt is round, with wise gray eyes and thinning gray hair that is totally lacking in direction, no matter how he combs it. Unlike his wife, Uncle Milt has always harbored a bit of the wanderlust and a pent-up desire to see those "faraway places with strange-sounding names." For over thirty years he piloted the ferry which runs between Whidbey Island and Port Townsend on the mainland. I can understand his longing to navigate more of the world than that brief thirty-minute crossing from shore to shore.

"What about playing cards?" Aunt Ivy asked, going down her mental checklist. "We'll need five decks if we're going to play 'hand and foot.'"

"I only brought three," Inez Roberts told her with a stricken look. "I knew I should have bought more when they were on sale last month."

"Inez, we're going on a cruise, not visiting a third world country," Charlie put in dryly. "I'm sure we'll be able to buy a deck of cards somewhere if we need one."

I smothered a smile as my uncle gave Aunt Ivy's floral carry-on another fruitless shove and grumbled, "I thought we were going to pack light."

"Why don't you put the blue case on its side and that little black one in the back?" she suggested.

The two men exchanged a knowing male look that plainly said her suggestion was ridiculous and would never work. Over forty years of married life, however, dictated they would be wise to at least try rather than argue. The suitcase in question was duly shifted and the black bag slipped neatly in the back, allowing just enough space for the last carry-on.

Charlie Roberts slammed the lid of the trunk with a good-natured shake of his head, then winked at me. "So, Lucy, what are you going to do with yourself for two whole weeks? Have wild parties every night?"

"She'll do what she always does," Uncle Milt huffed before I could answer. "What with working at the libraries and the old Alexander place, she probably won't even know we're gone."

I tried to ignore the sudden sting of my uncle's words. They weren't intended to hurt me. I knew that. Rather, it was the sharp edge of truth in his offhand remark that jabbed at me. *She'll do what she always does.* All the nameless longings I'd been struggling to quell suddenly rose to the surface in a floodtide of painful emotion.

Aunt Ivy took one look at me and her maternal instincts instantly came to the fore. "Lucy, are you all right?"

I slipped on a ready smile, wishing she weren't so perceptive of my every mood, but it has always been that way. She and Uncle Milt never had a daughter of their own, so I have been the recipient of their unstinting love nearly all my life. And though I've often wished I had at least one conscious memory of my mother and father, perhaps it was kinder that I was spared the trauma of their passing. I was not quite two when my parents were killed in a plane crash near Hong Kong. My father, Stephen Norris, was a foreign correspondent and rarely able to take my mother along on his assignments. The ten-day trip to Hong Kong was to be a sort of second honeymoon as well as business, and Mother had asked her brother if he and Aunt Ivy would take care of me. And care for me they have, sometimes a bit too protectively, but I love them too much to complain.

"I'll be fine," I assured her. "You know I will. And I expect you to send me a picture of you and Inez on the beach in your bikinis."

My aunt's mild blue eyes widened in horror at the mere suggestion, and Charlie Roberts let go a delighted chuckle.

"Inez bought herself a new swimsuit especially for the trip," he told me. "It has lots of blue and purple swirls. Should go great with her varicose veins."

Inez gave her husband a healthy shove as laughter filled the final moments of farewell, easing the sudden awkwardness that accompanied their parting.

Then they were gone, and I turned my steps toward the charming old bungalow that has been my home for nearly thirty years. A faint breeze, no more than a whisper through the tender new leaves of alders alongside the drive, suddenly made me shiver. *She'll do what she always does.* My mind couldn't let go of the words and all they implied. Most of the time I'm fairly content, but lately I've found myself wondering when, or if anything will ever change in the seasons of my life with its calendar of sameness.

This morning, for example, was the second Wednesday of the month, and every second and fourth Wednesdays, I drive out to the old Alexander home to clean and dust and make sure it is in spotless order. Ordinarily, this is a job I thoroughly enjoy. For twenty-one years, my aunt and uncle have been the caretakers of a stately old Victorian that sits on a scenic bluff overlooking Admiralty Strait and the mainland. I grew up working alongside them and listening to stories about Captain Alexander and his young bride who was terrified of the sea. The home has quite a romantic history, and I probably know as much about it as the Alexanders themselves. Other than an occasional phone call and the monthly check, we rarely hear from the present owners. This absence has become even more evident since they decided to open the home to the public.

For almost five years now, I've been in charge of scheduling and escorting tours through the place. There are dozens of historic homes on Whidbey, many built by sea captains who chose to retire here in the late nineteenth century. But the fact the Alexander house has remained in one family for over a hundred years and still has many of its original furnishings, including vintage woodwork and textiles, makes it especially unique. During any given month, I might have groups of architects, university students, preservationists, or interior designers coming through. Today, thankfully, there were no tours, and wouldn't be until the end of the following week.

The rest of my time is spent working for the Island County libraries. Three times each week, I go to the libraries in Langley, Clinton and Coupeville, where Lucy Norris becomes the "story lady" for several classes of elementary students. If my friend Peggy Gamble had her way, I would show up dressed as a modern version of the

"Story Princess," complete with glittering wand and gown. I much prefer to let the stories themselves take center stage. It always thrills me to see that special light in children's eyes when a book comes alive for them.

Much of my life seems to revolve around books. Tomorrow afternoon, it's my turn to host the monthly meeting of Coupeville's book club, where I'll head a discussion of Daphne du Maurier's *Frenchman's Creek*. Initially, some of the members had balked at the idea of reading such a dated classic instead of a novel from the current bestseller list, but I stood firm in my selection. *Frenchman's Creek* might not be as well known as the author's famous *Rebecca*, but I absolutely adore the lush tale of a privileged English lady and her adventures with a French pirate.

Casting aside the more bloodthirsty elements of the trade, I sometimes find myself lamenting the fact that piracy has fallen out of fashion. What a thrill it would be to spy a colorful pirate ship creeping stealthily along the Strait at sunset, instead of the Washington State ferry making its predictable crossing.

A loud honking overhead broke into my thoughts and glancing up, I saw a pair of Canada geese winging their way over treetops and newly plowed fields toward the shining waters of Penn Cove. Watching their effortless flight, restlessness and longing stirred within me yet again. How on earth could I resign myself to dusting and polishing hundred-year old furniture in a silent house that lived in the past, when this was *now* and the morning was calling, and if I didn't answer, something inside me would shrivel up and die.

She'll do what she always does. . . .

No! Not today. Mentally tossing aside my schedule and responsibilities, I walked toward the house to get my car keys and wallet. Five minutes later, I was driving north with the car windows down and my hair blowing in the breeze.

Destination was not a conscious thought or concern. I stopped once to watch a long-legged colt gambol across a grassy field beside its mother. Another time, I picked a handful of daffodils from the swath of sunny yellow growing near the roadside, exulting in the delicate drift of fragrance that colored the air. I refused to turn the car radio on, or put in one of my favorite CDs, needing only the music of the morning and the wind's timeless melodies.

Miles passed in a pleasant blur of beauty and blossom, verdant farms and forested hillsides. I drove straight through Oak Harbor, Whidbey's largest town, not wanting its urban sprawl to encroach on my mood. Soon I was nearing the island's northernmost point where its neighbor, Fidalgo Island is connected to Whidbey via a bridge over Deception Pass. The scenic pass and its seventy-year old bridge is a popular tourist site, yet somehow, the place never loses its sense of drama and visual impact.

Straight ahead, the massive steel girders spanned the deep gorge in a solid hand-clasp of metal arches and cantilevers, while far below, the restless waters made their own way. On impulse, I made a quick left turn into the parking area provided for those wishing to experience the wonders of the place on foot. On weekends, the bridge and adjacent State Park would be crawling with traffic and tourists, but today, being mid-morning and mid-week, I was pleased to find less than a half dozen cars.

Zipping up my windbreaker against the morning chill, I locked the car and headed for a forest trail leading down the steep hillside. Above me, traffic rumbled its way across the bridge, but the forest itself was cloaked in pleasant silence. Ancient firs and cedars whispered to red-barked madrona trees, and on the slope below, there were splashes of color where the sunny gold of Scotch broom clung tenaciously to the cliffside. Occasionally, a squirrel sent its scolding chatter to a hidden neighbor in needled branches high above, but that was all.

As far as I'm concerned, there's far too much noise in today's world. Too many grindings and grumblings of machinery, and the heart-hurting blare of boom boxes and car audio systems. It's difficult to escape it, or even find a place where silence is still permissible. Technology seems intent on magnifying sound in every human habitat, be it a movie theater, shopping mall or workplace. The poets of centuries past would have found it more than a little difficult to encounter a noise free sanctuary where inspiration could be fostered and expressed. Thoughts and feelings are quiet things, needing nature's nurturing air and tranquil moments in which to germinate and grow.

This morning, despite the peaceful surroundings, my own mood was far from tranquil. As I wound my way down the narrow trail, unrest churned inside me, not unlike the deceptive current swirling far below.

Was it only my life's simple routine that troubled me? Or something deeper. Had I become so accustomed to my insulated island life that I was afraid to enlarge those boundaries? But what else could I do? Move away from Whidbey and exchange the comfortable familiarity of my home for loneliness in a new location? At the moment, nothing seemed clear or right. All I really knew was I felt stuck in the stagnant middle of my life, without the rosy promise of a dream, or even the hint of one.

With the doomsday event of my thirtieth birthday only a few months away, I've made a conscious effort not to think about the encroaching passage of years. This isn't always an easy task, especially when Aunt Ivy is forever lamenting my state of "single blessedness,"

Journal Entry

Days pass, not without gratitude or goodness, yet there has been no delineation, nothing to distinguish one from another. Until now. Unexpected and unique, my life has a defining moment—one against which all else shall be measured and judged as 'before' and 'after.'

He has come. This morning I saw his ship, and with his coming everything has changed. My emotions are all at sea, no longer anchored in the safe harbor of routine. I feel as if I am on the brink of some grand adventure, waiting impatiently for the wind to change and breathe life into the eager sails of my desire.

Where once there was only the misty image of a dream, I now see his face in my mind. And having seen him, the dream is no longer satisfying. I want to know him in every way—from shared moments of quiet conversation to passion's flaming language in the night.

Will we meet again? I don't know. Foolish woman that I am, I don't even know his name. But I have felt the warmth *of his smile. Even now, it lingers in my heart like a caress. . . .*

Bronwyn McBride

CHAPTER TWO

Sensible Decisions vs. Inner Desires

Smiling softly, I walked back to my car and drove away, knowing the morning and I would never be the same. Common sense tried to insert the caution that it was unlikely I would ever see the man again. But even that couldn't prevent a warm stirring inside whenever I thought of the moment he had smiled and reached out to me. Seeing him and the tall ship was more than mere chance or serendipity—it was a miracle. My own private miracle. And I felt like celebrating. But how?

The answer came as I was driving back through Oak Harbor. I would stop by Peggy's home and take her to lunch. Not exactly an earthshaking way to celebrate, but it would have to do.

Peggy Gamble and I have been friends ever since the day our junior high gym teacher mixed up our name tags and locker assignments. That, plus the singularly important commonality that neither of us had any liking for our given names was more than enough to create a bond between us. Peggy and Lucy. The names are painfully old-fashioned without an ounce of glamour or allure, especially when compared to the likes of Tiffany, Brittany, and Brooklyn. But unlike other friends whose names and faces have dimmed with the passage of time, the bond between Peggy and me is stronger than ever. I was maid of honor at her wedding, and she staunchly insists that she will be the matron of honor at mine, even if we're both ninety-three and toothless.

I pulled up in front of the Gamble's modest frame home and parked my car street side, as the driveway was blocked by an assortment of toys, scooters, and Peggy's husband's current restoration project—a vintage Thunderbird convertible in bright cherry red.

With his curly brown hair, boyish grin and fondness for Western shirts, Gary Gamble is a pleasant enough man, but to be honest, I'll never understand what Peggy sees in him. The sign over his car repair shop proclaiming, "You won't gamble with Gamble," says it all. Easy going, dependable and totally devoted to Peggy he may be, but exciting or romantic? Never. Obviously, Peggy must feel differently, because she and Gary produced two healthy sons in record time, and lately she's been making motherly noises that strongly hint she'd love to start baby number three.

In a way, I both admire and envy her. I don't know many women who would give up a scholarship to a chefs school in Paris, along with the opportunity for a lucrative career, in order to marry a simple man who comes home every night with grease on his clothes and grime under his fingernails.

And yet, Peggy often tells me I've done the same thing—given up the chance to continue my own education to work in the library system on Whidbey and help an aging aunt and uncle whose sons do little more for their parents than make a perfunctory visit every month or two.

I gave a quick tap on the back door and poked my head inside. "Hello, hello!"

"I'm in the laundry room," came a voice quavering with emotion.

I entered the small laundry/sewing room off the kitchen to find my friend standing in front of an ironing board, iron in hand and tears streaming down her cheeks.

"Peggy, what's happened? What's wrong?"

"Nothing," she answered with a sniff, and set the iron down to grab some tissues from a box on the nearby counter. Dabbing her eyes, she gestured to the portable TV. "I was just watching *Roman Holiday*. The ending always kills me."

I smiled and shook my head. My passion for books has its equal in Peggy's love for old movies and film stars. She still has scrapbooks filled with pictures of her favorite actors and actresses. I'm sure in her daydreams, Peggy sees herself as a domestic Doris Day, singing and cooking her way to happy endings. And there are some similarities in their appearance. Like the actress, Peggy is a madcap, sunny blonde with dancing blue eyes and a dazzling smile, although since the arrival of her two sons, her figure has become what Aunt Ivy would describe as "pleasingly plump."

I moved a stack of little boys' underwear off a chair and sat down. On the screen in front of me, Audrey Hepburn's luminous beauty was unmistakable, even in black and white. When the camera moved to a closeup of Gregory Peck's handsome features, Peggy gave a languid sigh.

"They don't make men like that any more. Will you look at those eyes—as deep and dark as beef bouillon!"

"Beef bouillon," I said with a laugh. "It's true. You can't get any more romantic than that."

She laughed good naturedly at my teasing and switched off the TV. "This is a nice surprise. What brings you my way? I thought you took care of the Alexander place on Wednesdays."

"I do, but not today. Today, I feel like celebrating, so I'm treating you to lunch. Can you get away?"

"Sure. The boys won't be home from school for a couple of hours. I can finish ironing these tablecloths any time." She unplugged the iron and ran a hand through her short blonde hair. "What are we celebrating?"

I hesitated, not sure how to begin, or even if I wanted to tell her about seeing the tall ship and the dark-haired man. It wasn't as if Peggy wouldn't understand, but somehow, the experience was still so new and tender, I felt as if I needed to hold it close for awhile.

"Lucy, what's happened?" she asked, giving me a close look. "Something's happened. You look . . . different." Her blue eyes widened and the pitch of her voice lowered to a dramatic whisper. "Have you met someone?"

"Yes . . . no . . . well, not really, but oh, Peggy, I'll never forget it. He was on a tall ship going through Deception Pass."

"Who was on a tall ship? What were you doing at Deception Pass?"

I laughed and shook my head, thinking I should know better than to try and keep anything from Peggy. "Well, after Uncle Milt and Aunt Ivy left this morning, I felt like going for a drive and—"

Before I could finish or even begin, a strident rendition of the *William Tell Overture* broke into our conversation.

Peggy sighed and reached for her cell phone. "Mark your place,

The ticking of the clock in the hall. The thump of the furnace coming on. The absence of familiar sounds was almost as bad. There was no evening news blaring from the living room, no rattle of pans in the kitchen with Aunt Ivy calling for Milt to turn down the TV and turn up his hearing aid.

I finally climbed into bed with a glass of milk and *Frenchman's Creek* for company. Knowing the tendency of book club members to occasionally veer off track, I'd prepared a list of discussion questions, as well as some background information about the author. But now, glancing through my notes, it sounded like a lot of romantic rubbish. Even the novel couldn't hold my attention. Instead of du Maurier's mysterious Frenchman, all I could see was the raven-haired man with his reckless smile and wind-burned cheeks. Once more he was reaching out to me, his smile hinting at adventures to come and his eyes promising even more. With a groan, I tossed the book aside and turned out the light.

MORNING DAWNED WITH lowering clouds and a light drizzle of rain. I welcomed the change. Gray skies were much less distracting than yesterday's tender blue. Whether from a small remnant of guilt or a renewed sense of duty, I attacked my obligations for the day with fierce determination, the first order of the day being my story hour at the local libraries.

Depending on their mood and energy level, my sessions with the children from the Island's elementary schools can range from exhausting to exhilarating. This morning was one of those lovely times that ranked high up the "exhilarating" scale. My rendition of George MacDonald's *The Princess and the Goblin,* had the groups of first and second graders totally wide-eyed and wiggle-free. And when I read the final chapter of Ernest Thompson Seton's classic, *The Biography of a Grizzly*, there were several boys, in addition to the girls, who were sniffling and wiping their noses. Not a bad feat for a rowdy bunch of ten and eleven-year olds.

Then it was back to Coupeville to prepare for the arrival of the book club. In honor of du Maurier's story and to create the proper ambiance, I set the table with Aunt Ivy's best rose-bordered china. Elaborate silver candle-sticks aren't my aunt's style, but she has some lovely crystal ones which would do nicely. And while the ladies from Coupeville might not be dining on "crab prepared in the French fashion," Aunt Ivy's chicken salad was perfection itself. Vases filled with fresh flowers—daffodils, hyacinth and soft pussy willows—adorned the living and dining rooms, filling the house with spring's haunting fragrance.

As I finished arranging the flowers, my thoughts drifted into a romantic idyll where I fancied myself the Lady Dona, awaiting the arrival of her lover. Carrying the illusion still farther, I wondered, as she had, what I should wear. Nothing in my limited wardrobe looked the least bit eighteenth century, and even if I did discover an elegant gown of creamy silk lurking in the closet, I doubt I'd have the nerve to wear it. Oh well. The least I could do was upgrade my usual attire of jeans and a tee shirt.

Flipping through the hangers, I took out a blouse of soft ivory muslin and paired it with a peasant-style skirt in hues of burgundy and copper. In place of Lady Dona's ruby earrings, I found a pair of garnet ones that had belonged to my grandmother. Old-fashioned, yet timeless, the earrings suited me well, the dark red glitter of the stones a compliment to my fair skin and hazel eyes. As for my hair, it was too long and thick to attempt Lady Dona's ringlets. A gold clip pulling the unruly brown waves back from my face would have to do.

CHAPTER THREE

The Sea Captain's Home

I made my escape from Coupeville and drove west with nary a sign of Norman Phillips on the horizon. Nor were there gray skies and drizzle. This morning's rain had given way to a golden afternoon with sunny patches of blue sky chasing away the few remaining clouds. Chasing away Norman Phillips might prove to be a bit more difficult, thanks to my aunt's well-meaning interference. But even that prospect couldn't spoil my enjoyment of amber sunlight spilling over plowed fields of rich black earth, some already sprouting the tender green of a new crop.

The drive from my aunt and uncle's home in Coupeville to the Alexander house is a pleasant one—but it is especially lovely in the spring. The moment I leave Highway 20 and take the simple country road which runs west across the island, I feel as if I've stepped back in time. Century-old farmhouses nestle in the shelter of ancient trees, looking much the same as they must have in Whidbey's pioneer days when a group of venturesome sea captains first discovered and claimed the island's fertile soil.

Foremost among them was Captain Thomas Coupe from New Brunswick, who had the distinction of being the first man to sail a full-rigged ship through Deception Pass. Then there was Captain Frank Lovejoy from the coast of Maine, Captain Kinney from Nova Scotia, and James Swift who had sailed the seas since he was a lad of fourteen. After years of navigating the Atlantic in the ship *Tecumseh,* Captain Joseph Clapp retired from sea-going life to become Coupeville's first postmaster. Now they all reside in the little cemetery on a hill, still within view of the sea and the lovely land they helped settle.

After driving due west for a few miles, the farmland ends in a dramatic bluff and rocky coastline, with stunning views of the Olympic Peninsula and the Strait of Juan de Fuca. It was here that a hardy Scotsman, Captain James Alexander first settled and built a home for his bride, Cecily Fairfield. Cecily, a delicate young woman some twelve years her husband's junior, had a lifelong fear of the sea; in particular that her beloved James would someday go to a watery grave. To ease her fears, Captain Alexander graciously retired to life on the land. Yet, it was Cecily who would leave him, dying shortly after the birth of their second child, a son they named Duncan James.

Heartbroken, Captain Alexander left the home and tragic memories behind him and moved to Seattle. Two years after his wife's death, he married a spinster schoolmarm by the name of Edith Blakeney. Edith was a practical woman with a kind heart, who was genuinely fond of her husband's two small children and much too sensible to be jealous of a dead wife. Rather than trying to change or eliminate all the memories in their Whidbey Island home, she found it much to her liking.

In 1922, young Duncan James married a Seattle socialite by the name of Priscilla Scott, and some ten years later, after the death of his father, Duncan inherited the home on the hill. This was a critical time in the home's history, and one that could have ended quite

Although I didn't speak or move, he must have sensed he was no longer alone, because he glanced up then and saw me. His mouth parted and a pair of remarkable blue-green eyes stared at me with the same sort of disbelief I was experiencing.

"Bronwyn?" he said in a voice like rough velvet.

"No . . . no, I'm Lucy."

Confusion wrinkled his brow and he got to his feet. "But aren't you the one. . . ?"

"I—I'm Lucy Norris."

"The Willoughby's Lucy?"

I swallowed and nodded. "They're my aunt and uncle . . . yes."

He came toward me through the golden haze and my grip on the railing tightened even more. No longer out of fear, but because my legs were suddenly so weak, I didn't think they would hold me.

"I'm sorry if I startled you," he began, offering a smile of greeting and apology. "I tried calling your aunt and uncle this morning, but didn't get an answer."

"My aunt and uncle are out of town," I said faintly.

He nodded then glanced around with undisguised pleasure. "It's been so long since I've seen the place, I just decided to come by. I hope you don't mind."

"Seen the place?"

His smile and eyes met mine. "I'm Duncan. Duncan Alexander."

I've never been very good at concealing my emotions, and I'm sure the wonder and amazement flooding through me at that moment must have been clearly evident.

Duncan Alexander . . . the man on the tall ship. . . .

A look came into his eyes then, warmth and something akin to secret recognition that totally unnerved me. I glanced away and for the first time noticed the small clothbound book in his hand.

"Where did you get that?" I gasped.

"I was wandering around the house and found it on the window seat. Apparently, it's a journal belonging to someone named Bronwyn McBride. I assume you know her."

"Know her?"

"Well, yes, otherwise why would her journal be left here in the house?"

"Oh . . . yes. I—of course I know her. She's my—my cousin."

Those sea-blue eyes were measuring as a slow smile curved the corners of his mouth. "Your cousin."

"Yes, and I'll be glad to return the journal to her."

I reached out to retrieve it, but Duncan Alexander only smiled a rather wicked smile and started down the stairs, book in hand.

"Thanks, but I'd like to return it myself."

"But—but there's really no need," I called after him. "I'm sure she wouldn't want you to go to any trouble."

"It's no trouble. I probably shouldn't have, but I couldn't resist reading parts of the journal." He tossed a meaningful glance over his shoulder and said, "I'd like to meet this cousin of yours. She sounds like a fascinating woman. Do you mind giving me her phone number?"

I trailed after him, my voice light and breathless. "Well, I—I suppose I could but—I doubt you'll be able to reach her."

"Why not?"

I reached the bottom of the stairs where he stood looking at me with that decidedly wicked grin.

"Because . . . she's staying with some friends and—uh, she's going out this evening."

He nodded agreeably. "I see. Well, why don't you give me her number anyway, and I'll leave her a message."

I drew a quick breath. "I'm sorry. I don't know if that will work."

Instead of being dissuaded, he gave a short laugh. "No problem. If she's staying with friends, you could give me their number. Or better yet, give me the number of her cell phone."

"That's the problem!" I said more adamantly than I intended. "She doesn't have a cell phone. Bronwyn hates cell phones. And I have no idea when she'll be back—probably not until quite late. But when she comes in, I'll give her your message."

"I thought you said she was staying with friends."

"Oh, I did. I did. What I meant was, the next time I see her I could give her a message and have Bronwyn call you."

Duncan Alexander considered this for an uncomfortably long moment before giving me a short nod. "All right. Please tell your cousin that I'd like to have dinner with her tomorrow night at the Moonraker Inn in Langley."

"Tomorrow night?" I swallowed and said in a small voice, "I'm sure she'd love to, but she has a previous engagement. Something she can't get out of."

"Then we'll make it Saturday evening instead. Seven o'clock at the Moonraker." His mouth twitched slightly as he looked down at me. "And tell her I won't take no for an answer."

I sighed and glanced down, unable to meet his eyes. "I'll tell her."

"Good." Duncan followed me through the dining room to the kitchen and asked, "Do you have any plans for this evening?"

"Plans?"

"If you're not busy, I thought we could go somewhere and get a bite."

I suddenly found myself bristling at his casual invitation. Bronwyn

McBride was invited to the Moonraker Inn, while I was asked to go somewhere and "get a bite."

"I hope you can spare the time," he went on. "Since your aunt and uncle are out of town, there are a few matters concerning the house that I'd like to go over with you."

"Oh, I see."

"I haven't been to Coupeville in years," he said easily. "So any place you'd like to go is fine with me."

Still bristling, I was tempted to suggest he take a flying leap off the nearest Taco Bell. Then, looking past my silly pride, I noticed for the first time the lines of weariness in his face. And something else . . . a tight-edged strain to his bearded mouth that spoke of some deeper worry.

"There are several places we could go," I said, "but if you'd like something simpler—a home-cooked meal—I'll be happy to fix you something."

"You really wouldn't mind?"

"No, of course not."

His smile was warm, easing the tightness around his mouth. "I'd like that very much."

Thoughts of sitting across the table from Duncan Alexander suddenly prompted a wildly fantastic image . . . Lady Dona inviting the Frenchman to an intimate candle-lit supper . . . the lady and the pirate sharing an evening that would change the course of both their lives.

Then reality encroached on the romantic, jerking me back to the present. Business matters regarding the house. That was all Duncan wished to discuss with me. It was my cousin, Bronwyn McBride, that he found so fascinating, not plain little Lucy Norris.

CHAPTER FOUR

Memories and Candlelight

By the time we reached my aunt and uncle's home, the golden afternoon was fading into the soft grays and pinks of approaching dusk. Robins were singing their last songs of the day as I parked my car in the drive beside the house. Duncan Alexander pulled up behind me, and getting out of his car, glanced around with a smile.

"You know, most of the time when you come back to a place, it's totally different than the picture you have in your mind. But your aunt and uncle's home hasn't changed a bit. Everything's exactly the same—except for you." Once again I saw the glint of recognition in his eyes and that secret smile of amusement curving his mouth. "You're nothing like the little girl I remember."

Lips parted, I had no response to this amazing bit of information.

"You don't remember, do you," he said.

I shook my head. At the moment, his nearness was enough to blot out everything else, memory included.

"Tell me, Lucy, have you rescued any kittens lately?" he asked, reaching out a hand to me.

Memory flooded back even as warmth and color flooded my cheeks. . . . I was a scrappy little six-year old, all eyes, with a pointy chin and a dusting of freckles across my nose, and my plans to go fishing with Uncle Milt had just been spoiled by the arrival of the Alexander family.

Ordinarily, most of the business matters were taken care of by phone or letter, and once in a great while, Mr. Alexander might drop by to speak with my uncle. On this particular summer's day, it was not only John, but his wife and two children who arrived without warning.

Uncle Milt and Aunt Ivy dismissed the Alexander's polite apologies for intruding, and invited them in with a warmth and welcome befitting a long lost relative's sudden return from the dead. While my uncle settled John and Evelyn in the living room, Aunt Ivy scurried into the kitchen to prepare refreshments for the family. Duncan must have been nearly thirteen at the time, and his father explained with a rueful smile that his son preferred to wait in the car with his head buried in a book. I was instructed gently, but firmly, by Uncle Milt to take the Alexander's daughter upstairs to my room to play.

Caroline Alexander was two years older than I, and a silken-haired, blue-eyed blonde. Even at the tender age of six, I was painfully aware of the differences between us. In her dainty print blouse of pink and white, with spotless white shorts, Caroline was a vision of beauty and disdain, while I, in denim overalls and a tee-shirt, looked more like a big-eyed boy, except for the curling masses of woodsy-brown hair that Aunt Ivy was forever trying to tame.

Caroline was instantly bored with anything I offered her—my toys, my books and dolls. Each suggestion was received with distaste and a slight screwing up of her lovely mouth, as if she'd been forced to swallow some unpleasant medicine. Finally, in desperation, I'd asked if she would like to go outside and have a tea party with Juanita.

"Who's Juanita?" she wanted to know.

"My kitten."

"That's a stupid name for a cat."

"It's not stupid!" I shot back. "It's amazing."

Caroline had no answer for this and followed me outside to the backyard to see this "amazing" animal.

Juanita had been given her name by my uncle who found the half-starved, abandoned kitten wandering the ferry dock on the Strait of Juan de Fuca. Hence the name. Juan, however, upon closer examination turned out to be a Juanita.

The thin straggly kitten soon plumped out quite nicely, but she still had a bit of a wild streak in her. On this particular day, Juanita wasn't the least bit interested in having a tea party. She was even less enchanted with Caroline Alexander. After tolerating the girl's attentions for a few mewing moments, she wriggled out of Caroline's arms and scampered up the old hawthorn tree, safely out of reach. Juanita's haven quickly became a lofty prison, and the animal set up a frightened yowling.

I scrambled up after her, managing to climb as far as one of the lower limbs, before my shirt and my hair became caught in the tree's thorny branches. Clinging to the scratchy trunk, I couldn't move forward or back.

"Are you all right?" Caroline called from below.

"I'm stuck," I admitted, my voice quavering.

"I'll go get my father and your uncle."

"No!" The last thing I wanted was for the dignified Mr. Alexander or Uncle Milt to witness my humiliation.

So there we were—Juanita mewing loud protests on a limb and me stuck fast barely one yard away, with thorns pulling my thick hair.

"How are you going to get down?" Caroline wanted to know.

I had no answer. In my mind, I saw myself stuck in the tree forever, dying a slow, lingering death.

"Looks like you could use a little help," said a voice from below.

I glanced down to see Caroline's older brother grinning up at me. "Juanita's stuck," I told him with as much dignity as I could muster.

"Juanita's not the only one," he answered with a laugh and began climbing the tree.

"Hold still while I get your shirt and hair untangled," he said, leaning over me.

I grimaced and closed my eyes, but his fingers were amazingly gentle. Only moments later I heard him say, "There you go. Hang on to me now, and I'll help you down."

"What about Juanita?"

"Juanita can find her own way down," he said, not unkindly.

I opened my eyes to see Duncan Alexander smiling at me and reaching out an encouraging hand. The moment his fingers grasped mine, my fears simply melted away. Something inside told me I was safe.

Now, after all these years, that same hand was reaching out to me once more. . . .

"I'm amazed you still remember," I told him, feeling a shiver of emotion at his touch.

"Why wouldn't I?" he countered with a laugh. "That was the first time I got to rescue a maiden in distress."

I withdrew my hand and made a study of unlocking the front door. "I suppose you've had numerous occasions to rescue other maidens since then."

He shrugged and followed me inside. "I wouldn't say numerous. Some women don't want to be rescued."

I didn't know what to say to that, so instead, I mumbled something about making himself at home.

Duncan stood for a moment, hands in his pockets, his sea-blue gaze taking in the living room and all its homey familiarity with a sense of appreciation that surprised me. There was certainly nothing unique about the old floral sofa flanked with Aunt Ivy's plethora of pillows, Uncle Milt's favorite armchair, or the lamps on old-fashioned end tables, sharing space with African violets and framed photos. Yet I saw open delight in his eyes. He turned slightly to gaze at the large picture over the mantle of a clipper ship sailing across rolling green swells of the sea, and something in his profile struck me as hauntingly familiar. The broad forehead with that dark hair falling away in unruly waves. The strong nose and rugged line of his bearded jaw. Then I knew. The profile of the man before me was one I had seen before—in the portrait of his great-grandfather, Captain James Alexander.

Duncan turned in time to catch my fascinated gaze and I felt my cheeks burn.

"I'm sorry—I didn't mean to stare, but I couldn't help noticing how much you resemble your great-grandfather."

"In more ways than one," he said. "I'm afraid I inherited his love for the sea, as well as his looks."

"And is that a bad thing?"

"There are those who think so," he answered quietly. Then, shrugging the matter aside, he turned to me with that heart-shaking smile. "I don't know how much use I'd be in the kitchen, but if you'd like a fire, I'll be glad to get one going."

"Thank you . . . a fire would be nice," I said and made a hasty retreat.

Safely out of range of those eyes and that smile, my thoughts ran rampant, keeping pace with my swiftly beating heart. How could this be? Only last night I was eating my supper in solitude, my thoughts weaving a lonely pattern of longing around the face and smile of a man on a tall ship. And now that very man was in my living room—the great-grandson of the sea captain and his bride.

I leaned weakly against the counter and tried to steer my thoughts toward culinary matters. Better concentrate on getting supper ready or I'd be no use at all. Aunt Ivy's recent stockpiling gave me several good choices. I passed over today's chicken salad, along with the roast beef from Sunday's dinner in favor of a big pot of potato soup. That, topped with crumbled bacon bits, grated cheese and a fat dollop of sour cream, would make a hearty supper. And to accompany the soup, thick slices of French bread with pats of butter and Aunt Ivy's strawberry jam.

But what to drink? My aunt and uncle had simple tastes, and as a rule, served ice water or herbal tea with meals. Morning coffee and an occasional soft drink were the strongest stimulants to be found in the Willoughby household. Although Aunt Ivy rarely mentioned it, growing up with an alcoholic father had resulted in a strong aversion to any and all alcoholic drinks. For the most part, Uncle Milt respected her feelings, although I knew for a fact he might sneak an occasional can of beer with his friends.

I gave the soup a quick stir, then left the kitchen to ask Duncan Alexander about his choice of beverage.

Once more, I entered a room to discover him reading unaware. This time it was my notes on *Frenchman's Creek* that held his interest. In my hurry to leave the house after book club, I'd left them sitting on the coffee table. Something about the intentness of his concentration and the slight smile playing about his bearded mouth started my heart pumping double time.

"They're just my notes," I said unnecessarily. "I had book club here this afternoon."

He glanced up at me and there was a certain lift in his voice. "*Frenchman's Creek.* Very romantic and—very revealing."

"Revealing?"

He didn't elaborate, simply looked down at the notes with an enigmatic smile. I wanted to snatch them out of his hands, but instead, stood frozen to the spot, a pulse hammering away in my throat.

A moment later he set the pages down and said casually, "I guess I'd better get that fire started, unless there's something else I can do to help."

"No—nothing. Supper's nearly ready. I just wondered what you'd like to drink."

"Whatever you're having will be fine," he said, and getting up, crossed to the fireplace to crumple some newspaper.

A log fire was burning brightly, filling the room with its crackling warmth when I returned some ten minutes later, to tell him supper was ready.

Duncan followed me into the dining room and stood for a moment, surveying the scene—the linen tablecloth with Aunt Ivy's best china, and my centerpiece of spring flowers balanced on either side by pale green tapers in crystal candlesticks. There was a sparkle of amusement in his eyes as he turned to me, and for a moment I felt as if I'd been transported into the pages of du Maurier's novel. I could almost hear him say with a mocking smile, *Is it wise of you, do you think, to put all this temptation before a pirate?*

Only he was not a pirate and I was by no means a titled English lady, nor was there a button-mouthed servant named William to wait upon us. Duncan Alexander and I were alone in this intimate setting.

"I—uh, hope you like potato soup," I said, and with those homely words, the magical spell of romance crumbled around us like the bacon bits garnishing the soup.

Duncan gave an approving nod. "Everything looks great, but—the lighting's not quite right."

"The lighting?"

He nodded again and went back to the living room, returning moments later with a box of matches. "No point in wasting all that electricity, when you've already provided a much better source of illumination," he said and proceeded to light the candles. Then he reached for the light switch on the wall behind him and flipped it off.

"Much better," he pronounced with satisfaction, and sitting down, turned his attention to the soup.

I sank into my chair in a breathless heap, tongue-tied and all too aware of the devastating effect that candlelight lent to his face. Watching the play of light and shadow across those rugged features, I tried to think what Bronwyn McBride would say if she found herself in such extraordinary circumstances. Surely something more captivating than, "How's the soup?" or, "Would you like some jam?"

"Will you be here long?" was all I could come up with.

Duncan savored another steaming spoonful before answering. "Only a few days. I had a trial run on the *Chalcedony*, which took us through Deception Pass and down to Lake Union."

"Oh, is that her name?" I blurted out. "I mean—that's a wonderful name. One of Whidbey's early sea captains had a ship by that name."

Duncan smiled and nodded. "Yes, I know. The first *Chalcedony* was a famous northern trader in her day and the *Chalcedony II* is patterned after her. If all goes well, she'll be racing in the Tall Ships Challenge later this summer."

"Will you be sailing with her?"

My question went unanswered as his expression shifted to one of quiet intensity. "It was you on the bridge yesterday morning, wasn't it."

"Yes."

A thread of silence wove its subtle spell around us, then he smiled into my eyes and I felt it once again, the same surge of inexpressible joy that had filled me the morning before. Those warm currents of joy must have loosened my tongue, because suddenly I was telling him, "When I saw the *Chalcedony* coming toward me, with her sails so white against the sky . . . it was like a dream. And you . . . the expression on your face. I don't know when I've seen anyone so full of life and so completely unafraid. I've always loved the sea—yet in some ways it terrifies me."

"I don't know any seaman who doesn't have a healthy respect for the ocean," he said gently. "Have you done much sailing?"

"Not really . . . I—I haven't had much opportunity. Most of what I know is from books rather than experience."

"There's nothing wrong with that. When I was younger, I used to read everything I could get my hands on about the sea and ships. But it wasn't enough. I guess sailing is in my blood."

"Like your great-grandfather," I put in with a smile.

"I suppose so."

There was a tentative, almost cautious note to his voice, as if by admitting to the fact, he would incur censure or disapproval. A shadow clouded his sea-blue eyes, and he glanced away.

My heart began an erratic pounding as I watched him, and suddenly I found myself saying, "Sometimes, when I'm working at your great-grandfather's home, I find myself thinking about him—wondering if he ever regretted giving up his life at sea after he married Cecily. I'm sure it must have been hard for him at times, knowing that she feared the very thing he loved so much. Even though they loved each other—still, it's sad that she couldn't have shared that part of him."

"Maybe he tried to share it, but she didn't understand—or want to," Duncan said quietly.

"Maybe. I think fear keeps people from understanding a lot of things. Especially something as mysterious and powerful as the sea. Even though I've had little experience with sailing, there's something about ships and the ocean that calls to me. I don't know why, but it does. It always has."

Across the glow of candlelight, Duncan's eyes met mine as he quoted softly, "*So comes to us at times, from the unknown and inaccessible solitudes of being . . . the rushing of the sea-tides of the soul. . . .*"

I nodded in quiet wonder that he should know one of my favorite poems by Longfellow, as my voice joined his on the last lines. . . . "*And inspirations that we deem our own are some divine foreshadowing . . . and foreseeing of things beyond our reason or control.*"

Neither of us spoke for a moment, but when he smiled at me, I knew that a door to knowing him had just opened wide.

The rest of the evening became an intimate voyage through

Duncan Alexander's life. The familiar surroundings of the room ceased to exist as I sailed with him from one ocean to another, feeling the winds of discovery on my face, exploring exotic ports of call, then sailing off to the next destination. The light in his eyes, the excitement in his voice gave me free passage into his world. Passage that I eagerly accepted.

I stood with fourteen-year old Duncan on the deck of the old sailing ship, *The Star of India,* and felt the thrill of the ship's wheel beneath his hands. I went with him on his first voyage onboard a sail-training ship, suffering through miserable moments of sea-sickness, along with the weak-kneed fright of climbing aloft for the first time. I was there during the silent midnight watches, a thousand miles out to sea, as his awe-filled gaze took in the silvery canvas of night, with constellations burning quiet paths across the sky.

I worked alongside him as he patiently taught troubled teens the exacting discipline and knowledge required to sail a multi-ton craft with some 11,000 square yards of canvas. And I heard the raw pain edging his voice when he talked of his father's disappointment in his only son—that Duncan would choose a nautical career, charting his course across oceans instead of the prosperous sea of finance that his father had mapped out for him. There were other disappointments, glossed over in actual words, but scarring nonetheless. A fiancé, who preferred the tangible delights of what money had to offer, rather than his love.

Foolish, foolish woman, I thought, wondering how any woman could fail to recognize the treasure of being loved by this man.

Duncan had just begun to describe one night's experience during the blackness of a wild Pacific storm, when a sudden gust of wind rattled the windows. He paused, then straightened with the realization that the candles were burning low and the darkness of this particular night had completely enveloped the room.

He glanced at me and his voice, laced with sarcasm, couldn't hide the embarrassment on his face. "Well . . . nothing like holding someone hostage in their own home. I can't believe I've done this—talked half the night and told you things that—" He stopped abruptly and shook his dark head, as if he could somehow shake away the discomfiture of having revealed so much of himself.

My heart beat faster in a dance of secret joy, for I knew exactly what he'd been about to say . . . *things that I've never told anyone.*

"You're too polite," he went on, giving me an awkward smile. "Why didn't you stop me?"

"I wasn't being polite. I didn't want to stop you."

"Lucy, I—" He drew a sharp breath then shoved back his chair. "I had no idea it was so late. I appreciate the dinner and—and your patience."

The stiff formality of his tone found its way into my own voice. "You're welcome."

We stood facing each other, awkward silence filling the space that only moments before had been so warm and intimate.

"Uncle Milt and Aunt Ivy will be sorry they missed seeing you."

"Please give them my best. And tell them I enjoyed seeing the house again."

He was going. Of course he was going. The thought filled me with a heaviness so acute it resembled despair. Pasting the wretched semblance of a smile on my face, I walked with him to the front door.

"Thanks again for the dinner," he said, taking my hand in a friendly gesture. Nothing more.

"I'm glad you enjoyed it."

He paused on the porch steps and glanced over his shoulder. "You won't forget to give your cousin my message."

I stiffened and told him with a decided lack of warmth. "Saturday night, seven o'clock at the Moonraker."

"That's right. Goodnight, Lucy."

"Goodnight."

Journal Entry

Unfulfilled dreams are like the tender buds of flowers that never open, but wilt and wither on the stem. All the sweetness and fragrance remains tightly closed within itself.

So why do I go on dreaming? Why do I persist in sending out those fledgling, spring-like hopes into a world of cold drizzle and rain? And why is it, whenever I trip and stumble over the rough stones life conveniently places in my path, that I go blithely on, with my gaze on the far horizon rather than the ground?

Some might attribute this to my stubborn nature or even label it sheer foolishness, and perhaps they are right. Yet I do know this. There is something even sadder than a dream unfulfilled, and that is to never dream at all. That sounds impossibly sentimental, I know, but for me it is true. Never dreaming, or allowing for the possibility of the impossible in one's life, would be like living in a world without rainbows and star-light. No matter how fierce the storm, afterwards there is that delicate promise of the divine arching across the sky. And even the blackest night cannot alter the fact that somewhere in the heavens, stars are shining.

And if I believe that, which in my heart of hearts, I truly do—then somehow, sometime, I must also believe that I will see him again.

Bronwyn McBride

Chapter Five

The Broken Pitcher

It was three minutes past five and not four-thirty the following afternoon, before I heard Peggy's mini-van gunning up the drive. Despite her madcap ways, Peggy Gamble is one of the most prompt people I know and takes pride in arriving exactly on time, which to her way of thinking is usually five minutes early. That she would be over thirty minutes late in picking me up was more than unusual. It was unheard of.

I hurried outside and climbed into the passenger seat of the van. "Have you had one of those 'joys of motherhood' days?" I asked, hoping to lighten her harried expression.

"Worse," she said and launched into a detailed description of her day from hell. Listening to her, I knew any problems of mine would have to wait. First, the washing machine had gone on strike and refused to drain or complete its cycles, so Gary didn't have his work clothes ready. Then, right in the middle of baking the perfect cream puff shells, she'd gotten a call from the boys' school. Gavin's teacher didn't want to alarm her, but he'd had a slight accident on the playground and could she please come and pick him up. The cream puff shells, instead of coming out golden brown, had become burnt offerings to the oven god, and Gavin's "slight accident"—going down a slide head first—had required eight stitches in his chin.

"Are you feeling all right?" she asked now. "You seem a little tired, or preoccupied."

The truth of the matter was, after my evening with Duncan Alexander, I had scarcely slept at all. I was tired and edgy, and the last thing I felt like doing was serving canapés and goodies to a bored group of beautiful people at Marius Charbot's cocktail party. If it hadn't been for the fact that backing out now would be devastating to Peggy, I would have gladly cancelled.

"I guess I'm still a bit nervous about this whole cocktail party thing," I said, thinking that was as good an excuse as any.

"Lucy, I told you, there's nothing to it. Other than keeping the trays filled, you'll be practically invisible."

"Oh, well, that's something I'm very good at—being invisible."

Peggy frowned and gave me a close look, but before more questions could follow, I asked, "What road did you say we're looking for?"

"Manitou something—lane or grove."

"I think I see it just ahead."

Charles Bastian's directions to the Charbot home had taken us onto a winding forest road near the seaside village of Langley. Private lanes branched off on either side, cloaked in the shade of old growth forest. An occasional mailbox beside a secretive lane was the only indication of man's presence in this woodland domain. The homes themselves were not visible from the road.

Peggy slowed the van as we approached one such lane leading into the depths of the forest. Nailed to the bark of a shaggy red cedar was a small metal sign, scarcely noticeable to the casual passerby, but clear in its message nonetheless: *Manitou Grove—Private Drive—No Trespassing.*

The road wound steadily upwards through "tunnels of trees," as Peggy liked to call them—graceful archways of lacy alders sharing the darker green of fir and cedar. Shadows of late afternoon were deep under the canopy with only speckles of sunlight finding their way to the forest floor.

"It doesn't seem quite fair that one man should own all this," I said, gazing at the pristine beauty on either side.

Peggy gave me a smiling glance. "That's my friend, wanting to share with the entire world. I know what you mean though. What do you want to bet, Mr. Charbot only comes here once or twice a year, if that?"

We drove for perhaps another half mile, with the road climbing steadily in a series of zigzag curves. Near the top, the trees began to thin, and after rounding one last curve, the forest suddenly opened up, offering a sweeping vista of sea and sky and the distant Olympic mountain range. Dominating the hilltop was a magnificent log home. Two stories high, with pointed gables, balconies and wide windows that embraced the expanse of its hilltop setting, the place was stunning. Massive whole logs supported a covered porch that ran the entire length of the house, and there was a chimney of gray river rock climbing a far wall. The landscaping was on a scale equally as large, with terraced walls of boulders, and curving walkways bordered with evergreens and wildflowers.

"Good heavens, it's a hotel, not a house," Peggy said, braking the van to stare at the log home.

"I assume the servant's entrance must be around back," I told her with a grin.

It was. Along with a four-car garage, a guesthouse and a vine-covered walkway leading to the main house. Peggy parked beside a small van bearing the insignia of the Moonraker Inn, then looked at me with a nervous sigh.

"Okay, Lucy, there's only one thing we need to remember."

"And that is?"

"That Marius Charbot zips up his pants the same as everyone else."

I laughed. "Thanks, Peggy. I'll try to remember."

One of the employees of the Inn was there to greet us and ushered Peggy and me into the kitchen. Ron Bartoli was short and slender with spiky dark hair, clever brown eyes and an easy smile. Like me, he was dressed in a white shirt with black slacks and vest. The perfect uniform for invisibility which immediately labeled us as hired help rather than anyone of interest or importance.

Ron's familiarity and ease in showing us around indicated this was not the first event he had catered for the Charbots, and for that I was grateful. After explaining the kitchen layout, he helped us carry in the food and supplies Peggy had brought, then returned to his own duties of setting up the bar.

Peggy was truly in her element. Despite the rustic features of the home's design, the kitchen was state of the art with shining granite counter-tops, built-in ovens and a large center island. "I'm in heaven," she sighed, and happily went to work.

My own responsibilities were relatively simple, consisting of little more than "put this here" and "take that there," but having less than an hour before guests were due to arrive, added some stress to what would have been an enjoyable task. Trays in hand, I hurried back and forth from the kitchen to the great room and its adjoining dining area, feeling as if I'd been transported onto the pages of a glossy home magazine.

The great room was stunning in size and design, with a natural stone fireplace climbing one wall, another devoted entirely to windows, and a beamed ceiling at least twelve feet high. Hardwood floors and massive leather furniture joined the old world elegance of oriental rugs and fine artwork in a surprising marriage—European hunting lodge meets the Old West—the common denominator being money. The only drawback to all this stylish perfection was that everything seemed more than a bit untouchable. It was difficult to rid myself of the notion that if I moved a vase or *object d'art* so much as a quarter inch, alarm bells would instantly go off through the house.

By six forty we were nearly ready for the arrival of guests, but I had yet to catch a glimpse of our host and his wife. In a far corner of the great room set aside for the bar, Ron Bartoli was arranging the last of the wine glasses. Peggy was putting the finishing touches on the hot artichoke dip, and thankfully, nearly all the food had been transferred from the kitchen to lovely silver trays and chafing dishes in the dining area.

As I approached the food table with its opulent spread, I couldn't help comparing the lavish offerings to last night's simple dinner with Duncan Alexander. In contrast to my centerpiece of spring flowers, the Charbot table had a tall crystal vase filled with white roses and lilies with golden throats, the sides of the vase trailing foliage, glossy and darkly green. Duncan and I had dined on Aunt Ivy's rose-bordered china, whereas tonight's guests were offered small plates rimmed heavily in gold. Potato soup was simple fare compared to the platters of smoked salmon and braziers filled with spicy Swedish meatballs. Accompanying this was an artfully arranged assortment of fine European cheeses, crackers, vegetables, and tomato aspic ringed with caviar.

I smiled then, remembering Duncan's enjoyment of the meal and the richness of our conversation. Would I trade all this lovely opulence for the evening we had shared? Never.

Searching for an empty spot to put the salver of éclairs and chocolate-covered strawberries I was carrying, I found my gaze lifting to a pair of forlorn dark eyes that looked down upon the feast from their framed boundary on a far wall. The painting was nearly life-size in proportion and larger than life in its emotional impact. I'd been drawn to it from the moment I entered the dining room, but couldn't justify giving it closer examination until now.

The artist's subject was a young peasant girl wearing a simple skirt and blouse with a colorful shawl around her shoulders. She was sitting on a stone wall near a cistern, with hands clasped. On the dusty ground near her bare feet lay an earthenware pitcher, its base cracked and broken. The artist's technique was masterful, his brush-strokes so true in their portrayal, that I felt sure if I were to reach out and touch the girl's hand, soft flesh would meet mine rather than canvas. Yet it was the haunting expression in her dark eyes that held me captive. In their depths, I felt silent anguish, remorse and shame. Why shame? Surely, the emotion in that lovely young face must have been caused by something more tragic than the loss of a broken pitcher.

I moved closer to discover the artist's name and saw the scripted signature of *William A. Bouguereau.*

"Magnificent, isn't she?" came a deep voice just behind me.

I started and swung around with a surprised jerk that upset the contents of my dessert-laden tray. One of the éclairs and a few strawberries tumbled to the floor, but I managed to save the rest by clutching the tray to my chest. That same moment, strong hands reached out to steady me, and I glanced up into a face of sheer masculine perfection. The man was at that polished forty-something age, with a smooth gloss of dark hair, classic features, and eyes that glittered like black onyx. I tried to swallow my embarrassment, knowing this had to be none other than Peggy's Louis Jourdan look-alike and our host, Marius Charbot.

"I—I'm so sorry. This is totally my fault. . . ."

"It's no one's fault," he said, his smile charming and slightly amused. "Please, allow me."

He took the tray out of my hands, and I quickly bent down to retrieve the runaway strawberries. Thankfully, the éclair hadn't spilled its creamy filling on the rug, but in trying to save the tray, the front of my vest was now smeared with a gooey mixture of whipping cream, chocolate and strawberries.

"Please excuse me," I murmured, giving him an embarrassed smile. "I'd better take care of this before your guests arrive."

"Of course."

He nodded agreeably, the glitter in those dark eyes more amused than anything else, as I backed away and made a hasty retreat to the kitchen.

Peggy took one look at me, and her eyes widened. "Lucy, what on earth?"

I dumped the éclair and strawberries in the sink. "Don't ask, just point me in the direction of the nearest bathroom."

"Down the hall, first door on your right."

Praying I wouldn't run into our host again, I skulked down the hall between the kitchen and great room, then dived inside the bathroom without thinking to knock.

Kneeling before the porcelain throne, retching in miserable dry heaves, was a lovely woman with hair like pale blonde silk. I knew immediately who she was. All the elements of a young Princess Grace were present in the woman's classic beauty, although her present situation was far from regal.

"I'm so sorry—I didn't mean to intrude."

She glanced up briefly, the loveliness of her features diminished only slightly by the sick pallor of her skin. Beads of perspiration dotted her brow. Before she could speak, another wave of nausea hit and she bent over the toilet once more.

Hearing those dry heaves and seeing the pathetic way she clutched her stomach, I couldn't just leave her there. I took a washcloth from the towel rack, moistened it with cool water and leaning down, pressed the cloth gently to her forehead.

"Thank you. . . ." she got out, trying to catch her breath.

"Is there anything I can do?"

"No . . . no, it'll pass," she said after a moment.

I looked at her then smiled, suddenly realizing the likely source of the problem. Goodness knows I had seen Peggy in similar circumstances often enough during the early months of pregnancy.

Giving her a supporting hand, I helped Mrs. Charbot to her feet. "If you like, I'll be glad to get your husband."

The hand on my arm instantly tightened. "No! No, please . . . don't say anything about this to my husband!" Her blue eyes were pleading as they met mine. If it weren't so preposterous, I would have sworn I saw fear there was well.

"If you're sure—"

She straightened and drew a ragged breath. "Yes, I'm sure." Seeing my doubtful expression she managed a smile and insisted, "Really, I'm much better. I appreciate your help, but there's no need to bother

Marius. Not with our guests arriving. . . ." She glanced in the mirror, frowned at her reflection, and gave the silken hair a careless swipe. "Heavens, I look a sight. I'd better go upstairs and make some repairs."

"I have some repair work of my own to do," I said, gesturing to the stained front of my vest. "I'm afraid I had a run-in with some éclairs."

We smiled at one another, and I was struck once more with the woman's classic beauty. She turned to go, then paused, the look of pleading back in her eyes.

"You won't say anything about this?"

"No. . . ." I shook my head, puzzled at the urgency in her voice.

"Thank you."

And with that, she was gone.

Peggy was arranging a swirl of almonds around a tray with spinach and feta tartlets as I came back to the kitchen. She gave my freshly scrubbed vest and shirt a smiling thumb's up and announced, "This is the last of it. I am now ready for the onslaught of the beautiful people."

I took the tray from her and right on cue, the doorbell rang. Actually, doorbell is much too common a term for the mellifluous chimes that sounded through the house. As I carried the tray of tartlets into the dining area, I saw Marius Charbot's elegant figure coming down the stairs, heading for the entryway. I wondered briefly what excuse his wife had given for not being at his side to greet their guests. Granted, this one was a good ten minutes early, but not being acquainted with cocktail party etiquette, I had no idea what was considered the proper time to arrive.

Curiosity to see the 'beautiful people,' as Peggy was fond of calling them, had me lingering at the food table, smoothing an invisible wrinkle from the perfectly ironed cloth. My position near a far wall afforded only a partial view of the large entryway, and I edged a little closer.

Mr. Charbot opened the door, then stepped back in obvious surprise. His voice was less than welcoming. "Duncan! This is rather unexpected."

I gasped and ducked behind the concealing fronds of a large planter as Duncan Alexander entered the house without waiting to be invited in. I needn't have worried that he might see me. As the two men faced one another, their measuring looks and stiff dislike were far more palpable than any outward attempts at politeness.

In some ways, they were amazingly alike—both of them dark-haired, and an easy six feet in height (although Duncan was a good two inches taller), and striking in looks. In other ways, they were a study in marked contrast—Marius in his impeccable Italian suit of dark blue silk, with his suave elegance and finely chiseled profile; and Duncan, with that tousled mane of black hair, bearded jaw and rugged features. A black tee shirt and slacks with a jacket of brown leather emphasized the breadth of his shoulders and muscular build.

"Hello, Marius. I had business in the area and thought I'd stop by. How's my little sister?"

My jaw dropped as my mind did a startling bit of addition. Caroline Charbot was Duncan's sister—the bored little blonde of my childhood?

Marius remained near the doorway, making no move to invite Duncan inside, but his smile and voice took on an ingratiating warmth.

"Caroline's fine. Wonderful, in fact. I'm sure she'd love to see you as soon as she arrives."

There was a slight pause, as Duncan took this in. "She's not here?"

"I'm afraid not. Caroline had some last minute details to take care of in Seattle, but she'll be joining me tomorrow for the Art Fest."

"Looks to me like the festivities have already started," Duncan said, glancing across the great room to the bar where Ron had bottles of champagne on ice.

"Yes, actually, they have," Marius answered easily. "I'm hosting a small dinner party for some art dealers and out of town guests. They should be arriving any time, in fact." He gave the gold watch on his wrist a pointed glance and added, "I hate to cut this short, but tonight really isn't the best time for a visit. Why don't you give us a call, say, tomorrow afternoon?"

"I will."

The hard edge in Duncan's voice was unmistakable, and I found my pulse doing a nervous little dance. What possible reason could Marius have for blatantly lying to his brother-in-law?

I heard voices and laughter coming from outside, and the next moment a tall woman with a choreographed windstorm for hair, blew into the room on a cloud of cloying perfume. Dressed in form-hugging pants of raspberry silk and a skimpy lace camisole, there was a wraithlike slenderness to her body. Gold bracelets jangled a metallic melody on each wrist, as she reached up to bestow a welcoming kiss on her host. Behind her was a hawk-nosed man easily twice her age, and dressed as if he were half that.

"Marius, darling, it's been ages," the woman crooned.

Duncan stepped back as the two entered, his face a tight mask of frustration. "I'll see you tomorrow," he said and was gone before Marius could reply.

way, "The last painting of his to come up for auction sold for nearly four million."

"True," Frank acknowledged, finishing his wine with a gulp. "An amazing amount of money to spend for a picture of pristine peasants with clean feet."

Walter ignored the comment and continued to probe Marius for more details. "What makes you think *The Fairy Thorn* even exists, let alone that it's hidden in some rundown hacienda?"

"Oh, it exists," Marius answered smugly. "I happen to have a copy of the bill of sale from its last owner."

I half turned to see Walter stunned into momentary silence. Even Frank's bored expression had lifted. Once more, I saw the piercing look of a hawk on the hunt as he pressed softly, "You have the bill of sale?"

"I do. Six months ago, Caroline and I attended an estate sale near Monterey. We were told that several of the items came from an old hacienda outside Mazatlan. I happened to be looking for furnishings with a Spanish influence for the new inn in Carmel, so we bought several pieces. Caroline is much more knowledgeable than I am about these things," he said magnanimously. "When the pieces were delivered, it was she who discovered some correspondence and loose papers inside one of the desks. You can imagine how my curiosity was aroused when she showed me the receipt from an art gallery in New York City, dated 1902. The bill of sale was for the purchase of an original oil titled *L'epine de la fee*—the thorn of the fairy—by William Adolph Bouguereau."

Walter sputtered his amazement in profane terms while Frank went on with an incredulous frown, "But why Mazatlan? What would some Mexican want with a nineteenth-century masterpiece? That doesn't make any sense."

Caution urged me to move away, even as curiosity insisted that I find out more. Turning my back to the men, I stood plates in hand, reminding myself that I was nothing more than a background fixture; a servant whose opinion and presence couldn't possibly matter. As if to reaffirm this, two female guests got up from a nearby sofa, barely pausing in their animated chatter to hand me their gold-rimmed plates before heading for the bar. In that moment, I felt about as functional and non-human as a coat rack.

"The man who bought *The Fairy Thorn* was not Mexican," Marius was saying. "Richard Melville was the son of a prominent New York banker."

"But why Mazatlan?" Walter echoed Frank's earlier comment. "What would the son of a New York banker be doing in Mexico?"

"I wondered the same thing," Marius admitted, "and was curious enough to do a little research on Melville as well as the times. In the 1880s and '90s, Mazatlan was enjoying a golden age of prosperity, and Melville was one of many American businessmen who came to Mexico hoping to capitalize on the area's rich financial possibilities. Unlike those who made a killing and left, Melville decided to stay, and his motives weren't all profit based. He fell in love with and married Mercedes Delgado, the daughter of a wealthy land owner. The Delgados were the original owners of the hacienda and definitely belonged to old Spain. From what I could find out, Melville purchased the painting in New York, then had it shipped to Mazatlan as an anniversary present for his wife."

"You may have proof that the painting existed," Frank allowed, "but what makes you think it's still around—hidden somewhere in that hacienda, just waiting to be found—by you, of course."

"And what makes you think it isn't?" Marius countered with a smile. "Frank, my friend, stop playing devil's advocate long enough to remember a bit of Mexican history. The Revolution began in 1910 and Mazatlan wasn't exempt from all the unrest and violence. Two years after the trouble started, Melville sent his wife and children to live with some relatives in the states, while he stayed behind to pack their belongings. Unfortunately, he was shot and killed when bandits raided the hacienda. World War I followed on the heels of the Revolution, and the place was abandoned for years. The Delgado family managed to hold on to it until the mid thirties. That's when the hacienda was sold to distant relatives who turned it into a guest ranch."

Frank gave a skeptical snort. "Well, it's a fascinating story, Marius, but I still say the chances of that painting going unnoticed for a hundred years, let alone the odds of it being in that hacienda, are nothing short of astronomical."

I turned to see Walter's bald pate bobbing in reluctant agreement. Just as reluctantly, I retreated with my stack of gold-rimmed plates, casting a sidelong glance at Bouguereau's sad-eyed peasant girl on the way.

By nine-thirty, most of the guests had departed and at nine forty-five, silence descended once more upon the home. Caroline and Marius were very gracious in thanking Peggy for filling in at the last moment, and generous in their praise. I purposely stayed in the background, not wanting to intrude on her moment of glory.

During the drive back to Coupeville, Peggy talked nearly non-stop about the dinner party—how beautiful the home was, how handsome and charming Marius was, how romantic and attentive he was to his wife. Listening to her, I found myself becoming more and more tense. She was understandably enamored with the Charbots, and I didn't want to be the one to disillusion her. Besides, what did I really know about the man—other than the fact that he was charming, intelligent—and a very good liar.

For that matter, who was I to cast stones? At this point, my own faults and frailties kicked in big time, and thoughts of the following day left me with a sick feeling in the pit of my stomach.

"I'm so glad you could help me out tonight," Peggy was saying as we neared Coupeville. "I really owe you."

"No problem. I'm glad I could help."

We drove for a few moments while I tried to gather my nerve as well as my thoughts.

"Peggy?"

"Hmm?"

"There's something—that is—I've been wanting to ask your advice—well, maybe not advice exactly, but I need your help."

"Sure. What can I do?"

I drew a deep breath and said quietly into the darkness, "I . . . I need a kind of makeover."

"A makeover?"

"Yes. I need to look glamorous and beautiful . . . like a movie star."

She laughed. "Lucy, what are you talking about? Movie stars don't even look like movie stars any more. And you're already beautiful. You just don't know it, that's all."

"You don't understand. I need to look like someone else."

"Someone else? Do you have anyone in mind?"

"Yes . . . her name is Bronwyn McBride."

"Bronwyn—?" Peggy began, her voice totally mystified.

"McBride," I finished with a sigh.

"I've never heard of her. Who is she?"

"Well, actually, it's me. I'm Bronwyn."

"What?"

"I know it probably sounds a little confusing, but—"

"A little confusing?" Peggy put in. "Maybe I'm missing something. Can we go over this again? For starters, who's Bronwyn McBride and why do you want to look like her?"

"I told you, I'm Bronwyn McBride."

"But you already look like yourself!"

"I know, and that's the problem. I look like me, *not Bronwyn*. And Duncan will be taking Bronwyn to dinner tomorrow night!"

"Who's Duncan?"

I gave a helpless laugh and leaned back against the car seat with another sigh. "Oh, Peggy, I've gotten myself into a terrible, mixed-up, wonderful mess, and it could be that all the makeovers in the world won't solve it, but I've got to try."

Peggy pulled into my aunt and uncle's driveway and switched off the engine. "Tell me about this terrible, wonderful mess," she said. "I have a feeling I'm going to like it!"

CHAPTER SEVEN

Bronwyn

It helped to sit there in the dark and not have my foolishness displayed in the unforgiving light of day. Peggy said little throughout my pathetic attempt to explain, but her understanding was as tangible as a touch.

Complicated situations often have very simple beginnings, and my discovery of Bronwyn McBride was exactly that. Driving out to the Alexander home, I would sometimes stop at the old Sunnyside cemetery for a quiet walk. Situated on a grassy hilltop overlooking farms, fields and Admiralty Strait, there is nothing grim or morbid about the place. There are so many silent stories there, and a lovely, poignant kind of peace. Even the wind seems to blow more softly, whispering through wonderful old cedars, firs and holly trees.

On this particular day, I had stayed longer than usual, reading the quaint sayings on headstones and imagining the lives of those long ago souls who made Whidbey Island their home. I remember the lilac trees were in bloom, and the blossoms ran the gamut of color, everything from white and pale lavender to deepest purple. The air was filled with their heady sweetness. Even now, the smell of lilacs reminds me of the day I found Bronwyn.

I was wandering about an older section of the cemetery where the grass grew long and thick and many of the headstones were so worn that the names and dates were undecipherable. I'd stopped to admire the lavender poem of a wisteria vine curled around white marble when I found her.

Bronwyn McBride, beloved wife of
Edward Ian McBride
Born: 1816 Died: 1871
She was bonny & brave to the end.

The headstone was tilted at a crooked angle where the ground had settled and shifted over the years, but there was something about the saying that touched me. *Bonny & brave to the end.*

"Even her name seemed to call out to me," I told Peggy. "Bronwyn McBride! Somehow I knew that she was a woman who'd lived a life full of passion and adventure and love—all the things I've longed for and thought I would never have."

"Oh, Lucy," Peggy said softly.

"I know that must sound totally strange. It does even to me, but somehow, in my mind, Bronwyn became the kind of woman I'd always wanted to be—someone beautiful and confident and daring. A woman who was free to express her innermost dreams and desires. And so, whenever I was feeling frustrated or restless—or just plain stuck as Lucy—I began keeping a journal as if I were Bronwyn McBride. It was so much easier to be free with my thoughts and feelings when I was Bronwyn, instead of Lucy the librarian."

"Oh, Lucy," Peggy said again with a long, drawn-out sigh.

"I thought no one would ever know, but the other day I left my journal at the Alexander house and Duncan found it."

"Who's Duncan?" she demanded.

"Duncan Alexander. His parents own the house, but I haven't seen them for years. Anyway, I went out to finish cleaning yesterday, and there he was—sitting on the window seat reading Bronwyn's—I mean, *my* journal."

Peggy was silent for a moment, taking this in. "Okay, maybe I'm a little dense, but why is this so terrible? I mean, Duncan doesn't know you're Bronwyn. Why didn't you just politely yank the journal away from him?"

"Believe me, I tried," I said with a shaky laugh. "But he wouldn't give it to me. He wants to meet Bronwyn."

"Oh dear."

"It gets worse. Duncan has a dinner date with Bronwyn at the Moonraker Inn tomorrow night."

"What? Good grief, Lucy, how did that happen?"

"I was desperate! He kept asking questions about Bronwyn, wanting her phone number—and—and how he could get in touch with her. I sort of panicked and told him she was my cousin."

Even the near darkness of the car couldn't hide the bulging whiteness of Peggy's eyes as she stared at me. "Lucy, my friend, you are in one mell-of-a-hess, as my father used to say."

"I know."

Peggy straightened up with a little shake of her blonde head. "All right. Excuse me for stating the obvious, but has it occurred to you, this whole thing could be solved by simply telling Duncan Alexander the truth."

"And totally humiliating myself."

couture, not clearance markdowns."

Peggy shrugged this aside. "What we need is taste and creativity more than money. I know the owner of a classy consignment shop in Anacortes. We should be able to find something there ... you are so disgustingly slender. Hmm. I'm beginning to see it all now. . . ."

"See what?"

"A little black dress—very Holly Golightly, with a touch of Catherine Zeta-Jones, and some strappy stiletto heels." She nodded, a pleased gleam in her eyes. "I like it."

I had a moment's vision of me tottering up to Duncan Alexander in stiletto heels pretending to be someone else, and was seized with complete, absolute terror.

"Peggy, I don't know if I can do this. I was crazy to even consider it. I don't know what made me think I could pretend to be someone else."

"Then don't pretend. Remember what you told me last night—about not lying because you really are Bronwyn? I think that's true. Inside you, there's a woman who's beautiful, confident and adventurous—but all these years you've been afraid to let her out. It doesn't really matter what her name is—Lucy or Bronwyn. She's there and she's real. And I think it's time you got to know her."

I drew a shaky breath and nodded. "Let's cut the hair."

There was a moment as I looked down at the clumps of brown hair scattered on the floor of the salon, when I felt slightly sick and highly tempted to call the whole thing off. All I had to do was tell Duncan Alexander that I was a fool and there was no Bronwyn. Two things stopped me. The most obvious one being that I had no idea how to get in touch with Duncan—not so much as a phone number or a place where he was staying. The other deterrent was more subtle, just a quiet nudge of a thought that slipped into my mind, bringing with it a sense of calm and confidence. *Bonny and brave to the end.* Thinking of Bronwyn, I knew I couldn't let her down. Somehow I had to live up to whatever strength and courage she had possessed. Cutting my hair was nothing.

"Were you thinking shoulder length?" Syd asked before going further.

"Shorter," I said.

In the chair beside me, Peggy gulped. "Lucy, are you sure—?"

"Shorter," I said again and smiled. "Could you do something like Audrey Hepburn in *Roman Holiday* or *Sabrina?*"

A sudden gleam lit Syd's eyes and she gave me an enthusiastic nod. "Yes! Absolutely!"

Twenty minutes later, I glanced from side to side, smiling at my newly shorn reflection in the mirror.

"Oh my gosh," Peggy said with dazed delight. "It's perfect! Your eyes look even bigger, and the shape of your face. . . ." She sighed and said again, "It's perfect!"

Syd was beaming. Grabbing a broom, she started sweeping away the remnants of the old Lucy. "What's next with the makeover?"

"A new wardrobe," I told her. "Peggy's taking me to a friend's consignment shop in Anacortes."

Syd gave me a wistful glance. "I'd love to go with you, but I have a ton of appointments this morning. Let me know how it goes, okay?"

"I will," I said, grateful that she hadn't asked too many questions. Peggy had told her that I needed an emergency haircut for a date with one of the world's most fascinating men, and naturally, that was enough.

Driving to Anacortes, I had to keep glancing in the visor mirror to believe that the gamin-like image was really me. And each time I felt a secret thrill. I liked what I saw. Hopefully, Duncan Alexander would like it as well.

When Peggy first mentioned her friend's consignment store, I'd had my doubts, but the Serendipity Shop was definitely high-end. Lou Ann herself was there to meet us, and entered into the selection process with enthusiasm and fashion savvy. Slender and tall, with streaked blonde hair and an engaging smile, she was the type of woman who could wear anything and look wonderful. Like today, with a simple top of lemon yellow, long legs clad in a pair of tight jeans, and chunky bracelets on her tanned wrists, she was the epitome of casual elegance. For a moment, just seeing her, I felt dowdy and small. Bronwyn McBride, however, envied no woman. She knew who she was. Armed with that knowledge, I entered the fray.

As the outfits and accessories began piling up on the counter I made a brief attempt to halt the buying frenzy that Peggy and Lou Ann had instigated.

"Excuse me," I inserted meekly, as Lou Ann held up a stunning pantsuit in ivory-colored silk to which Peggy gave wholehearted approval. "I thought we were looking for just one outfit, not an entire wardrobe."

"Your wardrobe's needed a major overhaul for ages," Peggy pronounced mercilessly, eyeing a gauzy sun dress with a fringed, gypsy-like shawl. "Bronwyn—I mean—*you* would look absolutely gorgeous in this," she said, blue eyes dancing.

"Yes, but—"

"If something doesn't work out, you can just bring it back," Lou Ann told me. "And Peggy's right. That dress was made for you."

I sighed, then laughed. "Add it to the pile."

AT THREE MINUTES past seven, Bronwyn McBride pulled up in front of the Moonraker Inn, and stepping gracefully out of her car, handed the keys to the valet with a smile that told him no other attendant on the planet was as lucky as he.

Heads turned. Eyes followed her as she walked confidently inside.

The décor of the Moonraker combined nautical charm with nineteenth-century elegance. On every side, guests were met with the gleam of polished brass, richly carved wood and stunning marine paintings.

I caught a glimpse of Bronwyn as she sailed past a gilded mirror—chin held high, dark brown hair framing a face with shining lips and hazel eyes, her figure an enticing silhouette in a form-fitting, black sheath. Draped casually around her shoulders was a *Pashmina* shawl in emerald green.

Seeing her confident reflection, no one would ever guess that my heart was pounding wildly and my hands, with their perfectly manicured nails, were ice-cold. Peggy had given me specific instructions for the entrance, and so far, I had followed them to the letter. "Walk in as if you own the place. Don't look for him. Let Duncan find you. Then watch the eyebrows! If he likes what he sees, they'll shoot straight up. The eyebrows never lie!"

I paused as a male voice, sounding slightly stunned, croaked, "Bronwyn?"

Turning slowly, I saw Duncan Alexander near the doorway of the dining room, staring at me open-mouthed. It required considerable effort on my part to keep from doing the same. Besides the fact that he looked devastatingly handsome in an open-necked shirt of dark blue with a sport coat and slacks of charcoal gray, I had one other thing to contend with. He had shaved his beard. The results were entirely capable of sending me into delightful oblivion, but somehow I managed to tear my eyes away from that strong, smooth jaw and the slight cleft in his chin.

Bronwyn gave him a practiced smile and said, "Hello," in a tone that was sultry and low.

Peggy was right about the eyebrows.

Chapter Eight

The Moonraker Inn

After that brief, breathy hello, Duncan and I found ourselves simply standing and staring at one another. My welcoming smile turned stiff and my throat was suddenly too dry for speech.

Duncan cleared his throat and his dark brows resumed their normal position. "The resemblance between you and your cousin is—uh, quite amazing."

I gave him what I hoped was a casual shrug and adjusted the soft emerald folds of the shawl. "People tell us that all the time. Lucy and I are really more like sisters than cousins."

"I can see that." He nodded and cleared his throat again. "Thank you for coming."

"From what Lucy told me, I understood this was a condition that had to be met before a certain item could be returned."

He laughed then, and his blue eyes gleamed. "Well put, Miss McBride. But I hope I won't be judged too harshly for wanting to meet the woman whose journal kept me awake half the night."

My heart nearly burst with the dazzling import of his words, but my reply was light and cool. "Are you sure it wasn't a sense of guilt, rather than my writing that kept you awake?"

He grinned at me with maddening enjoyment. "You inspire a good many emotions, but I assure you, guilt isn't one of them." Taking my arm, he led me toward the dining room. "Shall we discuss it over dinner?"

The Moonraker's dining room was brimming over with sounds and smells to entice and delight. Soft music mingled with the pleasant babble of human voices. Servers clad in neat black vests, slacks and white shirts were weaving among the tables with tantalizing platters of sizzling steaks, seafood, and baskets of hot rolls. Not only was it a Saturday night, but the Art Fest was in full swing, and the Inn had more than its usual share of out of town guests. As the seating hostess led the way to our table, a new worry pecked at the fragile shell of my confidence. What if I ran into someone I knew? The chance of that happening was not nearly as remote as I would have liked. It was one thing to try and convince Duncan Alexander that I was Bronwyn McBride. He had met Lucy Norris only once. Fooling someone who had known me nearly all my life was another thing altogether. I tossed a covert glance around the room, and recognized a few guests from the Charbot's cocktail party seated at a table for four. But it appeared that no friends or acquaintances from Coupeville had chosen to dine at the Moonraker this evening.

Our table was in a far corner, beside one of the large windows over-looking the water. Wonderful. At least we wouldn't be in the room's main traffic pattern. And too, the lighting was purposely subdued, providing guests with a sense of intimacy as well as stunning views of the Saratoga Passage and nearby Camano Island. Outside our window, the evening sky wore ribbons of thin cloud tinged with rose, and the water was calm blue silk.

Taking in the scene, I drew a deep breath, trying to calm my nerves. "It's a beautiful evening."

Duncan stood close behind me, and for the briefest of moments, I felt his hands on my shoulders as he removed the shawl and draped it across the back of my chair. "Yes, very beautiful."

Breathe . . . I told myself. Just keep breathing. Bronwyn is used to men's attentions. It means nothing. . . .

Our server arrived then, a young man of perhaps twenty, whose smile and name badge were both slightly lopsided. Taking a nervous breath, he presented us with an extensive wine list.

I handed the list back to him along with one of Bronwyn's warmest smiles. "Thank you, Troy. I'll just have water, please, with a slice of lemon."

Duncan smiled at me. "And I'll have the same."

As the young man stumbled through a memorized account of the menu's specialty items, I suddenly realized that I, or rather Bronwyn, might be the cause of his nervousness and the added ruddiness in his cheeks. This knowledge was not at all displeasing. In fact, it made me bold enough to give him more than my undivided attention. Truth be told, it was easier by far to meet the adoring, if awkward gaze of this young man, rather than Duncan Alexander's all too inquisitive eyes.

"What would you recommend?" I asked.

"The flame-broiled salmon is very good."

"The salmon it is then."

"And I'll have the steak and shrimp," Duncan said, handing him the menu. "Make that rare."

"Yes, sir."

"Oh, and we'd like the calamari appetizer," Duncan added,

turning to me with that slightly wicked smile. "I hope you like calamari."

"I adore calamari," I replied.

Once our server had gone, Duncan leaned forward and fixed me with an interested look. "Do you visit your cousin often?"

"Not as often as I'd like."

"I gather you're here for the Art Fest."

"Yes. Yes, I am."

And here it comes, I thought. All the questions about Bronwyn's life. Normal enough if I really were Bronwyn, but terrifying under the circumstances, even though I'd taken the time to prepare a few generic dates and facts.

"Tell me about your cousin," he said quietly.

I stared at him. "Lucy?"

He smiled, and those intense, sea-blue eyes held mine. "Yes, Lucy. What's she like?"

"Well, I—she's—well, what exactly do you want to know?"

"Mmm, a little bit of everything. It surprises me that she's not married."

"Oh, well, she's—she's fairly busy."

Duncan's mouth twitched slightly. "Too busy to get married? I know she must spend a fair amount of time helping her aunt and uncle with our family home, but what else does she do?"

"She—uh, works for the libraries here on Whidbey. Nothing very important. Among other things, she reads stories to the elementary school students."

"And why isn't that important?"

I moistened my lips and gave him an expressive shrug that meant absolutely nothing. "Well, of course it's important, but—I—I think

Lucy probably feels that what she's doing doesn't make much difference in the world. You know, in the larger scheme of things. Please don't misunderstand me. I love my cousin, but she does lead rather a small life."

Duncan was silent for an uncomfortably long moment, his gaze on the fading light outside our window. When he spoke, his voice was so soft I could barely catch the words. "Wordsworth wrote a poem about another Lucy. In some ways she reminds me a lot of your cousin. How does it go? *She dwelt among the untrodden ways . . . a Maid whom there were none to praise, and very few to love. . . .*" His glance shifted from the twilight scene to meet mine. "I can't remember the rest, except for the last few lines. *She lived unknown and few could know when Lucy ceased to be . . . but oh, the difference to me!*" He paused, and the smile that touched his lips was no longer mocking, but quite gentle. "Perhaps, like Wordsworth's Lucy, your cousin makes much more of a difference than she realizes."

My eyes stung with unshed tears, and I silently cursed myself for being every kind of an idiot. I wanted desperately to tell him the truth, no matter how foolish I might seem, or what he might think of me. But right now, the tears were so close, and my throat was so tight, if I tried to say anything at all I knew I'd be lost.

"Duncan? Duncan, what a wonderful surprise!"

I glanced up with a start to see Caroline and Marius Charbot making their way toward our table, and my frayed emotions tightened into a worrisome knot. What if they recognized me as the clumsy server from their cocktail party the previous night? If they did, my charade as Bronwyn would be very short-lived indeed.

At the moment, neither one was paying any attention to me. Caroline's beaming smile was focused solely on her handsome brother. More than beaming. Something in her expression suggested a drowning man who had just been tossed a life preserver.

Marius' expression held surface politeness, but the glitter in those dark eyes was far from welcoming. Sleek and suave in a dark pin-stripe suit, he reminded me of a well-groomed black panther. The exact opposite of his wife's ethereal image in a dress of floaty, pearl-colored chiffon.

Duncan got to his feet, responding to his sister's greeting with a brotherly embrace.

"It's so wonderful to see you," she said again. "Why didn't you tell me you were coming?"

"I tried," Duncan answered, giving Marius a pointed look. "I called this afternoon, but—"

"Yes, and I'm afraid that's my fault," Marius interrupted, offering Duncan a welcoming hand. His smile was flawless. "When you called we were out with some friends of mine, art dealers from San Francisco. With the auction tomorrow, my focus has been more on business than it should."

"I'm so glad we ran into you," Caroline went on, taking her husband's arm. "We'd love to have you join us for dinner, wouldn't we, Marius?"

"Of course." There was no hesitation in his reply, but no warmth either.

Duncan stiffened slightly, then turned to me. Before he could say another word, Marius' smile and charm descended upon me.

"I can see why Duncan would want to keep you to himself, but I do hope you'll consent to join us, Miss—?"

"McBride," I answered smoothly. "Bronwyn McBride." I met his gaze with what I hoped was a gracious, but vaguely disinterested smile. There was distinct male interest in the look he gave me, but not the slightest hint of recognition. The previous night's uniform of "invisibility" had obviously blinded him to everything else.

Caroline Charbot glanced my way, taking note of me for the first time and a flicker of puzzled recognition registered in her lovely face. "Yes, do join us," she said. "I didn't mean to exclude you, but it's been ages since I've seen my brother."

Duncan smiled and put an affectionate arm about her slender shoulders. "It has been a long time."

Our server approached then, with a tray of deep-fried calamari. He glanced hesitantly at Duncan, but it was Marius who took charge of the moment.

"Mr. Alexander and Miss McBride will be joining us at my table. Would you please see to it that the extra places are set."

"Yes sir, Mr. Charbot."

Marius' table was in an alcove adjacent to and slightly elevated from the main dining area. A few steps above the common riffraff was how I'm sure he would view it, where the king could survey his domain, but not so far removed that the Inn's guests couldn't be afforded a generous glimpse of its handsome owner.

Marius immediately ordered champagne to celebrate the occasion, which I smilingly refused, as did Caroline.

"But how can I toast the two most beautiful women on the island, if you won't join me?" he complained.

Duncan's reaction was to sit stone-faced and silent, while Caroline looked suddenly nervous.

"I've always thought that a toast depends upon what's in the heart, rather than what's in the glass, wouldn't you agree?" I said, meeting Marius' dark eyes.

He chuckled and raised both hands in a gesture of submission.

before I saw the fleeting look in her eyes. The same look I had seen the night before when she practically begged me not to tell her husband about the bout with nausea.

"Even so, I refuse to talk about art and Bouguereau all evening," she went on. "Especially when Duncan's just arrived—not to mention our dinners."

"You're right," Marius agreed with an easy laugh. "I promise not to mention Bouguereau for the rest of the evening, but only on one condition."

Caroline's smile was a bit forced. "And the condition would be?"

"That Bronwyn and Duncan join us tomorrow afternoon for the auction, as our guests."

"That's a wonderful idea!" she said warmly, and turned to her brother with more than mere hopefulness in her eyes. The silent pleading I saw there bordered on desperation. "I do hope you can come."

"I'd love to," Duncan assured her, "but I'm not sure if Bronwyn has other plans."

I drew a shaky breath as my "tangled web" became more complicated still. "I have no special plans. It sounds delightful."

"It's settled then," Duncan said. "Thanks for the invitation, Marius."

Marius raised his glass and answered, "My pleasure," but his dark-eyed glance was focused solely on me.

Chapter Nine

Salvaging the Night

I don't know when I have experienced a more unnatural and uncomfortable evening. For the most part Duncan was stiff and silent, volunteering little to the conversation and responding to any direct questions with bare-bone answers. Caroline's smiles and laughter were a shade too bright, and Marius' charm slipped from smooth to slimy with each glass of champagne downed.

True to his word, the artist Bouguereau was not mentioned throughout the meal, but that didn't prevent Marius from discussing the upcoming auction and his current business dealings. Caroline made an occasional attempt to change the course of her husband's one-sided conversation, but somehow, Marius always managed to shift the subject back to where he wanted it—on himself.

Curiously, as Bronwyn, I had no difficulty responding to Marius' ego-inflated verbiage with the appropriate quip or question. It was obvious the man found himself so fascinating, it was beyond his ability to imagine someone else might feel differently—especially if that someone happened to be female. And this evening, I was the chosen recipient of his verbal narcissism. I was already regretting the reckless

Outside the Inn, Duncan paused long enough to ask, "Did you leave your car with the valet?"

My car. He was sure to recognize it as Lucy's. My mind shifted into high gear, trying to come up with a reasonable excuse that would keep Bronwyn's persona intact.

"Yes, but I'm in no hurry. I don't know what you had in mind, but I'd love to take a walk."

He gave a slight nod and the grip on my arm lessened slightly. "Good idea."

Away from the Inn, the evening air was soft with fragrance and blossom and a faint hint of the sea. I drew a welcome breath of its coolness, grateful to leave the stifling warmth and smells of rich food behind, as well as the pretense and forced politeness of dealing with the Charbots.

The Moonraker had been built on a steep, curving edge of shoreline, with the little town of Langley spread out below and the watery arms of the Saratoga Passage beyond. Not far from the Inn's southern side, an asphalt path wound down the hillside to a sheltered cove and pebbly beach. Halfway down, the steepness of the descent leveled out into a grassy knoll and here, a rustic bench and picnic table had been tucked against the hillside. I knew the spot well. Since Langley's library was barely a block away, I often visited the place for my lunch break or a short walk. Attempting the steep path in near darkness, wearing three-inch heels presented something of a challenge, but I silently assured myself that Bronwyn was up to it.

Duncan's hand on my arm was firm as we headed down the path, and there was still a bit of anger evident in his touch. My own emotions were a tangled mixture of frustration and disappointment. The evening had turned out nothing like I had hoped or imagined. Instead of enjoying Duncan's company, I'd had to play the role of adoring guest, catering to Marius Charbot's vanity and none too subtle attentions. A small light bulb of realization suddenly lit up inside me. Might Duncan's sullen silence throughout the evening have something to do with Marius' attentions to Bronwyn? Along with the obvious dislike of his brother-in-law, was there perhaps a smidge of jealousy motivating his behavior? However pleasant the possibility might be, I couldn't dismiss the feeling there was something else— some deeper worry—and the source of that worry centered on his sister Caroline.

I stumbled suddenly and pitched forward as my right foot encountered a skiff of sand and pebbles. Duncan quickly stepped in front of me, and reached out to grab my arms. His swift reaction did more than prevent a potentially nasty fall. All in an instant I was pulled close against him, and my flailing hands now rested on his chest.

"Are you all right?" he asked, his voice a shade huskier than usual.

"Yes, I think so."

It was a strange moment, colored with conflicting emotions. We stood there on the path, facing one another in the near darkness, his hands still gripping my arms. Looking up at the dark blur of his face, I wasn't sure whether to curse or bless those three-inch heels. Mortified as I was by my clumsiness, I couldn't help reveling in the warmth of his nearness and the feel of his taut, firm muscles beneath my palms.

His head bent closer and my lips parted in breathless anticipation of his kiss. The next moment he let go of me with an abruptness that was more stunning than my near fall.

"Those shoes of yours weren't made for hikes down a hillside," he said gruffly. "We'd better turn back."

"Actually, I think I need to sit down."

I forced my shaking legs over to the nearby bench and slumped down, wrapping the folds of my shawl more closely about me.

Duncan stood for a moment, not speaking, then joined me on the bench. "Are you sure you're all right?"

"I'm fine," I said, my voice sounding brittle in my ears.

The night's only sounds were the quiet lap of water pulsing against the shore, and an occasional car driving by in the distance. Far across the dark water, I could see the lights of the ferry as it made its nightly journey from the mainland to Whidbey. The white lights gliding across the blackness of the sea were like a caravan of earth-bound stars.

I turned my gaze from the night's soft beauty to Duncan Alexander's intimidating profile. "Are you still angry with me?" I asked quietly.

He didn't answer right away. When he did speak, his voice was tight with control. "And why would I be angry with you?"

"Oh, maybe because you think I'm foolish enough to be taken in by your brother-in-law's insufferable ego."

"And weren't you?" he demanded, turning to face me. "Taken in, as you said? It looked to me as if you were hanging on to his every word."

"I suppose it did look that way," I began, "but I was only giving him what he expected and—"

"What?" he exploded. "Just what kind of game were you playing? Marius couldn't keep his eyes off you all night. Don't tell me you weren't aware that he was coming on to you."

"I was very much aware," I said, my voice shaking a little. "And I was also aware how worried and uncomfortable your sister was. Look, I don't know what the problem is, but I do know it has nothing to do with me. If it didn't sound so far-fetched, I'd say that she's—" I broke off, tortured with what I knew and couldn't reveal from the cocktail party the previous evening.

"Go on," he urged, the anger leaving his voice. "What were you going to say?"

"Only that I think she's frightened—as well as desperately unhappy."

"Frightened. . . ."

He left the word hanging and I blurted out, "Of Marius! Couldn't you tell? Granted, he's nearly perfected the devoted husband act, but if you scrape away that smooth surface charm, I think you'd find something very ugly inside." I gave a little shudder that had nothing to do with the cool night air. "I'm sorry I gave you the wrong impression. Truly, I am . . . I—I guess I thought it might take a little pressure off you and Caroline if I kept Marius' attention focused on other things—" I broke off, realizing my response had been totally Lucy and not Bronwyn at all.

"And I'm sorry for blowing up at you like that," Duncan said, his voice gruff with embarrassment. "You might say this has been one hell of a night—not exactly what I had in mind. . . ."

I sighed and nodded. "It wasn't what I expected either."

"It's not too late to salvage what's left," he said and took my face in his hands.

For a first kiss, there was nothing very gentle or romantic about it. The frustration from "one hell of a night" was certainly there, along with fierce, male ownership, as if he were bent on claiming what was rightfully his. And I was. Lost in the rapture of the moment, conscious thought played no part in my response to him. All I wanted was for this swirling new universe of emotion to go on and on. . . .

Chapter Ten

Crumbs & Cake

A determined pounding combined with an annoying ringing jerked me out of an exhausted sleep and I turned over with a groan. I blinked and tried to focus sleep-glazed eyes on the clock sitting on my night table, while the insistent ringing went on, followed by more pounding. Seven-fifty. Who on earth could be here at this hour?

I grabbed my robe, and stuffing my arms into the sleeves, ran barefoot down the stairs. My heart was pounding almost as hard as the persistent knocking as my thoughts leaped from one potential tragedy to another. Had something happened to Uncle Milt and Aunt Ivy? From the sound of that frantic knocking, I was certain that someone must be dead or dying.

"I'm coming—all right, I'm coming!" I called and quickly unlocked the door.

Peggy Gamble stood on the front porch, looking something like a pretty pink Easter egg in hot pink sweats, with her hair in curlers and her face flushed with exertion.

"Peggy! What's wrong? What are you doing here?"

"What am I doing here? You promised you'd call me as soon as you got back from your date. Remember? I waited until after midnight, then Gary made me come to bed. Lucy, how could you do this to me? I've been dying to know what happened."

"Oh, Peggy . . . I'm so sorry. I know I promised I'd call, but—" I shook my head and raised both hands in a helpless shrug. "Come on in."

She bustled inside, curiosity bursting in her face.

"Let's go out to the kitchen," I said. "Have you had breakfast?"

"Breakfast! How am I supposed to eat anything? I left Gary and the boys in the middle of destroying my kitchen making pancakes and scrambled eggs. I would have called, but I had to see for myself if you were still alive or if you and Duncan had run off to Las Vegas."

I pulled out a kitchen chair and sank down with a groan, leaning both elbows on the table. "I don't know where to begin. I'm sorry I ever asked you about the make-over."

"Why? Did he recognize you?"

"No . . . no, he believes I'm Bronwyn," I said dismally.

Peggy went to the refrigerator and got out a carton of orange juice, then grabbed two glasses from the cupboard. After so many years, Aunt Ivy's kitchen was as familiar as her own.

"Well, isn't that what you wanted?"

"I thought it was, but everything's gotten so complicated."

"How complicated?" she asked, pouring us both a glass of juice. When I didn't answer immediately, she sat down and plunked the glass in front of me. "Lucy, whatever it is, you know you can tell me—you don't have to tell me—but unless you want me to die by inches, I think you'd better tell me."

"All right, but—"

"Did he kiss you?" she burst out before I could go on.

I shook my head and said miserably, "No . . . he kissed Bronwyn."

Her lips parted and a slight frown creased her brow. "But that's you . . . right?"

"Yes, but Duncan doesn't know that. I should have told him the truth right from the beginning. I hated lying to him. It was horrible. Which is really kind of interesting, because it was so easy to lie to Marius."

Orange juice sloshed against the sides of her glass, and her blue eyes widened. "You don't mean *the* Marius?"

I nodded. "None other. Duncan and I had dinner with him and Caroline, who also happens to be Duncan's sister."

Peggy slumped against the back of the chair, her eyes looking a little glazed. "And did they—did they know who you were?"

"No, they think I'm Bronwyn McBride, an art dealer from Seattle."

"What! Lucy, are you crazy?"

I shrugged and gave her a helpless grin. "I told you it was complicated."

"It's more than complicated. I'm starting to feel positively weak."

"There are some cinnamon rolls in the bread box. Help yourself."

"All right, and then I want you to start from the beginning—and don't leave anything out!"

Two cinnamon rolls later, Peggy leaned back against her chair and sighed. "So what are you going to do now?"

"What can I do? Duncan will be picking me up around three, and somehow I'll have to fake my way through a smarmy afternoon with Marius at the art auction."

"And then what? Are you going to tell Duncan the truth?"

"For rushing you away without a hello or telling you how beautiful you look."

"That's all right . . . I mean, thank you." Cheeks burning, I got into the car. Get a grip, I told myself. Bronwyn would never be flustered by a simple compliment. But it wasn't just the words or his voice. The man looked and smelled positively wonderful. A far cry from Norman Phillips' pudgy figure with that shuddering scent of mediciny mouthwash. I stole a sideways glance at Duncan as we drove away. Beige slacks and a tweed jacket in muted blues and grays; his white shirt a stark contrast against the tanned skin of his face and throat, not to mention the thick blackness of his hair. I drew a shaky breath and forced myself to look straight ahead.

Neither of us spoke for a few minutes. Coupeville's quaint nineteenth-century homes and outlying farms were behind us when he said without apology or preamble, "I suppose you couldn't help noticing that my brother-in-law and I don't exactly get along."

"He hides it better than you do, but yes, I noticed."

Duncan acknowledged this with a crooked smile. "The first time I met Marius, my gut feeling was that the guy was a liar and a phony. I could care less about his money and his hotels, and he knew it. That, plus the fact I was against him marrying my sister, didn't exactly put me in his good graces."

I sat very still, thinking, *Marius is not the only one who's a liar and a phony. Tell him. Tell him right now.* Instead I heard myself asking in a small voice, "Why were you against the marriage?"

He shrugged. "Believe me, I used to ask myself the same question. On the surface, it seemed like an ideal match. Caroline was head over heels in love, and even my parents were enamored with the man. Naturally, my father was impressed with Marius' financial assets, and my mother was totally taken in by his looks and cultured charm. I tried to tell myself I should be happy for my sister, but something about the guy just didn't feel right. Like I said, inside, I thought Marius was a liar and a phony, so I decided to do a little investigating." He paused long enough to give me a cryptic side-long glance, then said, "Up until ten years ago, Marius Charbot was Mark Cabot, a poor boy from the wrong side of New Orleans."

I stared at him, heart pounding, my clutched hands clammy in my lap. *Up until one day ago Bronwyn McBride was Lucy Norris, a poor librarian from Coupeville.* "Mark Cabot?" I repeated. "How on earth did you find that out?"

"It took some time, but it wasn't too difficult. Initially, all I knew about Marius' background was that he came from New Orleans and had been married once before. One of my tall ship cruises happened to take me around the Gulf of Mexico, and ended up in New Orleans. So while I was in port, I basically made a nuisance of myself and asked a lot of questions. One source led to another, and the pieces began to fall into place.

"Marius, or rather Mark as he was known then, used to work for one of New Orleans' pricier hotels and gaming establishments. His job and his looks gave him plenty of opportunity to mingle with the guests. He was especially popular with the women—wealthy older women. In a year's time, thirty-year old Mark had married fifty-something Rosalyn Sutter, a widow who was the sole inheritor of her late husband's billion-dollar hotel business. Rosalyn conveniently died five years later—and Marius Charbot appeared on the scene not long after."

My own deception suddenly seemed quite harmless by comparison, and I couldn't help asking, "How did she die?"

Duncan gave me a quick, telling glance. "I know what you're thinking. Believe me, when I found out about the woman's death, suspects anything—he's always been very possessive where Caroline's concerned—but ever since I arrived, he's made damn good and sure that I haven't had so much as five minutes alone with my sister. I went to the house Friday night and was told that Caroline was still in Seattle and wouldn't be arriving until Saturday."

"He was lying!" I burst out, then, as Duncan shot me a curious look, hurriedly amended my words. "I mean, he must have been lying. If Marius is that possessive, it doesn't make sense that he and Caroline would arrive separately."

"I agree, but there wasn't much I could do about it, except come back the next afternoon. This time, they were both gone. Marius' so-called chauffeur and all-purpose watchdog met me at the door and said they were out with friends, and he didn't know when they would return. Meeting them at the restaurant last night was a fortunate accident, but as you know, Caroline and I had no time to talk privately. If it hadn't been for Marius wanting to see you again, we never would have received that invitation to join them at the auction. Even so, I knew it wouldn't give me any time alone with Caroline, so I stopped by their house again this afternoon."

"What happened?"

"Marius answered the door and when I asked to see Caroline, he said she wasn't feeling well; that she was taking a nap. He hated to disturb her and would I mind postponing our visit until later this afternoon at the auction." Anger heated his voice and the muscles tightened in his jaw. "I felt like taking him out right then," he admitted, "but for Caroline's sake, I tried to keep my cool."

I felt my own anger rising, along with tight-edged worry. "You know he'll find a way to keep Caroline away from you at the auction."

"Yes, I know," he said heavily.

Chapter Eleven

Sugary Cottages & Lovely Nudes

Once more, Bronwyn McBride entered the Moonraker Inn, head held high, eyes shining, her demeanor poised and confident. But unlike the evening before, today's confidence was not part of an assumed persona. And the swarm of butterflies dancing inside me had more to do with euphoric afterglow than nervousness. Releasing a shaky sigh, I forced myself to concentrate on the task at hand. Only moments before, I'd left Duncan at the library, where he would wait ten minutes before making his way to the Inn's service entrance down a small alley on the north side of the building. Ten minutes should be ample time for me to find Marius and Caroline, do a quick meet and greet, and surreptitiously pass her the note Duncan had written. Then, while I entertained Marius, Caroline could slip away and meet her brother just inside the service entrance. If all went as planned, she should be back in plenty of time to rescue me from her husband before the auction started. A few minutes into the auction, I would make my excuses, bid the Charbots a fond farewell and meet Duncan in front of the library. And then? I had no idea. Whatever happened after that depended largely on Caroline herself.

I stopped briefly at the front desk to pick up a list of the various pieces on today's auction, then headed down a hallway toward the conference rooms. The auction was scheduled to begin in little less than half an hour, and the place was crowded with visitors, guests, and locals. Whidbey's annual Art Fest is a popular event with artists and art lovers alike, but this was the first year there had been a formal auction. Marius himself was sponsoring the event, with the Moonraker providing the venue for artists' works.

I was nearing the first conference room when the sight of Kathryn Parker, Langley's head librarian, brought me up short. Averting my face, I feigned interest in a mediocre marine painting of rocky shoals and flat, leaden sky. Thankfully, Kathryn was too absorbed in conversation with a patron to notice me, but her presence was an uncomfortable reminder. Besides dealing with the Charbots, the likelihood of seeing familiar faces in today's throng was yet another sticky problem. All I needed was for some friend or acquaintance to call out a greeting to Lucy while Bronwyn was occupied with Marius, and I would be faced with some very awkward explanations.

I waited until Kathryn had moved down the hall, then approached the conference room. Standing beside the open doorway was a huge hulk of a man with a shaved head and a bristly goatee and mustache. There was an aggressive, cocky look of self importance in the way he stood, legs slightly apart, with those beefy arms folded across his massive chest. Put him in a pair of outrageous tights instead of tan slacks and a golf shirt, and he'd be an ideal poster child for the World Wrestling Federation. Casting that occupation aside, I decided he must be part of the Inn's security force. What on earth was he expecting? I wondered, noting the glint of suspicion in his eyes as they flicked over the crowd. It wasn't as if there would be any Rembrandts or Picassos up for bid.

Apparently, I must have passed muster, because after giving me a brief, scowling glance, the man turned his attention elsewhere.

Inside the conference room, artwork in various mediums had been numbered and displayed on easels and the walls. Seascapes, landscapes, portraits and sculptures vied for viewers' attention on every side. Some works were obviously done by hopeful amateurs, but others were breath-taking in their scope and presentation. At the far end, a partition dividing the two conference rooms had been opened, doubling the available space.

I threaded my way through loosely woven clusters of art lovers, feeling the seconds ticking away as I searched for Marius and Caroline. The people in attendance were as varied and eclectic as the works of art themselves. Three-piece suits conversed with tee-shirts and faded jeans. Sedate women in polyester and pearls looked askance at the younger set with their bare midriffs and bottom-hugging jeans. In the midst of the melee, I recognized a few faces from the Charbots' cocktail party. The windstorm woman was there with bracelets jangling and that incredible storm-tossed hair. And as feared, there were others, even more familiar. At first glance, I saw several patrons of the library and students from the local high school. So far, everyone was either too absorbed in the art work or conversation with friends to pay me much attention.

Then I saw them. Marius was standing near a podium in the next room, engrossed in conversation with a bearded man who towered over him by several inches. As usual, Marius was the epitome of casual elegance in sleek navy and spotless white, while the bearded man at his side resembled a rumpled French beatnik from a bygone era. Not twenty feet away, Caroline and an elegant, fiftyish woman with stiff blonde hair were examining a fanciful painting of Shakespeare's fairy queen Titania and her dark lord Oberon.

I took Duncan's note from my jacket pocket and clutching it tightly, headed in Caroline's direction. All I needed was for the large faux Frenchman to block Marius' vision a few moments longer, and I would be at her side. I was close enough now that the women's conversation had shifted from wordless pantomime to audible sentences, modernism vs. academic realism being the topic of discussion.

"It's understandable that the Impressionists would create such a furor in the art world," the stiff blonde was telling Caroline. "Particularly when the craft of 19th century picture making followed basic principles of academic theory. . . ."

As yet, Caroline wasn't aware of my presence, but I swear Marius must have some kind of uncanny radar, because he stepped to one side and the next moment those dark eyes had me locked in their sight. All I could do was smile and nod. He acknowledged the gesture with a significant nod of his own and a lengthy stare that set my pulse pounding.

There was no time to hesitate or ponder my approach. Waltzing straight up to Caroline, I interrupted the two women with a smiling, "Hello. Don't you just love James Christensen's work? This is one of my favorites."

Caroline turned to me with a polite smile. "Bronwyn . . . hello. It's lovely to see you." She looked beyond me with a puzzled frown and I knew she must be wondering where her brother was. "Mrs. Abernathy, this is Bronwyn McBride, a friend of my brother's and an art dealer from Seattle. Bronwyn, Judith Abernathy."

Mrs. Abernathy pursed her thin lips and fixed me with a scrutinizing look; the expression in her clever brown eyes part curious, part disapproving that I had the temerity to intrude. "Miss McBride. Since you're an admirer of Mr. Christensen's work, might I assume that you have an opinion on modernism vs. classical realism?"

"I—uh, yes, of course, but I think an event like this lends itself to sheer enjoyment more than scholarly opinions." Out of the corner of my eye, I saw Marius heading our way and a shock of nervous panic shot through me. Taking Caroline by the hand, I pressed the folded note into her palm. "I'm sorry Duncan couldn't be here," I said, giving her a significant look, "but he sends his regards." Her blue eyes widened as she stared at me, and I went on quickly, "You look so lovely . . . just like a Monet watercolor."

"What's this about a Monet watercolor?" Marius asked, joining us with an engaging smile. "I thought he painted exclusively in oil. Have you made a discovery I should know about?"

"I—uh, was referring to your wife," I said, giving him an especially warm smile to cover my blunder. "And you made that discovery long ago."

"That's true, I did." Marius slipped an arm about Caroline's shoulders and acknowledged Mrs. Abernathy's presence with a gracious nod before saying, "Good afternoon, Bronwyn."

"Good afternoon, Mr. Charbot."

The dark eyes glittered and his smooth voice was slightly mocking. "I thought we agreed you should call me Marius," he said, then glanced around with casual concern. "And I thought my brother-in-law would be with you."

"Something came up. Some business matter that obviously couldn't wait," I answered with a careless shrug, then glanced from Marius to Caroline who was clutching the note tightly in one hand. "Rather than miss the auction, I decided to come by myself. I hope that's all right."

"Of course it's all right." Marius was quick to reassure me, and the look in his eyes said a good deal more. Turning to his wife, he went on as if her consideration was all that mattered. "Will you forgive me, darling, if I abandon you ladies for a few minutes? There are a few paintings that I especially wanted Bronwyn to see before the auction gets underway."

Caroline's answering smile was warm. "Please, go right ahead. I need to make a quick trip to the ladies' room, anyway. If you'll excuse me," she said and walked away.

I released a tense breath along with a silent prayer of thanks, and it took all my control not to watch her go.

"Mrs. Abernathy," Marius said, giving the woman a sugary dose of charm, along with a melting smile. "I was just discussing the merits of Arthur Hughes and other Pre-Raphaelites with that tall gentleman near the podium. My knowledge is sadly lacking in that area, but I'm sure he could benefit from your expertise."

"Do you really think so?" Mrs. Abernathy's rigid demeanor softened noticeably.

Marius nodded, adding in velvet tones, "You'd be doing me a favor."

Watching the woman sail away toward another hapless victim, I had to smile. "Now there's a lethal combination," I said. "I don't know which one to pity more—Mrs. Abernathy, or your friend, the giant Toulouse-Lautrec."

Marius tossed back his head and laughed and I felt his hand on my elbow. "Bronwyn, you have just saved me from an excruciatingly boring afternoon. Would you be very shocked if I told you how glad I am that Duncan had business elsewhere?"

I swallowed hard and thought, *Let the game begin.* "Not shocked at all," I answered, meeting his eyes. "Would you be shocked if I told you how much I've been looking forward to this afternoon?"

His dark eyes smoldered and the grip on my elbow tightened, then strayed to my arm. "Not shocked, but very delighted," he said softly.

Leaving Titania and her fairy court behind, Marius led me back to the first conference room. For a few moments the experience seemed slightly surreal, like the brush strokes of an Impressionistic painting. I was vaguely aware of interested glances and the turning of heads that accompanied our passage through the room. Pictures and portraits blurred and blended as we walked, seeming no more than splashes of color on easel and wall, while my senses reacted with prickly awareness to the oppressive touch of his hand on my arm and the velvet tone of his voice.

Marius paused beside a rather bland scene of a cozy country cottage, complete with picket fence and pink roses, and all in an instant, the surreal shifted into sharp-edged reality. Standing not two feet away were two teachers from Langley's elementary school, whose classes had attended my story session at the library only days before. Somehow, I managed to keep my attention on Marius, while my nerves jumped as if they'd landed on a live wire.

The two women glanced at, then through me, and moved on their way. I knew from their slightly puzzled expressions that my face looked familiar, but our surroundings and circumstances were completely foreign. And the flicker of admiration that I glimpsed in their eyes was obviously intended for the Art Fest's handsome host. Relief had me suddenly weak-kneed and grateful for Marius' supporting hand.

"What do you think of this one?" he asked, indicating the country cottage portrayed in all its bucolic sweetness. "Is it the type of thing one of your clients might enjoy? And please don't let the fact that the artist is a personal friend of mine influence your opinion."

I gave the syrupy scene a moment's study, not sure if he were testing or merely toying with me. "I suppose it has possibilities," I said. "Especially if the client happened to be a dentist and needed something innocuous for his office. No, better make him a doctor instead. This one is a bit too sweet for a dentist."

"Touché," he said, chuckling softly.

"Oh, but this one. . . ." My breath came out in a sigh of pure pleasure as I turned from the sugary cottage to a haunting watercolor. Moving out of ghostly gray mist, with the tips of its mast finding a stray shaft of sunlight, was a tall ship. The surrounding sea was a mysterious wash of muted color. Looking closer, I discovered the artist was one of the students at the high school that I'd often seen at the library, his arms loaded with books on seascapes and marine painting.

"This one appeals to you?" Marius asked with interest.

"Very much," I said, remembering the moment I'd seen another tall ship as it sailed beneath the bridge at Deception Pass.

"I have to agree, the artist shows promise," he allowed. "Is it one you'd consider for a client, or yourself?"

I hesitated, trying to conjure up a mythical client, and Norman Phillips suddenly came to mind.

"The particular client I'm thinking of probably wouldn't care for it. His soul is decidedly lacking in romance."

"But yours isn't."

My gaze lifted from the watercolor to meet Marius' dark eyes, my only answer an enigmatic smile.

"If you really like it, I'll make a point of bidding on this one," he said. "But it won't be for your client. Consider it a gift—from one romantic soul to another."

"That's very generous. I—I don't know what to say."

"You don't need to say anything. That charming blush says it all quite nicely," he said, leading me away from the watercolor to an earthy portrait of a near-naked woman surveying her lithesome body in a full-length mirror.

"And what about this one?" he asked, his voice slightly mocking. "Does it speak to you?"

I cleared my throat. "Well, the flesh tones are quite lovely."

Amusement danced in his dark eyes. "As I said, you have a most becoming blush." Then, moving a step closer, his gaze grew increasingly intent. "I know this must sound like I'm handing you a line, but—I still can't get over the feeling I've seen you somewhere before."

"Really? I can't imagine where."

The next moment his dark brows shot up and the grip on my arm tightened. "I know where I've seen you!"

"You do?" My heart plummeted somewhere in the region of my stomach, and I braced myself for the thudding possibility that my little charade was over.

Marius nodded, his smile sleek with satisfaction. "Bouguereau painted you over a century ago. It's amazing, really, the resemblance between you and the woman in one of his paintings. *Evening Mood.* Since you enjoy Bouguereau's work, I'm sure you must be familiar with it. It's one of his most famous nudes. The combination of innocence and sensuality, with the promise of passion . . . it's all there."

Along with weak-kneed relief, I felt an uncomfortable wave of disgust. Words were beyond me. It was all I could do to manage a faint nod. Thankfully, the wind-storm woman chose that moment to blow our way. Ignoring me completely, she took Marius' arm in a chummy grip.

"Marius, darling, I've been looking for you everywhere," she cooed. "I can't find those wicked little sketches you told me about." Giving me a pointed little smile she said, "You don't mind if I borrow Marius, do you?"

Marius disengaged himself with a polite smile that was totally lacking in warmth. "You might try looking near the end of the main hall," he told her. "Now, if you'll excuse me—"

I felt a moment's pity for the woman, seeing how quickly he had literally taken the wind out of her sails.

"Now then, where were we?" he said after she had drifted away into the crowd. "Ah yes. I believe we were discussing the provocative resemblance between you and one of Bouguereau's lovely nudes."

"Thanks for the compliment," I said carelessly, "but I don't think you've seen enough of me to make a fair comparison."

Leaning closer, his voice purred in my ear, "My dear Bronwyn, that is a minor technicality which can easily be rectified."

After putting more than my foot in it, I thought it best not to reply to this last comment. Especially when my "charming blush," as he put it, was probably all too evident.

Taking my arm once more, Marius moved through the crowd, turning now and then to acknowledge the smile or nod of some acquaintance.

A young man and woman edged past us, their pale faces and dark clothes stark sermons of the Goth culture.

"They don't look very happy, do they?" I commented, hoping to steer the conversation onto safer ground. "It makes me wonder why anyone so young would want to wear a shroud of darkness on a day like today."

Marius said nothing. Instead, he paused beside the bronze

sculpture of two bull elk, their horns locked in fierce combat. "I'm flying to Mazatlan the day after tomorrow," he told me, his gaze intent on the sculpture.

"Oh. Business or pleasure?"

"I'd like to think there's the possibility of both." Reaching into his jacket, he took out a pen and small business card, then wrote something on the back. "Caroline and I will be staying in the penthouse at El Cid, but you can reach me at this number any time." Dark eyes glittering, he placed the card in my hand and closed my palm around it.

I stared blindly at the battling elk, feeling the edges of the card sharp against my palm. Where was Caroline? If she didn't return soon, I wasn't at all sure how much longer I could go on playing this nerve-tangling game of innuendo. Then, from who knows where or why, an image suddenly came to mind, and I saw the Lady Dona with twelve men seated at her banquet table. Laughing and flirting, plying them with sweet wine and even sweeter smiles, Dona kept them enthralled, detaining the men from their deadly mission to capture her lover. I drew a determined breath. If Lady Dona could handle a dozen loutish Englishmen bent on murder, surely I could manage one Mark Cabot from the sleazy side of New Orleans. Every minute I spent with him was one more minute Duncan would have with Caroline.

"The prospect sounds intriguing," I said, forcing myself to meet his gaze. "But I really don't know if I can manage to get away."

His hand lightly caressed my arm. "If you can manage to get away, I think I could manage to make it worth your while."

Over Marius' shoulder, I saw the frowning approach of the security man who had been guarding the entrance.

"Mr. Charbot, could I see you for a minute."

"Not now, Rafferty."

The big man gave Marius a respectful nod, but stood his ground. "I'm sorry to interrupt, but there's a problem you should know about."

"Whatever it is, I'm sure you can handle it," Marius answered, cold dismissal in his voice.

The man gave me a cursory glance and shrugged. "Yes, sir." He turned as if to go, then said, "Would you like me to arrange for an extra seat next to you and Mrs. Charbot at the auction? Duncan's here and he's been having a nice long talk with your wife."

Marius stiffened and for the briefest of moments, I saw the mask slip. Anger, black and seething, roiled to the surface, altering the handsome canvas of his face. Then he was back in character, all politeness and control.

"Thank you, Rafferty." Turning to me, he managed a stiff smile then glanced at his watch. "I'm sorry to rush off, but I think I'd better remind Caroline that the auction's about to start." His smile broadened but lost none of its stiffness. "Once she and Duncan get talking, they lose all track of time. Will you excuse me, dear?"

"Of course."

And with that, he turned and followed the man Rafferty into the crowd.

Chapter Twelve

The Key

Troublesome questions teased and tormented my thoughts as I watched the two men go. Rafferty. What was it Duncan had called him? *Marius' chauffeur and all-purpose watchdog.* How much had he seen and overheard? If the man's frowning expression were any indication, Duncan and Caroline might be facing a very unpleasant confrontation when he and Marius arrived on the scene.

For a long moment, I stood there in the crowded room, not knowing what to do, while nerves and worry pounded a jerky rhythm inside me. Then the auctioneer took his place at the podium, announcing the auction would begin shortly, and asking guests to please take their seats. I joined the slow-moving masses as those planning to attend drifted into the adjoining room where rows of folding chairs had been set up. Finding an empty chair on the aisle near the back, I sat down with a tense sigh. There was nothing to do now but wait.

Not five minutes later, Marius and Caroline made their entrance, walking straight past me on their way to the front of the room. Marius was all poise and polish, acknowledging the small burst of applause that greeted their arrival with a nod and smile, but his grip on Caroline's arm was tight as a vice. Caroline's public persona was perfectly in place, ever gracious if slightly remote, with that air of refinement a bit on the cool side. But there was something in her eyes and the way she stared straight ahead with a brittle sort of concentration. In an unguarded moment, I thought I saw her chin tremble. Then her head lifted proudly, and I wondered if I had only imagined it after all.

As the Charbots took their seats near the podium, I glanced over my shoulder toward the exit door and saw Rafferty leaning against the back wall, a look of smug satisfaction twisting his bearded mouth.

Sheer determination kept me in my seat as the chairman of Langley's Arts Council gave his welcoming speech, and when Marius' dark-eyed glance found mine, Bronwyn managed a little smile and slight tilt of her head. Inside, my stomach was churning and I wanted nothing more than to run out of that room and find Duncan.

Three paintings and an unidentifiable object of twisted metal had been auctioned off before I felt I could leave without attracting any undue attention. Looking neither to the right or left, I made my way to the exit and walked past Rafferty without giving the man a second glance.

Once outside, I turned away from the Inn and headed down the walk-way which would take me to the library. My hurried steps were in sharp contrast to the leisurely pace of strolling couples, laughing teens and ambling clusters of senior citizens who passed by. The activities of the Art Fest had brought Langley's citizens out *en masse*, transforming what ordinarily would have been a sleepy Sunday afternoon. Cars were parked in every available spot along the curving stretch of road, and when I reached the corner where Langley's small library sat amidst a bower of blossoming trees, there was no sign of Duncan.

I stood for a moment, my thoughts darting from one worrisome possibility to another. Then a gray sedan approached from a side street, and worry faded into relief when I saw Duncan behind the wheel.

"The only parking place I could find was a couple of blocks away," he explained, reaching across the seat to open the car door. "Have you been waiting long?"

"No, I just got here."

"Are you all right?" he asked as I got inside.

I am now, I thought, meeting his concerned glance with a nod and a little smile. With him, I felt safe again. Safe and certain that somehow, all would be well.

"We need to talk," he said, "but not here. Are you hungry?"

I nodded, suddenly realizing that part of the weakness I felt was due to hunger as well as relief. In fact, I hadn't had anything to eat since that glass of orange juice with Peggy early this morning.

"I'm open to suggestions," he said. "Do you know a place nearby where we won't be interrupted or overheard?"

"Most of the restaurants will be pretty crowded, but we could go to a deli and pick up some sandwiches and drinks. I know several places on the drive back where we could stop and eat in the car, if that's all right."

He gave me a grateful glance. "It's more than all right."

Ten minutes later, we were parked on a secluded side road a few miles outside Langley. Behind us was the protective shield of old growth forest; to the right, a small hollow, thick with ferns and rotting logs. And off to the left, a fenced pasture where three horses grazed.

Except for an occasional car passing by on the main road, the silence was profound.

There was something infinitely calming in the simple act of sharing a meal. Hoagie buns stuffed with thin slices of roast beef, cheese, and tangy mustard. Salty potato chips and sweet clusters of green grapes. Simple fare that tasted like food for the gods. We fell upon the food as if half-starved, drinking in the peaceful silence of the place, along with our Diet Cokes, and postponing any conversation or discussion until the last morsel was gone.

I felt Duncan's watchful glance on my face as I stuffed the wrappings and empty cans into a sack and put them aside. When I met his gaze, he said nothing for a long moment, just raked a hand through the tangled darkness of his hair.

"It's hard to know where to begin," he told me with a frustrated sigh. "None of this is your problem, and here I am, dumping a mess of dirty laundry in your lap."

"You're not dumping. And I want to help . . . if I can."

The worry in his eyes softened as he looked at me. "You already have," he said quietly, and reached for my hand.

I smiled at him, feeling a warm surge of happiness as his long fingers closed around mine, then glanced down, afraid he would read too much in my eyes. "I hope you had enough time to talk with Caroline."

"Enough to know that I need to get her away from Marius, and soon. I was trying to convince her to leave him when he and Rafferty showed up."

"What happened?"

"Not much. At least on the surface. One look at Marius' face told me he was furious, but I knew he'd never risk making a scene in public. Instead, he managed to make Caroline feel guilty because the auction was about to start and he couldn't find her." Duncan blew out a tight breath and shook his head. "Watching her walk away with him was not a good moment. Especially after what she told me." He gave me a careful look. "Are you sure you don't mind if I do some more dumping? There's a lot I need to sort through."

"Very sure."

He nodded. "All right, then."

Calmly, deliberately, making no attempt to varnish or water down, Duncan recounted his sister's situation; how in recent months her concerns had grown into suspicions, and vague doubts had become fears.

"What Caroline thought was loving concern and protectiveness, was in fact, Marius' obsessive need for control," he told me. "The situation had escalated to the point where Caroline realized she was being watched and followed by Marius' chauffeur, Duke Rafferty."

"But why? What is Marius afraid of?"

"That's what Caroline wants to know. She's worried it might have something to do with Philip Delaney's death."

"Philip Delaney?"

"Marius' business partner and financial advisor. Two weeks ago, his body was found in San Francisco Bay. Apparently, he'd been reported missing for almost that long before the body was discovered. The news treated it as a suicide, but from what Caroline told me, Delaney's death is still under investigation."

Whispered comments from the cocktail party came back in a worrisome flood. *Poor Philip . . . the police said it was suicide, but one always wonders . . .*

"Does Caroline believe it was suicide?" I asked.

Duncan shook his head. "She doesn't know, but she has enough doubts to make her afraid. A few days before he disappeared, Delaney came to Caroline and gave her the key to a safe deposit box. He said he wanted her to have it in case anything happened to him. That could mean one of two things—either Delaney was contemplating suicide, or he was fearful that his life might be in danger. To make matters worse, Delaney had a meeting with Marius at their home in San Francisco the same night he supposedly jumped off the Bay Bridge."

I blew out a tight breath. "Do the police know about this meeting?"

"Yes, and they questioned both Caroline and Marius. According to Marius, Delaney seemed agitated and worried that evening. Marius told police he'd been concerned about the man's mental and emotional state for some time. That Delaney had been drinking heavily in recent weeks and wasn't himself."

"And did Caroline agree with that?"

"Basically, yes. She wasn't present during the meeting, and she didn't know about his drinking, but she agreed that Delaney was definitely worried about something. After their meeting, she overheard the two arguing as Delaney was leaving the house. You already know about Marius' plans to purchase an old hacienda outside Mazatlan. Caroline said he's become obsessed with the idea. Well, Delaney was totally against it. He told Marius the place was too rundown and too far away from the tourist business to be profitable, but Marius refused to listen."

And I knew why. Bouguereau's *The Fairy Thorn.* Aloud, I said, "Did Caroline mention any of this to the police?"

"Actually, yes, which is quite amazing considering that Marius was present at the time. Marius just brushed the whole thing off, and said it was nothing. That it wasn't unusual for the two of them to butt heads from time to time over business decisions. Obviously, the police must agree with his story. At least, there's no evidence or motive strong enough to indicate otherwise."

"But what about the key to the safe deposit box? Surely the fact Delaney wanted Caroline to have it means something. Did she give it to the police?"

"No, unfortunately. She knows she should have, but Caroline had her own worries at the time." Duncan's grim look softened. "That was the week my sister found out she was pregnant, and in addition to being very sick, she was terrified to tell Marius. He'd made it clear from the start of their marriage that he didn't want children."

I nodded, remembering Caroline's frightened expression at the cocktail party, and how she begged me not to say anything to her husband about the nausea. "It's frightening to think he has that strong a hold on her."

"He may have in the past," Duncan answered, "but I think that's beginning to change, or she never would have sent me that note asking for help. And she wouldn't have given me this. . . ." Reaching into his jacket pocket, he took out a small metal key. "Caroline's been carrying it around for weeks, wondering what was inside that box, and more than a little afraid to find out. She was actually on her way to the bank one afternoon when she discovered Rafferty was following her. So she changed her plans and asked me to find out instead."

My gaze lifted from the metal key to Duncan's somber face. "What are you going to do now?"

"Getting Caroline away from Marius is my first priority. But how and when. . . ." He gave a frustrated shake of his head. "I'm sure they'll be busy for the rest of the evening, what with the awards banquet and the reception afterwards. Then, too, it might not hurt to let Marius think I'm out of the picture. I told him I had a meeting this evening with some folks in Port Orford, and technically, that's true. But first thing in the morning, I'll be on their doorstep to get Caroline and take her to our parents' home in Seattle. Once I know she's safe, I'll turn the key over to the police in San Francisco, and they can handle things from there."

"It sounds like you have everything all worked out," I said, but my tone wasn't convincing.

Duncan's dark brows narrowed. "Something's bothering you."

I lifted my shoulders in a tentative shrug, not wanting to give voice to the unpleasant possibility that had occurred to me, but his probing look gave me no option. "What happens if Caroline won't come with you? Like this afternoon—what if she's too afraid to leave him?"

Duncan acknowledged this with a short nod, his fingers thrumming a frustrated rhythm on the steering wheel. "My sister's been spoiled and pampered most of her life, but I'd like to think there's still enough strength in her to face Marius and do whatever needs to be done. Besides, there's more than just Caroline's happiness at stake here. She has a child to consider, and I'll be damned if I let Marius put either one of them in jeopardy."

Seeing the determined set of his mouth and the fierce caring in his eyes, I said softly, "Caroline's very lucky to have you."

Duncan shrugged my words aside with a crooked grin and shake of his dark head. "I don't know about that, but she's stuck with me. Shall we go?"

I nodded, feeling a painful little tug inside as he started the engine and turned the car toward the highway. I wasn't ready to go. Not now, or ever, but I might as well face the fact that my part in the whole affair was basically over and done. And it was only a small role after all. The time had come for Bronwyn to go off stage and let the key players carry on.

NEITHER DUNCAN NOR I said much during the drive back to Coupeville. His thoughts were obviously focused on his sister's problems. Mine were less altruistic. By the time we pulled into the drive, shadows were lengthening and the hush of evening could be felt in the air. I stole a glance at the somber planes of Duncan's face as we walked across the lawn to the front porch. Already, he seemed miles away.

My determination to face the moment of parting added a false cheerfulness to my voice. "Will you let me know when Caroline's at your parents' home?"

"Of course I'll let you know." He took me in his arms for a brief hug and kiss. "I'll call," he said and walked back to his car.

I stood on the porch, watching with a frozen sort of pain as he backed the car out of the drive and onto the street. As he had on the morning I'd first seen him, Duncan raised a hand to me and I offered mine. Then he was gone.

For the next hour, I administered doses of sensible advice to my aching heart and restless mind. I took off the lovely silk pantsuit and put on a pair of old sweats, assuring myself that it was a relief to have the game over and done with. Bronwyn was gone and Lucy was back. No more pretense and no more lies. But there had been no pretense when Duncan kissed me. He may have thought he was kissing a woman named Bronwyn, but it was Lucy's heart and soul that had been freely given. Lucy who had come suddenly alive, loving every moment spent in his presence. And he would never know. But perhaps that was just as well. He had more than enough to worry about right now, and even if he did remember to call, who's to say whether I would see him again. At least now, I was spared the humiliation of having to explain my foolishness.

Going downstairs, I went through the usual evening rituals. Porch light on. Curtains drawn. I checked phone messages on the answering machine, and found there were only two. One was from Norman Phillips, expressing his disappointment that I hadn't been home when he came by and assuring me he'd try again soon. I groaned and erased the message. The other was from Peggy.

"Hello, my friend," came the cheery voice. "This is just a small reminder that you promised to call. I've been thinking about you all day, and I hope you're having an incredibly wonderful time. I'll be up late, so call me, okay? Bye." Then, with an irrepressible giggle, "I mean it, Lucy, a.k.a. Bronwyn. Whoever gets this message, call me!"

It took another hour before I was sure that my emotions were under enough control that I could talk to Peggy without crying or saying something totally stupid.

"Lucy!" she squealed. "How did it go!"

"Fairly well. It's been an interesting day."

"Fairly well? An interesting day? What kind of answer is that? Is Duncan still there?"

"No. No, he's gone," I said flatly. "And he—" I drew a steadying breath. "Peggy—so much has happened, it's hard to know where to begin. And right now, I'm so tired I can hardly hold my head up."

"Is everything all right?" she asked, her voice clearly worried.

"Yes and no. Duncan has some serious problems that involve his sister, but I'd rather not go into it on the phone. I'm fine though. Really. We need to get together soon, and I'll tell you what I can."

"Are you sure you're all right? You don't sound like yourself."

"I haven't been myself all day," I answered with a tight little laugh that threatened to turn into a sob. "Thanks for everything, Peggy. I'll call you tomorrow."

I LAY SLEEPLESS for a long while, listening to the night breeze rustling through the leaves of the old hawthorn tree outside my window, and watching moon shadows creep along the wall. Where was Duncan? Still in Port Orford, or somewhere closer by? Were his thoughts occupied solely with Caroline and Marius, or might I have a place, however small, in the midst of much more serious problems?

My throat was aching with the need to cry, but I flatly refused to allow any more self-indulgent lapses into "poor me." It had been an amazing day. A disturbing day. A day of revelation and deep concerns. And now that it was over, I felt a strange sense of unreality about it all. As if it had happened to someone else. Then the thought came to me with a poignant little twinge—it had happened to someone else. Bronwyn McBride. The experiences of last night and today, Duncan's kisses and Marius' unwelcome advances—all of it belonged to her, not me. By tomorrow, Bronwyn would be gone and Lucy Norris would take up the pieces of her predictable, patterned life.

Turning on my side, I watched the invisible fingers of the breeze tease the pages of the book that sat on the lamp table near my bed. Is this how *she* felt, I wondered. When Lady Dona left the Frenchman's side after their tumultuous time together, and returned to her old life, is this what she felt? This dull deadness inside, with a heavy aching that went beyond tears? Yet, even as my mind asked the question, I felt salty wetness trickling down my cheeks.

Chapter Thirteen

Names on a Passport

I'd been out of the shower just long enough to rub myself dry and slip on a robe when I heard the soft chimes of the doorbell, followed by an urgent knocking. I ran downstairs with wet hair and bare feet, glancing at the hall clock on the way. Barely nine. I should have known Peggy wouldn't wait for a phone call. She must have left home right after sending Gary to work and getting the little boys off to school.

I unlocked the door and whatever I had been going to say came out in a startled gasp. "Duncan!"

The shock of seeing him was magnified ten-fold as I wondered who he thought he was seeing—Bronwyn or Lucy. The next moment, my own concerns ceased to matter when I took in the expression on his face. Agitation coupled with anger hardened his features, and there was stark worry in his eyes.

"I'm sorry to bother you," he said, running a restless hand through his hair. "I should have called, but—"

"Duncan, what's happened?"

He slowly shook his head as if reeling from a blow. "Caroline's gone. When I got there this morning, they were all gone."

"What?"

"Everything was locked up. She's gone."

I reached for his hand and drew him inside.

"I never should have waited," he went on, self-blame mixed with anger heating his voice. "Damn it, I should have known Marius would pull something like this. I should have gone straight to their house last night—"

Without a word, I wrapped my arms around him and held him close.

"She's gone," he muttered, his face buried against my neck. "And I don't know where he's taken her."

"It's all right," I said softly. "I do."

"You what?" Duncan's head jerked up and he pulled back to look at me.

I answered his startled look with a smile of calm assurance. "I know where he's taken her. Why don't we go out to the kitchen and talk about it over breakfast. Would you like some toast and coffee?"

Like a man sleep-walking, he followed me from the living room into the kitchen. "But—how do you know?"

"Marius told me," I said, going to the cupboard for a loaf of bread. "They're flying to Mazatlan tomorrow morning, so we have plenty of time to come up with a plan."

"Mazatlan? What are you saying? What plan?" he said stupidly.

"To get Caroline back, of course." I put two slices of bread in the toaster then turned to face him. "Marius gave me his card at the Art Fest yesterday and told me where they'd be staying."

Duncan's dark brows narrowed and his voice was a husky growl. "Marius propositioned you. Didn't he!"

bronzed features, with that shadow of dark stubble defining his chin and jaw.

He glanced up then and our smiles met in a wordless moment of shared wonder.

Peggy cleared her throat and announced, "Well, I guess I'd better be going," all the while sending me a vast range of signals, everything from significant looks and nods to raised eyebrows and potent glances. All of which basically translated to the same thing: *Call me! We need to talk!*

After she'd gone, there was an awkward moment when I wasn't sure what to say or do. I busied my hands with taking the breakfast plates to the sink, and putting the carton of eggs in the fridge. Duncan sat at the table, staring at nothing, a thoughtful frown creasing his brow, and I knew the worry was back.

"Can I get you anything else?" I asked.

"No thanks." He shook his head and managed a smile.

Going to him, I put a hand on his shoulder. "It's going to be all right," I told him softly. "I don't know how yet, I just know it will. And I want to help."

Duncan took my hand and pressed a warm kiss into the palm. "And I don't want you anywhere near Marius—not in Mexico, or anywhere else."

I met his stubborn look with a smile and a kiss, inwardly more determined than ever. "All right, then. Let's talk about something else. The key to that safe deposit box, for example. Whatever's inside must be very important if Delaney was desperate enough to give the key to Caroline. Did she tell you anything else about it?"

"Not the contents, just the name of the bank in San Francisco where Delaney had the box."

"Well, that's a start. There's a computer in my uncle's study, and you're welcome to use it."

"Excuse me?"

I sat down in the chair next to his and turned to face him. "If we're going to find out what's in that box, we'll need to get airline tickets to San Francisco and a place to stay—not to mention the address of the bank. But then, you probably know San Francisco, so that won't be a problem. Marius and Caroline won't be in Mazatlan until tomorrow afternoon at the earliest, so that gives us almost two days to learn what's inside the box and make our plans."

"Lucy, you're not going to Mexico."

"But you will take me with you to San Francisco."

Duncan shook his head and let out a groan. "Good grief, girl, you make my head spin."

"Do I?" I said delightedly.

"Among other things," he said, with a look that turned my insides to butter. "Come here . . . no, on second thought, stay right where you are. If you get any closer, I won't be able to think straight."

"Duncan, I want to go with you to San Francisco."

"What about your job at the library? I don't expect you to just drop all your responsibilities for my sake."

I smiled and gave a little shrug. "There's nothing so urgent in my schedule that a few phone calls can't take care of." *I can always say that the Lady Dona has taken to her sick bed with an infectious fever, and requests that no one but her faithful servant William tend to her needs.*

Duncan fixed me with a measuring look. "Are you sure about this?"

"Very sure."

"You don't have to go. You know that, don't you?"

"Yes, I know that."

"And you understand we're talking about San Francisco—not Mexico."

I nodded, trying not to smile because his expression was so earnest and so determined, and I wanted nothing more at the moment than to climb onto his lap and kiss him until we were both senseless. Instead, I asked casually, "Were you thinking of flying out tomorrow morning?"

"Initially, yes, but I don't think that will work. Even if we caught an early ferry at Clinton, we'd still be facing commute traffic all the way to Seattle. We'd be lucky to get a late morning flight, and that wouldn't put us in San Francisco until mid-afternoon."

"So we might not make it into the city before the bank closes? Is that what you're worried about?" I asked, loving his use of pronouns.

"That's only one of the problems. I may have the key to that box, but there's no way the bank will allow me to open it. In order to do that, someone with a vested interest and proper identification would have to be present—and that someone is Philip Delaney's widow."

"You're right. I hadn't thought of that."

"Assuming we can get hold of her," he went on, "who's to say she'll be willing to help? Delaney's been dead, what—barely three weeks?"

"And who's to say she won't? We can face that when the time comes. Right now, the only thing we really need to decide is when we're leaving for San Francisco."

His dark brows lifted slightly, and the firm line of his mouth eased into a reluctant smile. "How long will it take you to make those phone calls?"

"Not long at all." I tried to keep my tone calm and businesslike, but my heart was soaring.

"If I can book us a flight, could you be packed and ready to fly out by this afternoon? I'd like to be in San Francisco tonight."

I nodded happily and caught my breath. "I'll be ready."

While Duncan was on-line making flight reservations, I called Kathryn Parker at the library and announced that I needed a week off. Kathryn was stunned into momentary silence. In all the years I'd worked for the library, I rarely called in sick and I'd never asked for a day off, let alone an entire week. She was so stunned, in fact, that she agreed. I quickly thanked her and hung up before any questions could follow. Next, I cancelled the two tour groups scheduled to go through the Alexander home at the end of the week. They weren't happy about it, but after some minor protests, they agreed to reschedule. What else could they do? It wasn't their house. Last of all, I phoned Peggy, knowing this call would be the most difficult. Peggy knew me too well for any flimsy fabrications or excuses. There was nothing I could do but tell her straight out what the plans were.

"What? You're going where?" she squeaked.

"San Francisco. And then Mexico, but Duncan doesn't know that yet."

There was a moment's silence. "Lucy, are you getting married? I thought people only went to Mexico for divorces."

"No, you goose, I'm not getting married. This has nothing to do with me. Duncan's sister is in trouble and needs his help. And he needs my help, even though right now, he thinks he doesn't want it."

"What kind of trouble?"

"I—I really can't go into that. After we get back, I'll be able to explain. Would you have time to check on the house while I'm gone?"

"Sure. No problem."

"Oh, and could you take in the mail? I'll leave a key for you in the flower pot by the back door."

"Lucy?"

"Yes?"

"Are you sure about this? I mean, you hardly know the man."

"Peggy, it's like I've always known him, even if we did meet only a few days ago." I sighed and admitted, "I know that sounds totally crazy. . . . "

"Crazy for some, not for you," she said, and I could hear the smile in her voice. "But you've got to promise me something."

"What's that?"

"Be sure and pack that killer sundress."

"Peggy, I love you."

"I love you, too. Be careful, girlfriend."

"I'll be fine. Things might get a little sticky, but I'm sure there won't be anything really dangerous. Nothing we can't handle, anyway."

"You forget, I've seen Duncan. And I saw the way he was handling things this morning."

"Peggy!"

She laughed. "Sorry, I couldn't resist. How long will you be gone?"

The magnitude and tremulous uncertainty of what I was about to do suddenly washed over me, and my stomach reacted by taking a queasy nosedive. "I don't know. A few days, maybe. I'll be in touch."

THE SEA WAS awash with silver and sparkling coins of sunlight danced on the swells as the ferry left Whidbey Island for the mainland. Duncan and I stood against the rail of the top passenger deck, as gulls dived and swooped alongside us. Their shrill cries seemed to mock the motorized progress of our crossing, while they were free to choreograph their own mercurial dance above the waves.

Glancing over my shoulder, I watched Whidbey's gentle hills and forests grow smaller and smaller against the watery horizon, while wisps of cloud blurred the island's shape into dreamy softness. My mind touched briefly on the thought that I was leaving behind much more than the boundaries of my island home. Today I had willingly exchanged the safety and sameness of my life for uncertainty and the unknown. Adventure beckoned and anticipation danced inside me, as free as the gulls' flight alongside the ferry.

Duncan put an arm around my shoulders, pulling me close against his side and I smiled up at him. No longer looking behind, I turned my face into the wind and whatever might lie ahead.

CHAPTER FOURTEEN

The City by the Bay

A few moments after takeoff, the exhilaration and excitement that had carried me recklessly along suddenly ebbed then abandoned me altogether. I hadn't flown since I was seventeen when Peggy and I decided to treat ourselves to a trip to Disneyland. Despite common sense and every positive statistic known to man, I couldn't rid myself of the fact that a plane crash had robbed me of my parents' lives, and it was that stark fact which haunted me now. Pulling my seat belt a little tighter, I stared out the small oval window into a vaporous sea of gray, feeling wave after wave of doubt, trepidation and sheer naked fear. What in heaven's name was I doing? What sort of madness had possessed me that I would leave my job and every shred of common sense behind to fly to San Francisco with a man I hardly knew? It was more than reckless. It was ridiculous. I was deluding myself to think that I could help Duncan with his family's problems. He was an intelligent man and more than capable of helping his sister. I had no right whatsoever to come barging into an affair that was clearly none of my business.

Self-recrimination rose inside me as the plane rose higher in altitude through swirling rivers of cloud. I kept my face turned toward the window, not wanting to look at Duncan for fear he would read every miserable emotion.

Above the jet engines' muffled roar, snatches of conversation coming from the row in front of ours indicated I was not the only one struggling. A young woman somewhere around my age was trying to deal with the needs of three small children. The oldest was a little girl of perhaps four or five, with bouncy brown curls and just now, a pale face tinged a sickly greenish-gray. Squirming in his mother's arms was an infant of no more than three or four months, and buckled in the seat beside her, an energetic toddler was bent on freeing himself from the restraints of his seat belt.

"Mommy . . . I feel sick. . . ."

"You'll be fine, Amy. Here, eat some crackers. Ryan, keep your seat belt buckled!"

"I don't want crackers."

"I need to go potty!"

"In a minute, Ryan—no, keep your seat belt on!"

This domestic duet of comfort and complaint was accompanied by the infant's fussy cries and intermittent moans from the little girl.

"Mommy, my tummy hurts."

"Amy, honey, please try to eat a cracker."

"I need to go potty—now!"

Listening to them, I decided it was high time for my own petty concerns to take a back seat. Leaning forward, I spoke through the gap between seats. "Can I help with anything?"

The mother glanced over her shoulder, reluctance warring with gratitude in her weary features.

I smiled and stood up. "If you like, I'll hold the baby while you take Ryan to the lavatory."

"Thank you." Getting up, she handed the fussy infant back to me, then, grabbing the toddler in her arms, made a beeline down the aisle toward the rear of the plane.

"Mommy!" The little girl cried out in real distress.

Before I could say or do anything, Duncan was out of his seat and moving quickly beside the frightened child.

"Your mother will be right back," he told her in gentle tones. Then, "I've got a surprise for you, but you have to guess which hand it's in."

"What kind of surprise?"

"It wouldn't be a surprise if I told you. Now guess which hand?"

I smiled as the child studied Duncan's closed fists, her discomfort momentarily forgotten. She pointed to his right hand which opened to reveal a stick of chewing gum.

Sitting down, I turned my attention to the chubby little fellow in my arms. Even if he hadn't been wearing Baby Gap denims and a shirt emblazoned with red and yellow race cars, there was no mistaking the infant's gender. Bald, with the barest whisper of blond peach fuzz on his round little head, he reminded me of an indignant baby Buddha. At the moment, he'd stopped fussing long enough to fix me with an unblinking stare that plainly said, "Who are you and what do you think you're doing?"

I smiled into his wary little face and began singing a nonsense version of "Rock-a-bye-baby," complete with actions and silly sound effects. My undignified performance was rewarded with a toothless grin. Naturally, this called for a repeat performance, and when I bent my head to nuzzle his soft little chin, I heard his chest-deep chuckle.

"You keep that up and I might become insanely jealous," said a voice from the seat in front of me.

Glancing up, I discovered Duncan observing my actions with a teasing glint in his eyes. "Mind if we join you?"

"Please do."

Turning to the little girl, he said, "Amy, how would you like to meet a special story lady?"

The next thing I knew, Duncan had escorted the child to our row and buckled her into the middle seat between us.

"If you'll tell Amy a story, I'll be glad to handle the competition," he told me and held out his arms.

"Are you really a story lady?" Amy asked as I passed her little brother to Duncan.

I nodded. "Have you ever heard the story about Princess Amy with the bouncy brown curls?"

She giggled and shook her head, and I was relieved to see some healthy color returning to her cheeks. "Is that me?"

"Someone just like you," I said, and proceeded to give her a shortened, personalized version of *The Princess & the Goblin,* where Amy was the Princess Irene and her baby brother was Curdie, the miner's son.

The mother returned mid-way through the story and took in the scene with some surprise. After thanking us, she tried to coax Amy back to her own seat, but the little girl would have none of it.

"The story lady hasn't finished. I want to hear the rest," she pleaded.

Her mother gave me a hesitant look. "You and your husband have been so kind. I don't want to bother you."

"It's no bother," Duncan said, giving me a wink and a smile. "And I'm with Amy. I want to hear the rest of the story."

By the time the plane began its descent into San Francisco, the Buddha baby was sound asleep in Duncan's arms, and Amy, too, was sleeping peacefully, her curly head and warm little body snuggled against my side. In the seat in front of us, Ryan and his mother were busy putting dinosaur stickers into a book.

I glanced out the window where pale color, saffron and dusty rose, lingered in a twilight sky. Below us were the jeweled lights and distinctive skyline of San Francisco. When the flight attendant announced our imminent landing, I felt a stirring of excitement inside, rather than worry or fear. Turning away from the window, I found Duncan watching me with the barest hint of a smile.

"No more second thoughts?"

I stared at him. "You knew?"

His smiling silence answered the question, but there was no censure in his eyes, and I knew all over again that I adored this man and would gladly follow him anywhere.

Following a man, however—whether it be across the world or into a neighboring state—does entail a few minor details, such as accommodations. And it was this particular detail which occupied my thoughts as Duncan and I made our way down the concourse toward the baggage claim. I was totally out of my element, and I knew it.

The sound of a cell phone chiming out, "Scotland the Brave," interrupted my thoughts and Duncan reached for the small phone attached to the belt of his jeans. "That'll be Roger," he told me. "We're staying at his place tonight."

Opening the phone, he said without preamble, "Hey Rog, where are you? That's great. See you shortly." He pocketed the phone and reached for my hand. "Roger'll meet us at the baggage claim."

"And he doesn't mind that we're—well, just dropping in?"

"I've known Roger for years. He's more like family than a friend. He'd be offended if we stayed anywhere else. I think you'll like him," he said, then added, "And I know he'll like you." The warm certainty in his voice touched a chord inside me that instantly calmed my concerns. "You two have a lot in common," he went on and proceeded to tell me a little about his friend; that Roger was an architect, specializing in the restoration and preservation of old homes.

"And is there a Mrs. Roger?" I asked.

Duncan shook his head. "Not any more. He and Jill have been divorced for a couple of years now."

"Oh."

"He never should have married her, and probably wouldn't have if he hadn't been on the rebound." A fleeting expression tightened his features, one that I was coming to know. "Roger's been in love with my sister since we were in college," he confided, "but for one reason or another, never felt he was good enough for her. I think Rog would have asked Caroline to marry him if she hadn't met Marius."

He fell silent, and it wasn't difficult to fill in the rest.

We reached the baggage claim area where rotating metal carousels were surrounded by searching clumps of passengers, each trying to distinguish his or her black suitcase from all the others riding the luggage merry-go-round. I'm not sure what I expected a thirty-seven year old divorced architect to look like, but Roger Lawder was a pleasant surprise. Close to six feet tall, with a lanky build and sandy brown hair, there was nothing particularly striking about the man until he smiled. Then it was impossible not to feel the impact of his honest warmth. The moment he took my hand and wrapped that wide grin around me, I knew he was a man you could count on. A man to be trusted.

"So you're Lucy," was all he said, but his sandy eyebrows shot up a notch and the tone of his voice was rich with unspoken meaning. Remembering Peggy's advice about eyebrows, I couldn't help smiling.

The drive from the airport to Roger's apartment consisted mostly of catch-up conversation between the two men, who hadn't seen each other for several months. Even so, I didn't feel excluded. Roger was openly delighted with my interest and connection to the old Alexander place and had an easy way of making me feel as if I were a qualified expert on Victorian houses, when it was clearly the other way around.

Dusk had deepened into night and the city was alive with lights by the time we reached his apartment. I found myself drinking in all the sights and sounds with quiet wonder. Part of me was still trying to believe that I was really here, driving through this fabled City by the Bay which had hitherto existed for me solely in the pages of a book.

Roger's apartment was on the eighth floor of a newish brick building, a few blocks up the hill from Pier 3 on the Embarcadero. Despite its glamorous location, the apartment itself was fairly small. The kitchen and living area consisted of one long room divided by a half-wall of painted cabinets. The furnishings were an eclectic blend of the present and the past. The kitchen was functional and fairly nondescript, but there was a marvelous antique hall tree in the entryway. In the living room, brass lamps on glass end tables framed a black leather sofa that faced an entire wall of windows with a breath-taking view of the city and the bay.

Off the living area were two bedrooms and a connecting bath. One of the rooms had been turned into an office of sorts, with a computer desk and chair, a futon couch, and an entire wall of bookshelves. A second wall was devoted to framed photographs of grand old nineteenth-century homes. The main bedroom was barely large enough for its king-size bed, lamp table and oversized dresser.

"The bedroom is yours, such as it is," Roger told me, depositing my suitcase inside. "Duncan and I will toss a coin over who gets the couch and who gets the futon."

I smiled my thanks, hoping my feelings of awkwardness with the situation weren't too apparent. Turning to go, my glance collided with a framed photo on the bureau, and I caught my breath. Blue skies and white sails and Duncan manning the wheel of a tall ship. Bare-chested and bronzed by the sun, with black hair blowing in a stiff ocean breeze, the expression on his face mirrored the joy I had witnessed that morning at Deception Pass.

"I took that a couple of years ago, on a Caribbean cruise," Roger said, his glance following the direction of my gaze.

"It's wonderful," was all I could manage.

Roger gave me a smiling glance, and we returned to the living room where Duncan was standing beside the wall of windows, staring out at the night.

"Are you okay?" I asked, moving beside him.

He gave a short nod and put an arm around my shoulders, his sober gaze focused on the night scene outside. My eyes followed his and I found myself looking past the towering office buildings, and beyond the busy street scene on the Embarcadero far below, to the Bay Bridge. Seen against the night sky, its massive steel cables stretched across the span of dark water like gleaming ropes of pearls. The thrill of this stunning sight was marred by a troubling realization—that it was this very bridge where Philip Delaney had supposedly committed suicide.

Duncan gave my shoulder a little squeeze and it was almost as if he knew my thoughts, or perhaps his own were traveling along a similar line. "I'd better give Mrs. Delaney a call before it gets any later."

I remained by the window as he sat down on the couch and began punching in the number on his cell phone. In those brief seconds while we waited for someone to answer, the scene imprinted itself on my mind. Roger standing near the couch, all casualness gone, replaced by a rigid stance of waiting. And Duncan, his dark head bent over the slim phone. His eyes lifted to meet mine for the briefest of moments, but it was more than enough for me to feel the weighty burden of this call. And outside, stretching across the watery expanse of the bay, the bridge where a man had jumped to his death.

"Mrs. Delaney, this is Duncan Alexander—Caroline Charbot's brother. I hope this isn't a bad time to call. . . . Thank you." He drew a short breath and said, "I don't know if you're aware that your husband had a safe deposit box at the Bank of California, but I. . . ." He paused, listening for a moment. "I understand, but I thought you should know that Philip came to my sister a few days before he died, and gave her the key to the box. . . . No, he didn't say what was inside, but from what he told Caroline, I think the contents must be very important . . . that's right. Would you be willing to meet me at the bank in the morning?" Duncan paused, then said with absolute assurance, "No. Marius won't be there. He doesn't know about the box, and I'd like to keep it that way. That's one of the reasons my sister gave me the key. . . . Yes, thank you. Ten o'clock. I'll see you there."

Duncan pocketed the phone with a sigh that held both relief and weariness, and got to his feet. "I'm glad that's over. I wasn't sure how much to tell her on the phone."

"It sounded as if she had some concerns about Marius being there," I said.

"Very much so. I got the impression Mrs. Delaney is not at all fond of my brother-in-law." He turned an inquiring glance in Roger's direction. "Do you know if the bank is within walking distance from here?"

Roger nodded. "It's only a few blocks east of us. I'd drop you off on my way to work, but I have to go in early tomorrow."

"No problem. We don't mind walking." Duncan shoved both hands in his pockets and released another sigh. "I just wish we didn't have to wait until tomorrow to find out what's in that box."

"Have you guys had dinner?" Roger asked, making a tactful change of subject. "There are plenty of places we could go, but if you don't mind staying in, I make a wicked spaghetti sauce."

Duncan glanced at me and made a smiling attempt to mask his frustration. "What would you like to do, Lucy?"

The decision was an easy one. "It's already been a full day. If it's all the same to you, I think Roger's spaghetti sounds wonderful."

"Spaghetti it is," Roger pronounced and headed for the kitchen. "Duncan, why don't you use some of that restless energy and go to the deli around the corner for a loaf of bread. Oh, and maybe a nice bottle of Merlot," he called over his shoulder.

The tenseness around Duncan's mouth relaxed into a slow grin. "Anything else on your list?"

"Nope. That'll do it."

Duncan put both hands on my shoulders. "Want to come with?"

"Thanks, but I think I'll stay and give Roger a hand in the kitchen. "Try not to worry so much," I added softly. "She'll be fine."

He tossed a quick glance toward the kitchen where Roger was busy getting things out of the refrigerator, then bent his head to kiss me, long and hard.

"I needed that," he whispered.

I smiled and put a hand to his cheek. "So did I."

CHAPTER FIFTEEN

Lucy's Plan vs. Storming the Castle

The spaghetti was every bit as wonderful as Roger promised. In addition to the Merlot, Duncan brought back a bottle of sparkling cider which he presented to me with a smiling, "I hope this is a suitable vintage for mademoiselle."

"*Mais oui,*" I said, touched by his consideration. "An excellent choice, *monsieur*."

During dinner, Duncan and Roger reminisced and teased and tormented each other with the competitive banter that men mysteriously seem to enjoy. And while I might not be overly seasoned with worldly experience, I am female enough to know that much of the boasting and bravado was for my benefit. It was altogether flattering, as well as enjoyable to sit back and enjoy their male energy. Over the years, Roger had joined Duncan on several tall ship cruises, and listening to the two of them relive some of their experiences was like listening to two boy pirates describing their escapades at sea.

"You know, Lucy," Roger said, putting down his glass to give me a boyish grin. "Duncan may be a bigger guy than me, but I was always a lot faster at climbing the rigging."

To which Duncan countered, "Yeah, but you always stopped half way up, because you were so afraid of heights."

"I wasn't afraid of heights," Roger protested. "I stopped because you kicked me in the head trying to get past."

"I didn't kick you in the head," Duncan denied with a crooked grin. "I was trying to step on your hands, and your head just happened to get in the way."

In the midst of the tall tales and laughter, I had the sheer pleasure of studying the two men. Roger, with his easy-going manner and boyish good looks, had a laugh so infectious that one simply had to join in. His admiration for Duncan was readily apparent. But then, so was his own intelligence and his sharp architect's eye for detail. The thought came floating past as I listened to them, that if I'd been fortunate enough to have a brother, I'd want one exactly like Roger Lawder.

Duncan inspired no brotherly thoughts whatsoever. Whenever our glances met across the table, I felt a warm tide of emotion that left me breathless and floundering in its wake. It wasn't just his dark good looks and rugged frame, or those blue-green eyes whose depths could hold sunny laughter, storms, and all the mysteries of the sea. It was something more. Something inexplicable and so profoundly intimate, that my very soul felt naked in his gaze. When I no longer trusted myself to look into those eyes, I allowed myself the pleasure of studying his hands instead. Strong hands, whose long fingers had handled rough lines and kept a ship's wheel firmly on course. Hands that had touched my skin and left me weak with longing.

I picked up my glass of cider and took a steadying sip, waiting for the warm ache inside me to subside. When I dared glance up again, I found Duncan watching me with a little smile. He raised his glass in a silent salute, and I knew without a word being spoken, that he understood because he felt the same.

After dinner, when food and dishes were put away, the conversation shifted to more serious matters, as Duncan filled Roger in on the situation with Caroline and Marius and what had occurred over the weekend. That Roger was still very much in love with her, I had no doubt. Seeing the look on his face when Duncan mentioned Caroline was pregnant, tore at my heart. Damn Marius, I thought with sudden anger. Damn his ego and his slick sophistication and every last penny of his pride-fostered fortune. Roger was worth more than a hundred Mariuses. If only Caroline had seen that.

"Where's Caroline now?" Roger was asking. "Is there any way you can get in touch with her?"

"I don't know. They could be at their place here in San Francisco, or even the Inn at Carmel. All I really know, thanks to Lucy, is that she and Marius are flying to Mazatlan tomorrow." Duncan rubbed a thoughtful hand to his jaw. "Even if I knew where they were, I don't think it would be wise to contact her right now. For Caroline's sake, and until we know exactly what's in that safe deposit box, I'd rather let Marius think that I'm out of the picture."

"And then what?" Roger asked, the strain of helplessness showing in his eyes. "Seems to me it'll be a lot harder to get her away from him in Mexico than here. Why not just confront Marius and—"

"Confront him with what?" Duncan flung back. "Suspicions and innuendo? If things got ugly, Caroline might back down and refuse to come with me, the way she did yesterday at the Inn. She's frightened, Rog—of Rafferty as well as Marius. If you'd seen her face when she saw the two of them coming toward us. . . ."

Roger leaned back in his chair and blew out a frustrated sigh. "So how are you going to get her away from him? Do you have any kind of plan other than just showing up in Mexico?"

I looked at the two men on either side of me and spoke into the taut silence. "I have a plan—"

"Which is totally unacceptable," Duncan said before I could finish.

"But why?"

"You know why," he stated flatly.

"Well, I don't know why," Roger inserted, glancing at the two of us with an expression that was half-puzzled, half-amused. "What's your plan, Lucy?"

"Basically, it's pretty much the same as what we did yesterday at the Art Fest. Duncan and I would fly to Mazatlan, but of course, Marius wouldn't know that he was there. Then Bronwyn would give Marius a call, and—"

"Hold on a second," Roger interrupted. "Who's Bronwyn?"

"Well, actually, I'm Bronwyn—I mean, I'm not really Bronwyn, but Marius thinks I am."

Roger's puzzled glance shifted from me to Duncan, then back to me again. "And why does he think that you're this Bronwyn?"

"Because that's who I told him I was—but that part gets a little complicated."

"Trust me, Rog," Duncan put in meaningfully. "It gets more than a little complicated."

I ignored him and went on, "Like I said, when we get to Mexico, Bronwyn will give Marius a call. If I did no more than meet him for lunch, that would give Duncan the chance to get Caroline, and he could—"

"Hold on a minute." Roger put up both hands. "Sorry to interrupt again, but Mazatlan's not exactly a small place. There are probably more than a dozen hotels. Just how do you—or this Bronwyn person expect to get in touch with Marius?"

I hesitated, seeing familiar storm clouds brewing on Duncan's face. "I uh—Marius told me where he'd be staying. Then he—well, he gave me his number and sort of invited me to meet him."

"Invited you to—?" Roger stared at me, comprehension dawning in his face. "Are you saying what I think you're saying?"

"That my blasted brother-in-law propositioned her!" Duncan broke in heatedly. "That's exactly what she's saying. Now do you understand why this crazy plan won't work?"

Roger's mouth twitched and his sandy brows lifted. "I'm beginning to understand a lot of things, but I don't think Lucy's idea is crazy. And it makes a lot more sense than 'storming the castle.'"

Duncan glared at his friend. "No. It's out of the question."

"Could you excuse us a minute, Lucy?" Roger inserted mildly. "Duncan and I need to have a little discussion." He got up from the table and looking at Duncan, nodded in the direction of the bedroom.

Heated pieces of their discussion, if it could be called that, came back to me despite the closed door. I sat, smiling, in the small kitchen, as they argued back and forth, feeling more and more confident of the outcome. When they returned—Roger smiling and Duncan glowering—I knew I was going to Mexico. And so, it seemed, was Roger.

"Marius has never met him, so when you two get together for lunch or whatever, Roger will be somewhere close by," Duncan explained as we settled down to discuss details of the trip.

I nodded agreement to this, not wanting to admit my fears aloud, but suddenly very grateful that I wouldn't be dealing with Marius entirely on my own.

"Assuming all goes well, what happens after we have Caroline away from the bas—away from Marius," Roger said. "How are we going to get her out of Mexico?"

"Driving would be impractical as well as risky," Duncan answered. "And I have some concerns about flying. Mazatlan's airport is small, and that'd be the first place Marius would look for her. Getting Caroline onboard ship might be the safest."

"Since we're discussing transportation, I think there's something that needs to be—well—clarified." I cleared my throat, wishing the words didn't sound so stilted.

Both men turned to look at me and Duncan gave a quizzical shake of his head. "Such as?"

"Money," I said as nonchalantly as I could. "It was very generous of you to take care of my ticket to San Francisco, but I don't want you to think that I—well, that I expect you to pay for my airfare to Mazatlan. Or the hotel, for that matter. I have some savings and I'm perfectly willing to take care of my share."

Duncan's expression was slightly blank and he said nothing to this. Neither did Roger.

"You have more than enough on your mind without having to worry about money," I went on, hoping to ease his concerns and masculine pride. "I have no idea what all this'll cost, but I'm sure it's no small amount. And, well—please don't misunderstand—I think it's wonderful that you work for the tall ship cruise line, but it probably doesn't pay a lot more than my job at the library." I shrugged and said, "Anyway, I just wanted you to know that I can help with however much you need." I smiled at him and Roger, feeling much better now that money matters were out in the open.

Duncan's broad shoulders began to shake and he wiped a hand across his mouth. "Oh Lucy," he got out in a choked sort of voice.

For a moment I thought he was so emotional over my offer that he was trying not to cry. "It's all right," I began, reaching out to put a hand on his arm. Then I got a closer look at his face and realized he was struggling not to laugh. The struggle was short-lived, as he leaned back in his chair, no longer able to contain his laughter.

My chin lifted in spite of my injured pride, and I got to my feet. "Do you mind telling me what's so funny?"

Still chuckling, Duncan couldn't answer, so Roger filled in with a lop-sided grin. "I guess there's something that Duncan neglected to tell you. He doesn't work for the cruise line. He owns it."

"You own it?" I repeated in a small voice.

He nodded, adding with a grin, "But thank you for the generous offer."

Cheeks flaming, I had a moment of complete mortification, yet something in me couldn't play the part of indignant, offended female. Not when I saw the light shining in his eyes and the way laughter had eased the lines of strain and worry in his face.

"It's good to see you smile," I said.

Duncan got up from the table, and heedless of the fact that Roger was observing all this with interest, put both hands on my shoulders and drew me close.

"Want to go for a walk?" he asked softly.

"I'd love to."

"Have fun kids," Roger called, tossing Duncan a key to the apartment as I went for my jacket.

Duncan caught the key in one hand and gave his friend a pointed look. "Don't wait up for us."

A THOUGHT CAME to me as Duncan and I crossed the Embarcadero to walk along-side one of the piers . . . *She'll do what she always does. . . .* Ordinarily, I would be curled up in a soft chair, either reading a book or going over plans for my next story hour at one of the libraries. What would Uncle Milt and Aunt Ivy think if they could see me now? In San Francisco, walking hand in hand with the great-grandson of Captain Alexander.

Duncan gave my hand a little squeeze and glancing up, I found his eyes intent on my face. "What's making you smile?" he asked.

I drew a breath of misty, sea-washed air and looked around me. Behind us the city was alive with lights, the skyline forming a man-made constellation against the night sky. The sound and movement of traffic along the Embarcadero was somehow muted and secondary to the creak of ancient timbers and the dark wash of water nudging the sides of the pier.

"All this," I said simply. "Being here with you—that is, being in San Francisco—and everything that's happened. . . . I guess I—I can't help having moments when I wonder if it's all real." I called a halt to my stammering and turned away from him to lean against the fence that defined the end of the pier.

Duncan was silent for a moment before asking quietly, "Why did you come?"

"Why did I—?"

"Why did you come with me? None of this is your worry, you know. You could have been safe at home right now," he said, then asked again, his voice soft and intense. "Why, Lucy?"

Looking up at the dark blur of his face, I felt a nervous pulse begin to dance inside me. There were several answers I could have given him, easy surface responses that would have kept my deeper feelings safe from further probing and discovery. But I couldn't think of one.

"I've spent most of my life being 'safe at home,'" I told him, "reading about others' adventures and wondering if anything exciting or wonderful would ever happen to me. That's partly why I started keeping a journal as Bronwyn McBride. She wasn't afraid to dream or take risks. Whenever I wrote as Bronwyn, all the sameness in my life disappeared." I paused, then admitted with reckless honesty, "But that isn't why I wanted to come."

A salt-scented breeze stirred the night air, but its coolness wasn't the cause of my sudden shiver. "It's you," I said in a low tone. "You're why I wanted to come. That's all. . . ."

Duncan's response to this was a quiet, "Give me your hand."

"What?"

"Your hand," he said, and taking it in one of his, placed something hard and smooth in my palm.

The lights at the end of the pier were dim, but not so much that I couldn't recognize what he had given me.

"It's an agate."

He nodded, gently closing my palm around the stone. "I found it a few months ago when I was wandering a beach a few hundred miles from here. Somehow, walking a beach always clears my head and brings things to the surface. Things you might not want to face. Like loneliness. And what the hell am I doing with my life? Anyway, I was pretty much wallowing in some self-pity when I glanced down and saw it—still wet and shining from the tide. 'Something wonderful lying amidst the ordinary,'" he quoted softly. "Like you, Lucy."

My breath caught in my throat as I looked up at him. His hand tightened around mine and his face bent nearer.

"There'll be no more longing or waiting for the changing of the tide," he said. "I'm here now, and you have the 'precious stone of our meeting' in your hand."

Chapter Sixteen

Letters from the Dead

I had no idea how long we were gone, but it appeared that Roger had followed Duncan's instructions not to wait up for our return. When we entered the apartment all was silent, and the only light burning was a small one over the stove. Duncan locked the door then turned to me. His eyes were a mirror of my own emotions as we stood, smiling at each other in the dim entryway. Then, without a word, we were in each other's arms, wonder and delight finding new expression in every kiss.

"What time will you want to get up in the morning?" he asked, his mouth warm against my neck. "I'll be happy to give you a very personal wake up call."

I laughed softly and held him closer. "Mmm, I don't know—after tonight, I might not be able to sleep at all."

"That makes two of us," he said, with a few kisses for added emphasis.

"That makes three of us," said a voice from the den. "And unlike you two, Roger has to go to work in the morning."

I jumped in Duncan's arms, but he only laughed and called toward the doorway. "Sorry, man. Go back to sleep."

"Yeah, right," came the tired groan.

After the day's amazing events, it took some time for my mind and body to wind down enough to relax, let alone sleep. But it wasn't merely a strange bed and unfamiliar surroundings that kept me wide-eyed and wakeful. Lying in the darkness, fingering the smooth shape of the agate Duncan had given me, I was too happy to sleep. Over and over, I heard his husky voice telling me, "I'm here now . . ." and my mind joyfully acknowledged what my heart had known all along. I loved him. No matter that the words had not been spoken, or that the chronology of this love was only a few days old. I loved him. The certainty was warm and glowing inside me. I smiled, thinking back over all my ponderings and puzzlings about love's long-awaited appearance in my life—its miracle and its mystery. It was really all so simple. Perhaps one did not discover love, so much as recognize it. And a part of me had known ever since that morning at Deception Pass. I smiled and burrowed into the softness of my pillow, thinking how the name of the place was the very antithesis of my experience. There had been no deception that morning. Nor would there ever be. I loved him.

Eventually, sheer fatigue won out, but it seemed I had no sooner drifted off, when I was awakened by the sound of Roger gargling in the bathroom. I turned over with a sigh, thinking I would probably have to forego Duncan's promised wake-up call.

Roger was out the door, toast and briefcase in hand by eight-thirty, with firm instructions to call him at his office as soon as we knew anything about the contents of the safe deposit box.

While Duncan made the flight reservations for Mazatlan, I packed my things and finished getting ready. I zipped my suitcase shut, realizing my wardrobe for a trip to Mexico was sadly limited. Only the "killer sundress" as Peggy described it, two pairs of capris, sandals, a sweater and a few tops. Hopefully, I wouldn't need more than that.

Leaving my suitcase in the hall, I went to the den where Duncan was at the computer. He glanced over his shoulder at my approach, and the silent message in his eyes couldn't be more plain: *Are you sure about this? It's not too late to back out.*

I gave him a smile brimming over with certainty and asked, "Were you able to get an early flight?"

"The earliest I could get is for eleven-thirty tomorrow morning. It's about a three and a half hour flight, so we should arrive in Mazatlan by mid-afternoon."

"That sounds good. At least this way, Roger can sleep in a little. I don't think he got too much sleep last night."

Duncan chuckled and reached for my hand that rested on his shoulder. "Neither did I," he admitted, and his smile was like the sudden appearance of the sun coming out of the clouds.

There was no sun in San Francisco this morning. A heavy marine layer had enveloped the city by the bay, adding a damp chill to the air as Duncan and I walked the few blocks from Roger's apartment to the city's busy financial district.

Duncan paused outside the bank's imposing edifice with its tall granite columns and classic architecture. "I doubt Mrs. Delaney's here yet," he said, glancing at his watch. "We're a good ten minutes early."

As we entered the bank's main lobby, he gave me a close look. "Is something bothering you? You haven't said more than five words the whole way here."

"I've been thinking about Mrs. Delaney. You have every reason to be here, but she doesn't know me. And I doubt she'll feel comfortable discussing her late husband's dealings with a stranger present.

I think things would go a lot smoother if you met with her alone."

Duncan's brow creased slightly. "You're probably right. Especially if the contents of that box are damaging to her husband in any way."

"Exactly. I'll just wait here and disappear behind the latest copy of the *Wallstreet Journal.* It should make fascinating reading."

All he did was smile and touch my cheek, but that was more than enough to send my heart skyrocketing somewhere high above San Francisco's foggy morning.

At nine fifty-eight, a sixtyish woman, impeccably groomed and dressed, entered the bank. Duncan had positioned himself near the main entrance, while I was seated a few yards away, seemingly absorbed in the newspaper.

Patricia Delaney was the embodiment of one of San Francisco's classic grand dames. Her light blonde hair was perfectly coifed, and she positively exuded class and brand names—from the beige linen pant suit, to the waft of Chanel No. 5 that reached me as she approached Duncan. In addition to a Prada handbag, the woman carried a quiet air of grief that made my heart ache. It was in her walk and the set of her shoulders, but most of all, in her eyes. A look that all the make-up in the world could not hide.

Mrs. Delaney extended a polite hand to Duncan and even managed a thin smile of greeting as he thanked her for coming.

"I've already talked to one of the bank officers," he told her. "Shall we let them know you're here?"

She gave a slight nod as Duncan took her arm.

They walked past me toward one of the teller windows, where a young Asian woman with porcelain skin and a smooth sheen of black hair was working. Giving Duncan and Mrs. Delaney a polite nod, she left her post to escort them out of the main room and down the hall toward the vaults.

I released a long breath and settled back to wait. Some five minutes later, the young woman returned and took her place behind the counter. Duncan and Mrs. Delaney did not follow. Sensing my gaze, she gave me a polite, "May I help you?" sort of glance. I offered a smile in return and resorted to the assortment of magazines strewn across a low table in front of me.

Ten minutes stretched slowly into twenty, then crawled towards twenty-five. Articles on global warming and atrocities in Iraq, political scandals and the latest celebrity gossip passed uselessly by on the printed page, while a part of my mind worried and wondered what was happening with Duncan and Mrs. Delaney. Unable to sit still a moment longer, I got up and left the room to stretch my legs and hopefully find a drinking fountain.

A short distance down the hall, I found an ancient brass fountain tucked into an alcove. The water coming out of the spigot in a tepid dribble tasted nearly as old as the building itself.

The sound of footsteps echoed on the marble floors behind me, and I straightened up to see Duncan escorting Mrs. Delaney toward the bank entrance. She was leaning heavily on his arm, her face chalky white and her eyes red-rimmed. In the space of half an hour, the woman had aged ten years.

I heard him say, "Will you be all right?" saw her stiff, answering nod and the way she bit down on her lower lip to stop its trembling.

Reaching into her handbag, she fumbled with the contents. "You'll call me?" she got out, finding a pair of dark glasses and putting them on.

He nodded. "I'll be in touch."

Then she was gone, walking briskly through the bank's revolving doors on that faint cloud of Chanel.

I hesitated, not sure if Duncan was aware of my presence, but the moment Mrs. Delaney had gone, he turned to me. All he said was, "Let's walk," but the tone of his voice was enough to stop any questions from being uttered. I took his hand and we left the bank without another word, walking out into the busy crush of cultures and noise of the city.

We walked down the narrow streets, through metal streams of traffic, past ancient apartment buildings, and modern sky-scrapers, with Duncan's tight grip on my hand and the grim set to his mouth conveying his inner anxiety. We had passed by the street which led to Roger's apartment building and were headed toward a small park where palm trees and the green flash of parrots brightened the morning air, when I finally stopped short.

"Duncan, please . . . what's happened? Can't you tell me?"

He glanced around, as if becoming aware of our surroundings for the first time.

"Did we pass Roger's place?"

I nodded breathlessly. "It's up the hill about a block."

He blew out a short breath and turned to face me. "I'm sorry, Lucy—" He broke off and shook his head.

"Shall we go back to Roger's?"

When he didn't respond, I touched his arm and said, "Please, Duncan—whatever it is, whatever's happened—you can tell me."

Taking hold of my shoulders, he looked down at me, and the quiet intensity of his voice sent a dark chill up my spine. "Lucy, I don't want you to go to Mexico. You can't go—not now!"

"Why not now?"

His grip on my shoulders tightened. "Because my brother-in-law's a murderer."

In the space of a moment, my mind flashed the image of Marius' handsome face at the Art Fest, with those glittering dark eyes and that polished smile. Marius . . . a murderer. Even as my emotions reeled with the thought, something inside knew it was true.

"It's bad enough that my sister may be in danger," Duncan went on, his voice ragged. "I'm worried sick about her—but to purposely put you in harm's way—I can't do that! Do you understand what I'm trying to tell you?"

My legs felt weak as water, but my voice was amazingly calm. "Let's go back to Roger's. We can talk there."

Seated on the leather couch, in the warm quiet of the living room, I couldn't bring myself to probe Duncan for any details about Marius. "Tell me about the safety deposit box," I asked him instead. "Mrs. Delaney looked very shaken as she was leaving."

Duncan reached into the pocket of his jacket and brought out a thick white envelope. "There wasn't much in the box," he said, tossing the envelope on the coffee table with a sigh. "Just two letters and a flash drive. One letter was to his wife, the other was for Caroline. There wasn't time to go over all the information on the flash drive. That'll be something for Mrs. Delaney and her attorney to handle—along with the proper authorities. Philip's letter to his wife was basically an apology—admitting that he'd been doctoring the books and profits of the hotel corporation for various reasons, including some pretty hefty amounts of blackmail money paid to Marius' former mistress. The letter to Caroline was longer and more detailed. Philip was very clear in stating that he believed his life might be in danger, and he wanted to warn Caroline."

"Warn her. . . ."

"That Marius has a nasty habit of getting rid of his wives and mistresses who didn't play according to his rules. Do you remember what I told you about the death of his first wife?"

I nodded. "That she was diabetic and had a problem with alcohol and anti-depressants."

"That's right, but apparently, Marius managed to aggravate those conditions and use them to his advantage."

"I'm not sure I understand."

"The main source of the problem was Marius' sexual indiscretions," Duncan said. "According to Philip, Marius was fairly discreet in the early years of his marriage to Rosalyn. If he played around, she wasn't aware of it. The real trouble started when she hired an attractive personal assistant and social secretary by the name of Denise Ashby. It wasn't long before Marius and Denise were involved in a pretty steamy affair. When Philip became aware of the situation, he warned Marius that if Rosalyn ever found out there could be some serious fall-out. And there was. Rosalyn got wind of the affair, but didn't know who the woman was. She'd finally had it with Marius' philandering and threatened him with divorce. That's when Marius turned on the charm and admitted he was weak, but insisted he'd never stopped loving her. He begged Rosalyn to forgive him and took her away for a second honeymoon. When he was confident that he was back in her good graces, he started seeing Denise again. But this time, he wasn't about to risk losing any of Rosalyn's fortune. On one hand, Marius was assuring Rosalyn of his undying love, and on the other, he managed to convince Denise that the only way for them to be together was to get rid of his wife."

I stared at Duncan, as the chilling reality of what he was saying sent an involuntary shudder through me. "Then Marius really was responsible for Rosalyn's death."

He gave a short nod and his mouth tightened. "I don't know how he and Denise did it—the letter didn't go into all the details—but yes, Marius was responsible."

"How would Philip Delaney find out any of this? I can't see Marius taking him into his confidence. That would be too risky."

"You're right. He didn't. But then, Marius didn't expect that his ex-mistress would come to Philip and tell all."

I shook my head, as if that would clear it of all the dizzying, sordid details. "Ex-mistress?"

"Marius promised Denise that they would be married after a respectable amount of time had gone by—at least a year—to keep tongues from wagging. And she agreed to wait. They could still see each other, of course, but very discreetly. Sometime during that year, Marius met my sister, and it wasn't long before Denise was discarded and forgotten. But she wasn't about to let Marius off the hook."

"'Hell hath no fury,'" I quoted softly.

"Exactly. When Marius refused to have anything more to do with her, Denise went to Philip and filled him in on all the ugly details. She told him she'd be willing to keep quiet—for a price. At the time, Marius and Caroline had only been married a short while, and he didn't want anything threatening his fortune or his marriage. So he told Philip to take care of Denise, and pay her whatever she wanted."

"And that's when Philip started doctoring the books?"

"Yes, but apparently, it wasn't the first time he'd done some creative juggling with the corporation's accounts. Before Rosalyn married Marius, Philip Delaney was her right-hand man, and she'd been very generous with his salary and bonuses. When Marius took over the hotel business all that stopped, so Philip started padding his salary and gave himself some hefty bonuses that Marius was unaware of."

I leaned against the couch with a sigh. "Good heavens, it's all so complicated."

"And it gets even more so," Duncan said. "After awhile, Denise wasn't satisfied with what they were paying her and demanded more. Naturally, Marius was furious and unwilling to pay up. Philip mentioned that Rafferty happened to be present when he and Marius were discussing what to do about her. It was Rafferty who told Marius not to worry, and suggested there were other ways to handle the problem. Two weeks later, Denise's body was found in an alley behind a New Orleans brothel."

I put a hand to my throat, feeling sick inside. "How long ago did all this happen?"

"Not long. Only a few months. Delaney was convinced that Rafferty and Marius had orchestrated the woman's murder, but he was smart enough to know he couldn't prove anything. And if he went to the police with his suspicions, the blackmail payments would come out and he'd incriminate himself as well. Then, about a month ago, Delaney decided to make a complete break with Marius. He made it clear in both letters that what he knew might not be enough to convict Marius for murder, but there was more than enough evidence on the flash drive to get Marius on income tax evasion. One way or another, Delaney was determined to bring him down, and he was ready to accept the consequences of his own involvement."

I shook my head. "Poor Philip. Those consequences turned out to be much worse than he imagined."

"On the contrary," Duncan put in. "Delaney knew exactly how dangerous Marius could be. He understood the risks, or he never would have written those letters and given that key to Caroline."

"So what do we do now?"

Duncan paused a long moment before answering and I didn't like the look that came into his eyes. Taking one of my hands in his, he said, "First, I'm going to give the police a call and let the detective assigned to the case know about Philip's letters. There may not be much they can do, but at least it'll be out of my hands. And then, I'm going to put you on a plane back to Seattle."

"But Duncan—"

"No buts," he said firmly. "I know you want to help, and I appreciate that—but the situation's changed."

I withdrew my hand, and got up to face him. "Nothing's changed—not as far as our getting Caroline away from Marius is concerned."

"The element of risk has changed," he argued. "Think about it, Lucy. We have an ex-wife, an ex-mistress, and an ex-business partner—all dead. I don't want you or my sister added to that list."

"I understand, but Marius has no idea that we know anything about him."

Duncan let out a long sigh. "Lucy, please—we've been through all this, and I don't want to argue."

"Neither do I, but whether you like it or not, you need my help."

He got to his feet and faced me, his eyes and voice hard in their determination. "Lucy, you're not going to Mexico!"

"You're right," I said, meeting his eyes with a determination that matched his. "I'm not going. But Bronwyn McBride is, and nothing you say will stop her."

Chapter Seventeen

The Inn at Mazatlan

Duncan was furious with me and I suppose he had every right. In his mind, I was being unreasonable, stubborn, and only contributing to the worries and problems he was already dealing with.

One's inner feelings make a very weak argument in the face of cold, hard logic, and I was sadly lacking when it came to giving Duncan a rational explanation for the near desperate knowing inside that insisted I had to go. There was more involved now than simply wanting to be with him. Much more. Yet words failed me whenever I saw the chilly distance in his sea-blue eyes, and we were left with a cold wedge of silence between us, where before there had been so much warmth and closeness.

Roger immediately picked up on the change in temperature when he returned from work. He came bursting into the apartment, eager to share the news that he'd been able to pull a few strings, and after talking with a friend of a friend, had gotten us accommodations at the Inn at Mazatlan, which was practically next door to El Cid, Marius' hotel. Roger was understandably puzzled by Duncan's less than enthusiastic reaction, but refrained from commenting.

The ensuing discussion about the contents of the safe deposit box did nothing to lighten the tension.

"I told Lucy that I wanted her out of this, that you and I could handle things from here," he informed Roger, as if I weren't present, instead of sitting two feet away. "But she feels otherwise."

The coldness in his voice cut through me, but I said nothing. Roger chanced a brief glance in my direction and gave a helpless shake of his head.

There was little else to say. Tight-lipped and somber, Duncan made a call to the police department and arranged a meeting with a detective on the Delaney case.

"I'm not sure how long it'll take," he said after hanging up the phone. "With any luck, I should be back in a couple of hours."

"I hope the police are in a listening mood," Roger commented, to which Duncan gave a brief shrug and was gone, without a word or a glance in my direction.

I moved to the wall of windows and stared out at the city, fighting back waves of hurt and determined not to cry. *I've lost him,* was all I could think. But whenever I considered not going to Mazatlan, just flying back to Whidbey to wait and wonder what was happening, I knew I couldn't do it.

Roger came up beside me and gave my shoulder a sympathetic squeeze. "It's okay, Lucy. Duncan's not really angry at you. He's frightened, that's all. And fear isn't a pleasant thing for any man to deal with, especially one like Duncan."

I sent him a grateful smile, but there was no way I could answer when my throat was constricted and tears burned hotly behind my eyes.

"There's a lot at stake here, and he knows it," Roger went on.

"When it comes to helping the people he cares about, Duncan's absolutely fearless. A few years ago, we were caught in a bad tropical storm off the Florida Keys. The crew were all young and for some it was their first voyage. The storm hit in the dead of night, when the ship was still under sail. Getting her tightened down would have been a test of courage for an experienced seaman, let alone those young kids. One of the crew members, he couldn't have been more than seventeen, was up in the rigging when he slipped and fell. That fall could've been fatal, but one of his feet got caught in the ropes. So there he was, hanging upside down, terrified and totally helpless. Before any of us could move, or even grasp what was happening, Duncan was climbing up after him. I still don't know how he managed to get the boy untangled and safely down from there, but he did."

Roger's arm came around my shoulders in a comforting hug. "There's a different kind of storm brewing now," he said. "And I don't blame Duncan for wanting to keep you safe and totally out of this mess. But for Caroline's sake—I'm glad you're coming."

Duncan returned some two hours later, and it didn't take two minutes to know that his meeting with the police had only added more fuel to his frustration. While not dismissing the letters entirely, the detective in charge basically said the contents were little more than hearsay. And before anything could be done about the allegations against Marius, it first had to be established that Delaney had actually written the letters. A handwriting expert would be called in and Duncan was assured the matter would be "looked into."

Other than explaining how the key to the deposit box had come into his possession, Duncan volunteered very little information, especially about our plans to go to Mexico.

Roger tried to lessen the day's tension by taking us to one of his favorite restaurants. The atmosphere was wonderful, and the food cooked to perfection, but my appetite was sadly lacking. So was the conversation. Poor Roger did his best to fill in the awkward spaces of silence, but even an excellent meal couldn't lessen the strain.

Duncan spent the remainder of the evening on the phone with a man named Morrison, who handled the scheduling for the various yachts and pleasure ships in his cruise line. Listening to the confident, capable way he discussed the matter, eliminating one possibility and considering another, I saw yet another Duncan. Someone who was very much accustomed to giving orders and having them carried out with no argument.

After some careful juggling and discussion, it was decided that the sailing yacht, *Isabel*, would be the best choice. The only drawback was, the yacht was returning from a pleasure cruise to Hawaii and the soonest she could reach Mazatlan's harbor would be sometime late Friday morning or early afternoon.

Duncan managed to control his impatience with the situation until after he and Morrison had ended their conversation and the arrangements had been confirmed. Then his worry and frustration erupted into restless pacing.

"Friday afternoon," he groaned, shoving both hands in his pockets and frowning at the jeweled lights of the city. "I hope to heaven that's soon enough."

"Actually, if you think about it, the timeline couldn't be better," Roger inserted calmly. "It's in our favor to let Marius think he has nothing to worry about. As far as he's concerned, you have no idea where Caroline is. Marius is probably feeling pretty smug and safe right now. Giving the guy a few more days of false security won't matter. Then, too, I don't know if you've thought about this, but before Lucy—I should say Bronwyn—" he corrected with a glance in my direction, "can set up a meeting with Marius, I'll need to contact Caroline and fill her in on what's happened."

Duncan's dark brows shot up a notch. "You—?"

"Who else? You certainly can't show your face around their hotel, and neither can Lucy, until after Bronwyn gets in touch with Marius."

Duncan's initial protest ended in a frustrated shake of his head. "So how do you propose to approach her?"

Roger shrugged. "I don't know, but it shouldn't be too hard. What's she going to be doing, other than some shopping and lazing around the pool? Probably, the easiest way would be to hang around El Cid, and orchestrate a nice casual meeting. That may or may not take a little time, depending on how close Rafferty sticks around."

Duncan's frown lifted and he gave Roger a consenting nod. "It sounds good."

I had to admire the calm way that Roger smoothed over Duncan's rough edges of worry, while my own contributions to the discussion were miniscule and basically useless. By evening's end, most of the plans and preparations were in place and Duncan's anxiousness had shifted to a steely sort of resolve. If he was still angry with me, he didn't show it, but I knew the distance was still there. Especially when he offered a cordial, "See you in the morning," with no goodnight kiss.

BETWEEN DUNCAN'S DISTANCE and the plane's turbulence, our flight to Mazatlan had to be one of the most miserable three and a half hours I have ever spent. More than one passenger had to avail himself of the air sickness bags provided. Strangely enough, I wasn't at all worried that the flight might be in peril. Rather, it was the thought of further humiliation rather than sudden death which concerned me. Knowing how strongly Duncan objected to me going to Mexico, the last thing I wanted was to add air sickness to his list of reasons why I shouldn't have come.

Glancing at the sea of slightly green faces around me, I drew a determined breath, staunchly telling myself that I would not be one of them. As the plane lurched and shuddered from yet another stomach-jolting round, I caught Duncan's watchful gaze on my face. Ignoring him, I stared stoically ahead and tried to concentrate on other things. Anything but my stomach.

Into my scattered thoughts came the vision of Lady Dona onboard the Frenchman's ship during a turbulent storm. Dona had made a wager with her lover, vowing she would not become seasick if he allowed her to sail with him on a dangerous voyage. If she did succumb, Dona agreed to forfeit her ruby earrings. Drawing a steadying breath, I relaxed my death grip on the seat's armrest. I might not have any ruby earrings to offer, but I was determined to perform as well or better than du Maurier's fictional heroine.

AND NOW, WE were here, walking across the hot tarmac toward the airport building in the blazing brilliance of a Mexican afternoon. In less than thirty minutes we passed through customs, picked up a rental car and were on our way.

Little was said during the drive from Mazatlan's airport to the city proper. I stared out at the foreign landscape, feeling no sense of glamour or excitement in the fact that Lucy Norris, who never went anywhere, was actually in Mexico. A dusty dry wind blew across dusty dry fields, and except for mesquite and grayish-green chaparral, no green softened the harsh desert landscape. I'd read about Mexico's poverty, but actually seeing the city's outlying housing developments, with row upon row of cement shanties liberally covered with graffiti, was still a sad introduction to a proud country.

To go from the wretched poverty of the *barrios* to the *Zona Dorada,* Mazatlan's impressive strip of resort hotels lining its beaches, was an even greater contrast. I had no preconceived notions as to what the Inn at Mazatlan might be like, but when we drove into a broad, circular drive beside a mammoth hotel some twelve stories high, I couldn't help staring.

Duncan left the car with a valet, and we entered the Inn's spacious lobby. The grandeur of Old Mexico combined with Mayan splendor was evident in the furnishings as well as the architectural design. I glanced around at the pleasing combination of white walls and polished wood, with tropical plants and a border of mosaic tile running along the balcony.

While we waited for Roger to register and get our keys, an attractive blonde sauntered by, tennis racquet in hand. Dressed in a sleeveless top and short shorts, the woman's clothes were an obvious compliment to her excellent figure as well as sun-tanned arms and legs.

She paused mid-stride to give Duncan an admiring glance and husky greeting. "Hi. Have you just arrived?"

Now that's a brilliant deduction, I thought, seeing as how we were standing in the lobby with suitcases in hand.

Duncan answered her query with a polite nod and smile.

"Good," she said. "I'll see you around."

Simple words, but I found myself fuming at the seductive promise in the woman's voice. I shot a few nicely aimed daggers in the blonde's direction as she walked by, swinging her hips as well as the racquet.

"Our room is just off the courtyard," Roger said, approaching us with key cards in hand, and led the way across the lobby toward some double glass doors.

Once outside, I blinked and stared. Palm trees swayed in a warm breeze, manicured lawns and shrubs were achingly green, and on every side, the brilliance of tropical flowers met my gaze in a rush of color and fragrance. Scarlet bougainvillea ran riot down the balconies and outside walls of the Inn, while fist-sized pink and yellow hibiscus and exotic Bird of Paradise grew in lush profusion along the paths and walkways. Near the center of the courtyard, liquid music from a stone fountain played on the soft air, while off to the right was a fair-sized swimming pool with lounge chairs and umbrellas flanking its curved sides. To the left, past the gardens and the fountain, was a restaurant with a red tile roof and open-air dining. Not far beyond the restaurant and the low-walled boundaries of the courtyard, I caught a shimmering glimpse of silvery blue sea.

We were walking past the fountain when a fat iguana that had to be a good three feet from head to tail, casually crossed our path. Duncan caught my wide-eyed look as the apple green lizard went jauntily on its way, and his solemn expression twitched into the semblance of a smile.

A number of guests were enjoying the courtyard as well as the pool. Three senior couples were engrossed in a game of cards at a table shaded by a large umbrella. The men were wearing outrageous tropical shirts and Bermuda shorts that revealed winter-white bony knees and legs, while their wives looked coolly confident in crisp cotton. There were a few families with children, and some tanned young women in bikinis, laughing and lounging by the pool.

For a moment, it all seemed strangely unreal; almost too beautiful, like the lavish set from one of Peggy's favorite old movie musicals.

I wouldn't have been at all surprised to see Esther Williams diving into the pool, while dozens of pool side maidens burst into song.

Then a movement high overhead attracted my gaze. Shading my eyes with one hand, I looked up to see the sharp curving wings and graceful flight of half a dozen pelicans riding the thermals. Pelicans. Something familiar in all this lovely strangeness.

While Duncan and Roger went to the Foreign Exchange across the street from the hotel, I unpacked my things and took a leisurely shower. Toweling myself dry, I gave myself a little reminder to send some praise Roger's way for our accommodations. I had no idea what strings he'd been able to pull, but our room was actually a two-bedroom suite with private baths, and a living room/kitchenette that had sliding glass doors opening onto a small patio and the courtyard. Duncan and Roger would share one of the bedrooms, while I had the luxury of a queen-sized bed and tiled bath all to myself.

I came out of the bathroom, the towel wrapped sarong-like around me, and felt the first stirrings of an evening breeze wafting through the open window. Languid and soft, it played over my skin with airy fingers. The sunlight spilling through the bedroom's sheer curtains was mellow and slanted, having lost its mid-day fierceness. I sat down on the side of the bed with a sigh, closing my mind to all the stress and tension of the past few days, and let my senses breathe in the beauty of this place . . . the golden light, the silken breeze, the spicy perfume of tropical flowers. It wasn't long before my thoughts drifted, then settled on Duncan, and I felt a sensual ache deep inside. I fell back on the bed in a delicious heap of wanton imaginings. It wouldn't hurt Duncan to forget about all the stress and drama for a little while. Tomorrow would come soon enough. What he needed was a pleasant diversion.

Smiling, I got off the bed and went to the closet. I slipped the "killer sundress" off its hanger and held it against me. Made of light cotton voile, with thin straps and a scooped neckline, the dress had a carefree, gypsy feel. Swirls of color—amber and turquoise, bright coral and sea-foam green—danced against a warm background of chocolate brown. The colors in the dress brought out the green and gold flecks in my eyes, and the matching shawl would be perfect to wrap around my shoulders when the evening air grew cool.

I stared at the confident, shining-eyed woman in the mirror and suddenly realized it wasn't Bronwyn McBride who smiled back at me, but the new Lucy. No, not new—the real Lucy, who had been inside me all along.

CHAPTER EIGHTEEN

Aphrodite Rising from the Sea

Duncan and Roger returned from exchanging dollars to pesos to find me sitting outside on the patio in full regalia, sipping a tall, frothy limeade. I was delighted to see that Peggy's eyebrow theory still held true. And the strangled sort of cough Duncan uttered was an added bonus. If I'd had any serious worries that he was indifferent to me, they were nicely quelled by his reaction.

Our dinner at Papagayos, the restaurant beside the courtyard, was wonderful—succulent shrimp and flame-broiled steak, crusty warm rolls, and fresh salad. My appetite returned with a vengeance, along with something else. I've never considered myself a flirt, but this evening, some wicked imp inside me took delight in plying Roger with questions about his current restoration project. I had no difficulty giving him the benefit of my smiles and attention, while occasionally tossing a casual glance Duncan's way.

By the time we finished dinner, the sun had set and the courtyard was a place of twinkling white lights and dreamy shadow. Near the restaurant entrance, members of a Mariachi band were warming up.

The soft strains of a guitar played on the evening air, and of course, there was a throaty marimba. Duncan was taking care of the tab when the band started to play "Spanish Eyes," and I couldn't help smiling. It was pure tourist hype, but in this setting, with the present company, it was completely wonderful.

A short distance away, a vine-covered gazebo with a wooden floor provided an intimate area for dancing. Already, two of the senior couples that I'd seen earlier in the afternoon were there, dancing cheek to cheek.

Roger followed the direction of my gaze and asked with a lopsided smile, "Would you like to dance?"

I experienced a momentary twinge of nervousness, realizing I hadn't danced with a man since the time Norman Phillips had taken me to the Senior Prom. Even now, remembering those doughy hands was enough to make me shudder.

Ignoring the narrow-eyed look Duncan sent his friend's way, I gave Roger an answering smile. "I'd love to."

Roger wasn't a wonderful dancer, but he was easy to follow. As we eased into the music's gentle rhythm, I felt myself relaxing.

"It's been years since I've danced with anyone," I admitted, not caring one whit that he knew.

"Me, too," he grinned. The grin broadened as he glanced over my shoulder. "But I doubt whether I'm going to have the pleasure of finishing this dance."

"Why not?"

Turning his face toward my cheek, he said in a low tone, "I'll give Duncan roughly another thirty seconds or so, before he comes stampeding over here and cuts in."

I pulled back a little to stare at him.

"You don't believe me?" he said with a chuckle. "I've known Duncan a long time. I've seen him drift in and out of love—mostly out—but I've never seen him like this."

"Really?"

Roger nodded and leaned closer. "What'd I tell you? Here he comes."

The next moment Duncan's tall presence was beside us. Rather than giving Roger a polite tap on the shoulder, his hand was more like a vice, prying us apart.

"Mind if I cut in?"

"Be my guest," Roger said, giving me a wink and a knowing smile. "Thanks for the dance, Lucy—what little there was of it."

Duncan's glowering expression relaxed into a grudging smile as he said, "Beat it, Rog," then took me into his arms.

We were both a little stiff at first, with an awkwardness that stemmed largely from uncertainty—what to do and what to say after a long day of tension and silence between us.

Looking down at me, he mumbled, "I'm sorry I've been such a jerk."

I met his eyes and said softly, "You're not a jerk."

We shared a smile and in less than a moment, everything was all right again. More than all right. We danced, not speaking, feeling the rhythm of the music blend in subtle cadence with the movement of our bodies. Desire flowed through the language of our clasped hands, and he pulled me closer. My breathing quickened as I felt his heartbeat speaking to mine, and my left hand moved from his shoulder to his neck, finding the thick darkness of his hair.

"This dance floor is getting far too crowded," he said, his lips warm against my cheek.

I glanced at the two other couples besides ourselves. "Much too crowded."

"Would you like to take a walk on the beach?"

"Mmm. . . . What about Roger?"

"Roger's a big boy. He can take care of himself."

Taking my hand, he led me away from the gazebo and through a vine-covered gateway that let us out of the courtyard, past the hotel boundaries. Straight ahead was a wide swath of sandy beach and beyond that, a lavender sea. The moon was a young crescent in a twilight sky, and only a small sprinkling of stars had made their appearance as we walked across the sand. Music from the hotel floated over my right shoulder, while the sea purred softly over my left, and the surf was little more than a gentle lapping against the shore.

Glancing around, the sheer wonder of it all flooded through me. I was in Mexico. I was in love. The mystery had not only happened—it was mine. Letting go of Duncan's hand, I impulsively took off my sandals and dropped them on the sand along with my shawl. I ran toward the water and gave a cry of pleasure as the silky rush of the sea washed around my feet and ankles.

Behind me, I heard Duncan's laughing, "Hey, wait for me!" and glanced back to see him discarding his shoes and rolling up his pant legs. Not waiting for him, I ran up the beach along the water's edge, loving the feel of hard wet sand beneath my bare feet, and the cool wash of the surf as it nibbled the shore. Seconds later, I heard splashing footsteps close behind me. Foolishly, I ran into the shallows, gasping as cool sea met warm flesh well past my ankles. Duncan's laughter, warm and rich, pursued me, and I half turned to see his rugged form barely an arm's length away. The next moment, I stumbled against an underwater stone and pitched forward with a startled yelp.

Duncan reached out for me, but my flailing arms caught his shirt, knocking him off balance, and we both went down in an ungainly heap.

He leaned over me, his voice breathless and unsteady. "Are you all right?"

I laughed and nodded, shivering a little as the sea swirled around us with a sibilant hiss. We were both drenched to the skin, and the thin fabric of my dress was like wearing nothing at all. When I tried to sit up, his arms came around me, and even the near darkness couldn't hide the light burning in his eyes.

His kisses were like the sea itself, a passionate force that met and hungrily embraced the land, withdrawing for a moment, only to come again . . . and again. . . .

It was some time before sanity returned, and even then, my voice, half-drugged with pleasure could only murmur, "Roger's probably wondering where we are. . . . What if he comes looking for us?"

"He wouldn't dare."

"But someone else might—come walking along the beach, that is."

He agreed with a reluctant groan, and lifting me in his arms, carried me out of the shallows and onto the sand. I was foolish enough to start kissing the muscled curve of his neck and throat, which resulted in yet another lovely delay.

It was fully dark by the time I glanced around the deserted beach, trying to see where I had left my shoes and shawl. Duncan must have eyes like a cat, because he located his shoes with no difficulty at all, while I moved stooped-back across the sand like a soggy bloodhound that has lost scent of its prey.

Duncan stripped off his wet shirt, and tossed it across one arm. "Need some help?"

"I can't remember where I left my blasted sandals and shawl. And I can't go back to the hotel like this. My dress is hardly decent."

"Delightfully indecent, actually," Duncan said, joining in the search. "Practically non-existent, in fact. Aphrodite, rising from the sea . . . wait a minute, here they are." He bent over to retrieve my things, and after handing me the sandals, wrapped the shawl around my shoulders.

"You are the most beautiful woman," he said softly. "Have I mentioned that lately?"

Lips parted, I slowly shook my head. Then I sneezed.

Duncan laughed and pulled me close for a hard hug. "I think I'd better get Aphrodite back to the hotel before she catches pneumonia."

We walked, arms around each other's waists, across the sand.

"It's hard to believe this is really happening," I murmured. "Any moment now, I'm afraid I'll wake up and find that it's all been a dream."

Duncan's steps slowed as we approached the low wall separating the hotel and its lovely courtyard from the beach. "Lucy. . . ."

"Yes?"

"When this is over—that is, getting Caroline safely away—" he stopped and cleared his throat. "Anyway, after things are more or less settled . . . I was wondering. . . ."

Shivering, I hugged the shawl closer about me and looked up at the dark blur of his face.

He blew out an unsteady breath. "What I'm trying to say

is . . . what would you think about coming back here for our honeymoon?"

My eyes widened and I half choked, "Our honeymoon?"

His mouth curved in the crooked grin that I loved. "You know, that traditional thing that happens after two people get married."

"Duncan . . . are you asking me. . . ?"

"In a roundabout, clumsy way—yes. I need to know if you—or Bronwyn—or both of you, would consider being my wife."

"I can't answer for Bronwyn," I told him softly. "You'll have to read about it in her journal."

He leaned closer, and cupping my chin with one hand, tilted my face up to meet his. "And what about Lucy? What does she say?"

"Yes," I whispered. "Lucy says yes."

ROGER WAS STRETCHED out on the sofa, remote in hand, channel surfing on the TV when we returned. His brows lifted slightly and there was an amused gleam in his eyes as he took in our bedraggled appearance—wet clothes and wet hair, with a liberal coating of sand.

"I take it the water's fine," he said dryly.

Duncan and I exchanged smiling glances and if it hadn't been for my sodden, shivering state, I think I would have burst from sheer happiness.

"You better get out of those wet things," he said softly.

I padded happily toward my room, still feeling slightly dazed. A hot shower successfully stilled the shivers, but I couldn't stop smiling. Warm and dry once more, I slipped on a white top and a pair of Capris, then rinsed out the killer sundress and hung it over the shower pole. After tonight's douse in the sea, it would never be the same. And neither would I.

My smile broadened when I remembered Peggy asking if I was going to get married in Mexico. I could almost see her wide-eyed look, followed by squeals of delight, when I told her that Duncan and I were engaged. She would probably press and probe, wanting to hear every detail about how it had all come about. Details that were far too dear and intimate to share.

I was blow-drying my hair when it came to me what I could tell Peggy. All I had to do was suggest the famous love scene between Deborah Kerr and Burt Lancaster in "From Here to Eternity," and her imagination would take care of the rest.

When I returned to the living room, Roger was still involved in some serious channel surfing, but Duncan was nowhere to be seen.

"Where's Duncan?"

Roger glanced up briefly. "He had a few things to take care of. He should be back in a few minutes."

"Oh." I slumped down on an easy chair near the couch, trying not to feel disappointed. Of course he had other things to do, and responsibilities that had nothing to do with me. It was unreasonable to expect anything else.

My nails drummed a restless rhythm on the arm of the chair, and I gave Roger a curious glance, wondering if Duncan had told him about our engagement. Probably not, I decided, unable to detect anything in his expression other than mild frustration, as he switched from a rerun of "Hawaii Five-O," to an episode of "Gilligan's Island."

I glanced at my watch and released a small sigh. It was barely nine. Much too early to go to bed, and there was no telling how long Duncan might be. Minutes dragged by as I watched Gilligan and the Skipper go through their mindless antics. I suppressed another sigh.

This was a fine way to spend my first evening in Mazatlan—get engaged, then watch reruns on TV.

"I can never remember what Gilligan's first name was," Roger commented. "Or even if he had one. I think they mentioned the Professor's name on the first episode, but I'm not sure."

"The professor's name was Roy Hinckley," I said. Getting up, I headed for the sliding glass doors that led to the patio, then paused, one hand on the door. "Do you know if iguanas are nocturnal? I'd rather not run into that lizard we saw earlier today."

"He's probably asleep under a rock. Don't worry, he wouldn't hurt a fly. Actually, that's not true." Roger grinned and corrected himself. "Iguanas are probably pretty deadly when it comes to flies."

On that cheerful note, I left the room and went outside. Beyond our small patio, the courtyard was unbearably lovely. The mariachi band had long since dispersed for the night, but the breeze was playing a haunting melody of its own in the palm trees. I leaned against the patio wall, still warm from its hours in the sun, and breathed deeply of the night air, trying to identify the elusive fragrance that teased my senses. Was it one flower, or the exotic combination of many?

I tried to shake off disappointment's weight with some stern logic. The trouble with me was, I was too much of a romantic. The mere fact that Duncan wanted to marry me should be more than enough, and yet . . . no words of love had been spoken. The passion of the moment, fueled by tension and worries of the past few days—was that what it was? Maybe he was already regretting asking me, and trying to figure some way of getting out of it.

"Lucy?" Roger poked his head out the patio doors. "Could you come here a minute?"

"Coming," I answered, thinking, *please, don't let it be more trivia questions about Gilligan.*

I entered the room to find Duncan standing beside the table with a huge bouquet of red roses in one hand, and a bottle of sparkling cider in the other.

"I thought a celebration was in order," he said, a pleased grin on his handsome face.

I blinked and swallowed hard, feeling sudden tears spring to my eyes.

"I would have been back sooner, but most of the shops were closed," he explained. "As it was, I had to bribe the guy at the flower stall. These were the last roses he had, and they were supposed to be for his girlfriend's birthday." His smile broadened. "It took some doing, but I finally convinced him she'd rather have some money from the Americano instead."

The tears were flowing in earnest now. I crossed the room in a headlong rush and flung my arms around his neck. "Thank you . . . oh, thank you."

"Darling Lucy," he said, kissing my tear-wet cheek.

"It's a good thing you came back when you did," Roger put in. "I don't think I could have kept quiet much longer."

"You knew?" I accused.

"Of course I did." Roger took the bottle of cider from Duncan and gave it a rueful glance. "What, no champagne?"

"Who needs champagne?" Duncan tossed back. "I have it on good authority that a toast depends on what's in the heart, not the glass. Isn't that right, Lucy?"

I smiled into his eyes. "I love you, Duncan."

"And I love you," he said, touching a gentle finger to my cheek.

Roger twisted the top off the bottle and gave us a wistful smile. "Well then, here's to love."

CHAPTER NINETEEN

The Meeting

If Roger had his way, he would have planted himself outside the door to El Cid's penthouse at first light. Discussing the matter over breakfast, his restlessness and concern for Caroline was only too apparent, but he reluctantly agreed with Duncan that it was doubtful Caroline would be out and about much before nine or ten.

It was barely eight o'clock and already the day promised to be a warm one. Duncan had chosen an outside table, well away from those occupied by other guests, and conversation was kept fairly generic until after the server had taken our orders.

"So what do you want me to tell her?" Roger asked when no one was within earshot.

"That all depends on the circumstances of your meeting," Duncan said. "If we're lucky and she's alone, tell her flat out that I'm here and I need to talk to her. Hopefully, she'll agree to meet me here at the Inn."

"And if she's not alone?"

"It's hard to say. If Marius and Rafferty are both in tow, it might be wise to wait for a better opportunity—one where you'd be able to talk with her alone."

"What if I were to play it as the chance meeting with an old friend, which it basically is," Roger suggested. "I could do a friendly meet and greet and see if I can get myself invited to lunch or something."

"That could work," Duncan agreed, "but how will we know what's happening?"

Roger frowned over his cup of coffee. "How about I tell Caroline and Marius that I've got to check in with my friends, then give you a call on your cell. A change of plans. I'll meet you later for golf, or whatever."

"That sounds okay, but it still doesn't give you much of an opportunity to talk with Caroline alone," Duncan said. "And no matter what's going on, you ought to check in with us every so often."

"What if Roger were to call, say, every half hour," I put in. "If nothing's happening and there's no sign of her, he could let the phone ring twice and then hang up. If the news is good he'd let it ring until you answer."

Duncan wiped a hand across his face and his serious expression collapsed into a crooked smile. "It's not as dramatic, I know, but I was going to suggest that Rog just send us a text." Leaning forward, he planted a kiss on my nose. "But he could still send the message every half hour."

Roger was on his way to El Cid a little after nine. The morning passed in taut half hour segments, with sparsely worded messages of "Nothing . . ." or "No sign of her . . ." fueling the frustration of waiting. Duncan seemed calm and quietly in control, but for a man used to action and hands-on involvement, sitting in a hotel room doing nothing had to be sheer torture.

When his cell phone rang at eleven-ten, only minutes after Roger's last call, we both jumped.

"What's up?" Duncan's voice was taut as a strung wire.

I watched his face as he listened intently. Finally, he gave a little sigh and said, "Don't worry about it, Rog. It's okay. No, I mean it. Why don't you head back here and we'll make whatever adjustments are necessary. Right. See you."

Duncan pocketed the phone and met my anxious gaze. "Caroline and Marius have left the hotel. Roger was just coming out of the men's room when he saw them heading toward the entrance. He tried to catch up, but Rafferty had a car waiting outside and the three of them drove off before Rog could do anything." He gave a fatalistic shrug. "Rog is furious and blaming himself, but it's just lousy timing, that's all."

"I guess there's no way of knowing when they'll be back."

Duncan shook his head. "No, but from the way they were dressed, Roger seemed to think it might be business rather than pleasure. Possibly something to do with the sale of the hacienda. Anyway, there's nothing we can do now until they return."

I put a hand on his arm. "Did Roger say how Caroline was?"

"Fine, as far as he could tell. Poor guy. This is a lot harder on him than I thought."

"And what about you?" I asked, searching his eyes.

"I'm sick to death of all the waiting," he admitted, "and I hate staying in the background. To be honest, I feel pretty damn useless, but I don't know what else to do."

"There's nothing any of us can do," I said. "Except wait."

"I DON'T KNOW if I should go back to El Cid right away," Roger confessed as the three of us enjoyed a bowl of nachos and guacamole outside on the patio. "I was beginning to get some suspicious looks from the hotel staff. I tried not to be too obvious, or stay in one spot for too long, but I think a few of them probably wondered if I was casing the joint."

Duncan smiled at his friend's use of slang. "Well, you can hardly blame them. You've always had that shifty-eyed, criminal look."

Roger relaxed a little and dipped another chip into the guacamole. "That's me. Good old public enemy number one."

"I have to agree with you though, about not going back to the hotel," Duncan said. "After lunch, there's something else I'd like you to do for me."

"What's that?"

"Take Lucy shopping."

Roger coughed on a mouthful of nachos. "Come again?"

"Look, there's no point in all three of us sitting around, doing nothing for the rest of the afternoon, or however long they're gone."

"But what about Caroline? What if she—?"

"Relax Rog, and let me deal with the what if's for a while. There's no reason why I can't phone the penthouse from here, and if Marius answers, trust me, I'll hang up rather than say what I'd like to. At least then, we'll know when they're back." Turning to me, he said, "There are a lot of open-air shops not far from the Inn. Buy yourself whatever you like. No limit."

"Duncan, that's very generous, but you really don't need to—"

"I do need to," he said in a tone that brooked no argument. "And

I want to. At the very least, I owe you a replacement for the dress we ruined last night."

I smiled a little and admitted, "I washed it out as best I could, but it's looking a bit ragged."

"Maybe that's just as well," he said, and the look in his eyes made my insides feel like warm butter. "I'm glad Marius will never see you in that dress."

BARELY HALF A BLOCK from the hotel, Roger and I came upon the Mexican version of a strip mall. What appeared at first to be only a shady alleyway between two huge hotels was actually a busy market place with a dozen or more covered stalls and booths. Everything from colorful Indian pottery and cheap souvenirs, to fine clothing, leather goods and exquisite silver jewelry was offered by smiling vendors.

Before leaving, Duncan had given me an obscene amount of money, with firm instructions to spend it on whatever I wished. This, however, was proving to be a difficult assignment. For one thing, I'd never had such a large amount of money to spend solely on myself. For another, it wasn't my money.

Roger and I wandered into a covered booth with canvas sides that had a large selection of women's clothing as well as typical tourist tee-shirts. I tentatively held up a white linen sundress with lace cutwork on the bodice and hem, took one look at the price tag, and promptly put it back on the rack.

After observing this same ritual of look, inspect, long for, and reject, Roger finally took me by the arm.

"Lucy, please! Do me a favor and buy something. If you don't,

Duncan will be majorly ticked at me, and you don't want that to happen."

"I know, but this is hard. It's not my money."

Roger shook his head at me. "What you need to do is approach this from a different perspective. Stop worrying about spending a little of Duncan's money—which, by the way, he has plenty of—and start thinking of giving him the pleasure of seeing you in something beautiful."

I smiled at him. "You know something, Roger? For a man, you have an amazing amount of insight."

"Yeah right," he said with a crooked grin. "If I'd had more insight and less hindsight, I never would have married who I did, and Caroline sure as hell wouldn't be married to that jerk Marius." He nodded toward a gorgeous off-the-shoulder blouse that I had just rejected. "Now be a good girl, and go spend some of my friend's money."

For the next hour, I did exactly that, with Roger trailing dutifully along, offering male opinions of yea or nay when requested, and never a complaint. We were coming out of a stall with wonderful leather goods when Roger suddenly froze and I heard his audible catch of breath.

"Across the way," he said in a low tone. "In the shop with the silver."

Following his gaze, I saw her—not fifteen feet away, idly examining some silver bracelets while the shop keeper, a diminutive Mexican man with eager dark eyes, was urging her to buy.

I glanced quickly around the nearby shops and stalls with their busy clusters of tourists. "I don't see Marius or Rafferty," I whispered. "Can we really be this lucky?"

Roger was still looking fairly thunderstruck and hadn't moved a muscle. I nudged his arm. "Come on. We might not get another chance."

As we threaded our way past a trio of sunburned, middle-aged women laden with packages, I wondered how to approach her. There was no time to choreograph the meeting, or fine tune any dialogue.

"Caroline. . . ." Roger was the first to speak as we entered the stall, and his voice was more than a little unsteady.

She glanced up at the sound of her name, and her eyes widened in surprise, then pleasure when she saw Roger. Dropping the bracelet, she stepped forward to meet him, a smile on her lips.

"Roger? I can't believe it! What are you doing in Mazatlan?"

He stared at her with his heart in his eyes, and all he could say was, "I came to find you . . . that is, Duncan and I came. And . . . and Lucy."

"Duncan's here?" Her eyes widened even more, then her gaze left Roger's face to meet mine in obvious confusion. "Bronwyn . . . you're with Roger?"

"My name isn't Bronwyn. It's Lucy Norris. My aunt and uncle are the caretakers of your parents' home on Whidbey."

"The Willoughbys?" she faltered. "I don't understand." A look of unease and faint suspicion crossed her face. "Then why did you say your name was Bronwyn? And how did you know where to find me?"

"Does the lovely *senorina* wish to buy the bracelet?" the little shopkeeper interrupted. "I give you a special price—especially for you."

Ignoring him, Caroline shook her head, still looking a little dazed.

"I'd like to see your silver," Roger inserted, suddenly coming to life. "I'm looking for a gift for my sister," he added, then nodded toward the rear of the shop, which was out of the way of tourists and passersby. "Why don't you girls go visit for a minute, while the gentleman helps me pick out a gift."

Taking Caroline by the arm, I drew her quickly to the back of the stall. "You asked how I knew where you were? Your husband told me, and gave me this. . . ." Opening my purse, I took out Marius' card and showed it to her.

Caroline stared at the card, with the phone number written plainly on the back, and nervously moistened her lips. "Are you saying you have some business with Marius?"

"Your husband's reasons for inviting me to Mazatlan have nothing to do with business. That's not why I came. I'm here with Duncan and we want to help you. He's at our hotel right now. If you'll come with us, he can explain everything."

"Lucy, Bronwyn—whoever you are—I don't know what all this is about but Marius is expecting me. I—I need to get back."

Seeing the growing apprehension in her face, I decided this was no time for niceties. "No, you don't. You need to listen to me. What this is all about is the key to a safe deposit box that Philip Delaney gave you before he died."

Her lips parted. "How do you know about the box?"

"I was with Duncan when he met Mrs. Delaney at the bank. One of the items in that box was a letter Philip Delaney wrote to you. He knew something might happen to him, and he wanted to warn you about Marius."

Her lovely face paled and fear stared starkly from her eyes.

"Caroline, please! Just talk to Duncan. He can help you."

Her gaze suddenly darted somewhere beyond me and she gave

a little gasp. "It's Rafferty . . . he's come to get me."

"Caroline—don't go!"

But she had already pulled away and was hurrying toward the shop entrance. Roger half-turned when he saw her, but it was too late.

I made my way to the open doorway in time to see Caroline walking swiftly down the crowded alley with Rafferty close by her side.

Chapter Twenty

The Phone Call

"I should go after her," Roger said as we watched them go.

"And do what? If she won't come willingly. . . ." I turned away with a frustrated sigh. "I tried to tell her about Delaney and the letter. I don't know if she believed me, but at least she knows Duncan's here."

Roger swore under his breath, and his expression was haggard. "She's changed," was all he said, but the look in his eyes made my heart ache.

I touched his arm. "Come on. We'd better tell Duncan."

It was mid-afternoon and the short walk from the market place back to our hotel was more than enough to make me feel slightly parboiled.

Roger gave my flushed face a concerned glance as we approached the Inn. "What we should have bought you was a hat. You're too fair to be out in this heat for long."

I had to agree, but I wasn't about to spend any more time or money shopping. "I hope Duncan likes what I picked out," I said, although that was the last thing on my mind at the moment.

"Trust me, he'll love what you bought." Roger's mouth curved in a sad little smile. "I spent nearly half what you did on one bracelet for someone who—oh well. Forget it."

As we crossed the Inn's courtyard, I spotted Duncan sitting on a lounge chair beside the patio's low wall. He was wearing a pair of khaki shorts, his chest and arms a healthy bronze, and his black hair gleamed darkly in the fierce afternoon sun. He straightened suddenly, catching sight of us, and raised an arm in greeting. My heart and breathing reacted as if they were on a wild rollercoaster ride, and I felt a sensual stirring in the region of my stomach. Would it always be this way, I wondered, giving him a happy wave. That the mere sight of him would evoke such strong emotions. Perhaps time would bring a gradual mellowing of our love, yet it was difficult to imagine anything sweeter than the fire blazing inside me now. A fire that put even the hot Mexican sun to shame.

"Been getting a few rays, I see," Roger said as we joined him on the patio.

"Not much else to do," Duncan answered with a shrug of those broad shoulders. Putting an arm about my waist, he planted a light kiss in my hair. "You're warm. Let's get you inside and out of the sun. How'd the shopping go?"

"Fine," I said and handed him the remainder of the money.

"What's this? I thought I told you to—"

"You gave me more than enough," I said, leaning up to kiss his cheek.

"I've never seen a woman who had such a hard time spending money," Roger commented, dumping an armload of packages on the table. "And the one thing we forgot to get was a hat." His voice had a false brilliance to it, and I knew he was trying to think of a way to introduce the subject of Caroline.

"So when do I get to see the goods?" Duncan asked, then gave me a closer look. "Is something wrong?"

"Nothing's wrong. But while we were shopping, we ran into Caroline. I told her you were here and tried to convince her to come back to the hotel with us, but she—"

"What happened?" he interrupted, looking from me to Roger.

"Lucy was talking to her when Caroline spotted Rafferty," Roger filled in. "The next thing we knew, she'd bolted out of there to meet him."

Duncan's lips parted, but he said nothing, just stood there with a tight muscle working in his jaw.

"I—it's probably my fault," I said. "Maybe I told her too much—or not enough."

Taking my hand, Duncan led me to the sofa. "Tell me exactly what happened," he said as we sat down. "Where you met her, what she said, everything."

When I finished, Duncan leaned back against the cushions and gave me an approving nod. "I'm glad you showed her Marius' card. My sister's been in major denial for a long time. She needed some shock treatment." Putting an arm about my shoulders, he pulled me close against his side. "Stop looking so tragic, my love. Her running away wasn't your fault. And it wasn't the first time. At least now she knows I'm here."

"If Rafferty hadn't showed up, I think Caroline would have come with us," Roger put in. "That guy is some scary watchdog."

Duncan considered this for a moment. "Do you know if he saw either of you?"

I shook my head. "I don't think so. Caroline and I were at the back of the shop when she saw him. And Roger was in front of us, but Rafferty wouldn't know him, or have any reason to think that we were together."

"That's good. I wouldn't want him to put Marius on the alert."

"So what do we do now?" Roger asked, his face showing the strain, despite his calm voice.

"I don't know that we have time to try and orchestrate another chance meeting," Duncan said. "While you were gone, I've been in touch with the *Isabel*. She'll be coming into port around eleven tomorrow morning, so whatever we decide, we've got to find a way to get Caroline on that ship."

Roger only nodded, his face a tight mask of worry.

I drew a steadying breath and spoke into the silence. "The way I see things, it's going to take all three of us to make this happen. Bronwyn will need to keep Marius occupied, and Roger—" I gave him an encouraging smile. "Rather than staying on the sidelines, I think you'd do much better providing some kind of diversion to get Rafferty out of the way."

Duncan's arm tightened around my shoulders, and I sensed his initial resistance to what I was saying. "I know how you feel," I told him, "but if anyone can calm Caroline's fears and convince her to leave, it's you—the brother she loves and trusts."

Seeing the warm blend of love and worry in his eyes, I reached up to kiss him. Held close against his chest, I barely heard the sound of the patio door sliding open, to gently close as Roger left us alone.

When I could breathe again, let alone talk, I murmured, "Try not to worry so much . . . somehow, we'll make it all work. Caroline will be fine."

Duncan drew back and took my face in his hands. "It's not Caroline I'm worried about. If anything happened to you. . . ."

"Nothing's going to happen to me," I said, trying to smile away his fears along with my own. "But I think it's time I made that phone call to Marius, and I—I just can't do it with you here. I can't play his ugly little game and pretend to be someone I'm not—not in front of you."

Duncan gave an assenting nod. "It probably wouldn't be a good idea to use the room phone, anyway. And you certainly can't use my cell. One look at the caller I.D. would be a dead giveaway."

"What about the lobby? It shouldn't matter if Marius sees that I'm calling from the hotel."

Duncan nodded then pulled me close for a hard kiss. "Hurry back, love."

THE VOICE ON THE line was brisk and businesslike, with none of the smooth honey or velvet tones I'd heard before.

"This is Marius."

"Hello . . . it's Bronwyn. I hope this isn't an inconvenient time to call."

There was a moment of silence, followed by a pleased, "Bronwyn? Are you in Mazatlan?"

"Yes. I'm sitting in the hotel lobby feeling quite amazed, as a matter of fact. Only yesterday, I was trying to convince myself that I had a hundred other things to do, but somehow, I couldn't remember what they were. I—I hope I'm not disturbing you."

He laughed, and the velvety voice was back full force. "To be honest, I find you very disturbing. Where are you staying?"

"We're practically neighbors," I answered lightly. "I'm next door at the Inn at Mazatlan."

"How convenient."

I drew a taut little breath. "I'm glad you think so."

"Do you have any plans for tonight?"

"Tonight?" I drew a shaky breath, thinking this wasn't at all in the plans.

"Yes. I'm having a little celebration dinner here at the penthouse, and I'd love to see you."

"Oh, and what are we celebrating?"

"At eleven tomorrow morning I sign the final papers for the purchase of the hacienda I was telling you about."

"Congratulations, that's wonderful. But I really hate to intrude."

"No one could ask for a lovelier intrusion," he said. "And it's nothing formal—just a casual gathering with some very stuffy bankers and lawyers who've been involved in the dealings for the hacienda."

"And Caroline?" I asked. "Will she be there?"

"Of course," he answered easily. "And I'm sure she'll be delighted to see a dear friend of her brother's."

I was grateful he couldn't see my face. "Who just happened to show up in Mazatlan? I wouldn't want to make things awkward for you."

He laughed again, a low chuckle that was smugly confident. "My wife isn't a problem that you need to be concerned with. But it would be very awkward for me—devastating even—if you didn't come. Seven-thirty?"

When I didn't answer immediately, he went on in a low tone. "Seeing a sunset from the penthouse is quite magnificent—but if you were there to share it, it would be unforgettable."

"Seven-thirty then." My voice was breathless from sheer nerves, but I'm sure he thought it was from the anticipation of seeing him again. "Do I need a special password to get in?"

"No password needed," he chuckled. "I'll just tell Rafferty to watch for the most beautiful woman in Mazatlan. Until this evening," he said softly and hung up.

I left the lobby and walked out into the sunny courtyard, feeling cold all over. Making my way to a stone bench near the fountain, I sat down with a shaky sigh, trying to get my emotions under control. I couldn't go back to the room and face Duncan the way I was feeling now. It didn't matter that Bronwyn had performed well and the call to Marius had achieved exactly what was needed. None of that could rid me from feeling slightly sick, and yes, more than a little afraid.

A penthouse party with bankers and lawyers. How in heaven's name was I going to pull this one off? And if that weren't intimidating enough, I had the tricky little trio of Marius, Caroline and Rafferty to deal with. I drew a long breath, trying to gather a feeling of calm from the fountain's liquid music, and the soft breeze playing through the palms. Nearby, I could hear the laughter of guests enjoying a lazy afternoon under shady umbrellas, or having a refreshing swim in the pool. Some were stretched out on lounge chairs, reading or napping, while others enjoyed chilled margaritas and nachos. On the beach, a group of sun-browned children had gathered to watch two para-sailors gliding high over the silky sea.

Everywhere I looked, simple pleasures met my gaze. No matter how stressful their lives might be at home, the vacationers here at Mazatlan were enjoying a delightful afternoon on the Mexican Riviera, while I was in this tropical paradise with my nerves tied up in knots.

I leaned down to retrieve a golden hibiscus blossom that had fallen beside the bench, and absently shredded its fragile petals. Somehow, while I was making my brilliant little plans to meet Marius for as brief a time as possible, it never occurred to me that he might have other ideas.

I didn't want to go to Marius' party. Truth be told, I never wanted to see the man again, let alone be a participant in his deceitful, underhanded games. What made me think I was capable of dealing with someone as twisted and dangerous as Marius Charbot? I seriously doubted whether Bronwyn McBride herself would be up to such a challenge.

Bonny and brave to the end. . . . The phrase quietly inserted itself into the cowardly jumble of my thoughts, and I instinctively straightened. All I had to do was say the word, and Duncan would gladly send me back home. I was the one who had insisted on coming to Mexico. The one who, only a scant week ago, had been longing for adventure and a little excitement to stir up the dull sameness of my life. Well, life had given me a heady dose of both elements. I couldn't back out now. Going to Marius' party might be an added challenge, but it didn't need to be terrifying. In fact, being in the company of some "stuffy bankers and lawyers" might provide some much needed interference from any unwelcome advances. And where was it written that I had to spend the entire evening in Marius' detestable company? If things got too difficult, I could always plead a headache and leave. Most important, going to the party would provide another chance to talk with Caroline. Remembering her frightened eyes and unspoken pleas helped diminish the last of my doubts and fears. I got up from the bench and discarded the shredded flower.

Bonny and brave to the end . . . . Despite my resolve, the phrase had acquired a slightly bitter taste and I couldn't help wonder exactly what that end might be.

SHADOWS WERE LENGTHENING in the courtyard and the brilliant clarity of late afternoon had softened to the golden hour before sunset, as Duncan, Roger and I sat around the patio table discussing the repercussions of my phone call to Marius. His dinner invitation had of necessity altered our own plans of going to Papagayos, to ordering some sandwiches and drinks from room service.

"Lucy, you don't have to convince me," Duncan conceded in a tight voice. "I know it's a great opportunity to talk with Caroline. But I don't have to like it."

"Let's face it," Roger put in. "This whole business with Marius is pretty dirty, but it will all be worth it once Caroline is safe onboard your ship."

"Agreed," Duncan said. "So let's take a few minutes to plan out exactly how that's going to happen. Naturally, any plans we make are dependent upon Caroline's decision to leave Marius." Reaching for my hand, he gave it an encouraging squeeze. "Assuming she agrees, you'll need to find some time during the party to let her know that I'll be waiting in front of El Cid at noon tomorrow. You mentioned that Marius will be signing final papers at eleven. I don't know how long that will take, but my guess is he'll want to meet Bronwyn soon after. Knowing Marius, he'll probably use seeing you at the party to arrange the time and place for tomorrow. It would be better—and a lot safer—if you could meet him at a restaurant, rather than have him pick you up here at the Inn."

"What do we do about Rafferty?" Roger broke in. "You can bet Marius won't want the guy trailing along when he meets Bronwyn, and that means he'll be sticking pretty close to Caroline."

"I know," Duncan agreed, "and that's where you come in. Lucy suggested a diversion of some kind, and I like the idea."

"You do?" I couldn't help staring.

Duncan chuckled. "Don't look so surprised, my love. What you said got me thinking that maybe we could create a simple wild goose chase to get Rafferty away from the hotel."

Roger's frown lifted and he leaned forward with interest. "What sort of wild goose chase do you have in mind?"

"What if Rafferty were to get a call from one of the lawyers handling the sale of the hacienda, about some important papers that Marius left behind, or forgot to pick up."

"I take it, that lawyer would be me?"

Duncan smiled and nodded. "That's right."

"Small problem," Roger said. "I don't know which law firm Marius has been dealing with, let alone the address of the place."

"No, but Rafferty does. He's Marius' chauffeur, right? All you have to do is tell him to come by and pick up the papers. As soon as he leaves the hotel, I want you to have the car ready and waiting outside El Cid."

Duncan turned to me. "There won't be time for Caroline to do any serious packing. That would only alert Marius and Rafferty. Just make sure you tell her to have her passport and whatever else she needs."

"I'll tell her." My voice was calm, in spite of the nervous little pulse beating in my throat. "Anything else?"

He nodded. "I've been thinking about your meeting with Marius. Most of the business offices are located downtown in Old Mazatlan, and that's probably where he'll be signing the papers. You might suggest having lunch someplace that's fairly close to the harbor. The Shrimp Bucket is popular with tourists and it's nice and crowded."

"The Shrimp Bucket," I repeated. "I'll remember."

"After that, make whatever excuse you have to—going to the

ladies' room, whatever—just get the hell out of there and grab a cab to the harbor. Okay?"

"Yes."

"I'll give you the address, but there isn't a cabby in Mazatlan that doesn't know where the harbor is. All the cruise ships dock there when they come into port." Duncan's mouth tightened as he looked at me. "I still wish we could come up with some other way. So much of this depends on you."

"It's all right," I told him. "We can do it."

"We?"

I smiled, my voice sounding braver than I felt. "Bronwyn and I. We'll be fine."

Chapter Twenty-One

Party at the Penthouse

The sun was low in the sky, gilding the sea with amber ribbons of light, and the first breath of evening was soft on the air as I stood outside the double doors to El Cid's penthouse. Situated high atop the massive hotel, with its own private balcony, the penthouse commanded a breathtaking view of Mazatlan's coast and the sea.

Hand poised to knock, I drew a steadying breath, wishing I could still the nervous flutter inside me. Bronwyn might look her glamorous best, but Lucy desperately needed another moment to quiet her nerves.

I was grateful now that Duncan and Roger had insisted on today's shopping expedition, or Bronwyn's wardrobe for the evening would have been sadly lacking. I smiled, remembering Duncan's stunned expression when I'd come out of the bedroom wearing one of the outfits I'd bought. Even Roger had uttered a low whistle of approval. The figure-hugging black slacks had a definite Spanish flair with their embroidered cut-outs on the outside seams. This, paired with a romantic off-the-shoulder blouse of white cotton and a sash of black and scarlet, made me feel slightly Carmenesque. Lips and nails were as scarlet as the sash, and whether from nervous excitement or a little extra shadow and mascara, my eyes looked enormous. I'd considered wearing a pair of gold hoop earrings, but decided at the last moment in favor of my grandmother's lovely garnet ones. The same earrings I'd worn when I first saw Duncan reading Bronwyn's journal.

"How do I look?" I'd asked.

The light burning in Duncan's eyes gave me my answer, but I still wanted to hear the words. As it happened, his response was passionately non-verbal. So much so, that I had to redo my lipstick and hair before leaving.

With a shaky sigh, I put the memory aside for future enjoyment, and knocked on the penthouse door.

I was steeling myself for either Marius or Rafferty to answer, but when the door opened, it was Caroline's startled blue gaze that met mine. There was a surprised moment when neither of us said a word.

"Bronwyn . . . or is it Lucy?" she said at last, a small edge to her voice.

"For tonight, it's Bronwyn," I told her. "Your husband invited me. Didn't he tell you?"

A slight frown narrowed her brows. "No . . . he didn't."

She looked beautifully fragile, yet elegant, with her blonde hair swept back from her face. Dressed all in white, with a sleeveless top that fell in soft folds around her waist, and loose-fitting trousers, the only color was her jewelry—a stunning necklace and earrings of silver and turquoise that brought out the blue of her eyes.

"Please don't say anything—" I began, then stopped at the sound of Marius' voice coming in a half-joking reprimand.

"Caroline darling, aren't you going to invite them to come in?"

The next moment Marius was beside her in the doorway. His lips parted and the dark eyes glittered when he saw me.

"Bronwyn . . . I'm so glad you were able to join us after all." His words implied a tentative arrangement. "You look lovely. Doesn't she, Caroline?"

"Yes," came the barely perceptible answer. "She does."

I gave them both a cordial smile, wondering what kind of story Marius would concoct to explain my presence in Mazatlan to his wife. I didn't have long to wait.

"I ran into Bronwyn at the bank this afternoon, while you were out shopping," he said smoothly.

"The bank," Caroline repeated.

"Yes. I'd just finished some business there when I saw her having a little difficulty changing dollars to pesos."

Caroline's brows lifted slightly. "I see."

And she did. We exchanged a wordless look, and I realized with a secret thrill that she knew Marius was lying. Turning to me she asked, "Is this your first trip to Mexico?"

"Yes, it is."

"Bronwyn's here to pick up some art pieces and Indian pottery for one of her clients, and I thought perhaps you could give her the names of some of the better shops." He put an arm around Caroline's slender shoulders, even as his eyes sent a dark message my way. "My wife has impeccable taste."

I nodded agreement to this, adding, "Any suggestions you have would certainly be appreciated—if it isn't too much trouble."

"No trouble at all," she replied.

"It's such a small world," Marius went on, confident that he'd provided his wife with a valid reason for my presence. "I told Bronwyn we couldn't have her spending her first night in Mazatlan all alone."

"Of course not," Caroline agreed, and ushered me inside. "Marius, why don't you introduce Bronwyn to our guests?"

These, thankfully, were relatively few in number. There was Señor Carlos Rodriguez from the bank, a round-faced, round-bellied gentleman in a tight blue suit, with a wine glass that seemed permanently attached to his right hand. And Señor Ortiz, the lawyer representing Louis and Maria Delgado, soon to be past owners of the hacienda. The Delgados were a handsome couple in their late sixties, who appeared quietly resigned to the sale of their property, and more than a little in awe of Marius' charisma and charm. Other than the Charbots and myself, there was only one other American present, a fairly nondescript man of medium height and build, with a thin-lipped mouth and shrewd brown eyes. Marius introduced him as "Mark Kohler, my valued legal advisor," and I knew with an uncomfortable little twinge, that this must be Philip Delaney's replacement. Despite his innocuous appearance, Kohler was glib and clever in a biting, sarcastic sort of way, and obviously bored with the evening's affair. His attitude toward the Delgados and Señor Rodriguez was clearly patronizing. Señor Ortiz, he patently ignored, as someone from the opposing team.

And of course, there was Rafferty, standing on the sidelines with those brawny arms folded across his even brawnier chest, and his narrow-eyed glance taking in the proceedings as if he expected one of the guests to try and make off with the silver.

The evening was not without its irony. Only days ago, I had been the invisible server for a cocktail party at the Charbot's log home, high on a forested hilltop. And now, here I was, an invited guest to a party at El Cid's top of the world penthouse. Instead of filling trays and removing dishes, I was the one attended by smiling, black-haired servers from the hotel.

The penthouse furnishings were definitely more casual than the elegant surroundings of Marius' home in Langley, but it was equipped with every imaginable amenity, including an outdoor pool and an indoor spa. Louvered doors folded back to reveal wall-to-wall windows, affording guests an unobstructed view of the sea and Mazatlan's lovely beaches.

After the necessary introductions had been accomplished, Marius led me to the buffet table, making sure that my plate received a generous sampling of the various offerings. Among other things, there was an abundance of shrimp, green mountains of guacamole, and chips and salsa ranging in temperatures from fiery to molten lava. At the bar, Marius teasingly offered to introduce me to the questionable delights of tequila, knowing full well I would refuse. Something in his voice and eyes told me that he'd already sampled some of the potent drink.

Across the room, I caught Caroline's watchful gaze on the two of us and wondered what she must be thinking.

"Excuse me, Marius, could I speak with you a moment?"

Mark Kohler approached the table, and before Marius could object, I gave him a smiling glance and said, "The Delgados are looking a little lost. If you'll excuse me, while you two talk, I think I'll practice my deplorable Spanish."

Marius agreed affably, saying, "You didn't tell me you spoke Spanish."

"I don't," I answered with a smile and turned away.

For the next forty-five minutes or so, I managed to keep well out of his reach, listening to portions of a heated discussion about offshore pollution between Señor Ortiz and Louis Delgado, and a debate over the financial merits and moral pitfalls of Mazatlan's *Carnival* season, which had recently ended. I complimented Señora Delgado on her beautiful Madonna-like smile and asked about her family, which resulted in a deluge of grandmotherly bragging that was part English and part Spanish.

I was hoping for an opportunity to talk with Caroline, but her duties as perfect hostess kept her fairly well occupied, and Marius or Rafferty always seemed to be close at hand.

Señor Ortiz was giving me an enthusiastic account of Mazatlan's economic conditions as well as some of its history, when I felt a hand on the small of my back and knew immediately who it was.

"Excuse me, *por favor.*" Marius gave Señor Ortiz the full benefit of his brilliant smile. "If I might borrow the lovely señorita for a few moments."

Nodding and smiling, Ortiz backed away and headed for the bar, while Marius took my arm and led me purposefully out of the living room and onto the balcony.

The sun had set, but the clouds hovering near the horizon still held a blush of deep rose, while the sea and sky slowly darkened from evening's azure to the deep sapphire of approaching night. Looking south, I could see the palm-covered courtyard and grounds of the Inn at Mazatlan, and my heart beat uncomfortably when I thought of Duncan waiting there, wondering what was happening.

Marius led me along the narrow balcony until we were around the corner and out of sight of the living room. "Well, what do you think of all this?" he asked, gesturing to the panorama stretching away on every side.

I leaned against the balcony's metal railing and concentrated on the darkening sea far below. "The view is stunning. It takes my breath away."

"*You* take my breath away," he said softly, one of his hands caressing my shoulder. "I never thought I'd be jealous of that old buzzard Ortiz, but whatever he was saying, you certainly seemed to find him entertaining."

I smiled, intensely aware of that hand on my bare shoulder, and tried not to shudder. "Señor Ortiz was giving me some of the history of old Mazatlan—including a rather graphic account of the yellow fever victims who died in the 1870s."

Marius gave a low laugh and turned me to face him. "My beautiful Bronwyn," he said softly, "I'm getting very tired of sharing you with a crowd. This party shouldn't last more than another hour. And then. . . ." His voice trailed off, and the look in his eyes couldn't have been more plain.

My voice was amazingly steady in spite of my pounding heart. Putting both hands on his chest, I said, "Marius . . . please . . . I'm not trying to be coy. We both know why I came to Mexico, but I . . . I really was thinking of making it an early night." His hands tightened perceptibly and I went on, my voice softly pleading. "There was so much to do before I could leave. I had hardly any sleep last night."

He hesitated, and I sensed he wasn't used to being denied or put off. His words confirmed this. "Patience has never been one of my virtues," he said, the voice as velvety as ever, but there was a frightening hardness in his eyes. "To be honest, I have a difficult time waiting for something I want—especially when it's something—or *someone*—that I want very much."

My throat went dry and I had no reply to this. All in a moment, I knew this man was entirely capable of murder. That he would stop at nothing to get what he wanted. I glanced down, unable to meet those glittering dark eyes.

One of his hands moved from my shoulder to stroke my collarbone, his touch now feather light. "What about tomorrow then?"

"I thought you had papers to sign."

"That will all be taken care of before noon. We could do lunch, and then I'll show you Mazatlan. How does that sound?"

I released a shaky sigh and nodded. "It sounds perfect. Where shall I meet you?"

"The bank offices are in Old Mazatlan near de Marzo. Why don't I meet you in front of the cathedral in the main plaza. Twelve o'clock."

"Twelve o'clock at the cathedral."

"You're trembling," he said, sounding more pleased than concerned.

"It's getting a little chilly."

"Liar," he chuckled, and had the audacity to lean down and kiss my shoulder. "Let's get you inside."

In my eagerness to do exactly that, I failed to see Señor Rodriguez talking with Mrs. Delgado beside the open doorway. He turned as I turned, and we collided breast to breast with a startled *oomph*, the contents of his ever-present wine glass spilling down the front of my white blouse.

I gave a little gasp and Señor Rodriguez broke into a flood of Spanish, mingled with embarrassed apologies in English.

I smiled into the man's flustered round face, hoping to ease his chagrin. "I'm so sorry. This is totally my fault."

Glancing up, I saw a strange expression cross Marius' face—one half-puzzled, and half-recognition, as he stared at me. The next moment Caroline was on the scene, calmly taking the situation in hand.

"We'd better soak that blouse before the stain sets," she said, and gestured to one of the servers. "Carlos, could you get me some club soda from the kitchen? Quickly, please. Thank you." Turning back to me, she added, "Club soda is my secret weapon for getting out stains, especially wine."

"Thank you. I'm sorry to be so much trouble."

"It's no trouble," she said, as one of the black-clad servers quickly mopped up the spilled wine, and Carlos hurried over with the club soda. Smiling her lovely smile, she took the bottle from him. "If you gentlemen will excuse us?"

Avoiding Marius' gaze, I followed her out of the room and down a hall to a bathroom that was all gilt and marble and mirrors.

Shutting the bathroom door behind us, she poured the club soda into one of the twin basins, while I pulled the wet blouse over my head. I handed it to her, then reached for a towel to sponge my wine-splattered bra.

"Thank you for not giving me away," I said, uncertain how to begin. "I've been hoping for a chance to talk with you all evening."

"Have you?" Her tone held the slightest edge.

"Despite how it may look, yes. The only reason I accepted Marius' invitation was because I needed to talk to you."

She said nothing. Her blue eyes held confusion and a bit of hurt.

"Caroline, you heard Marius' lies when he met me at the door. I didn't run into him at the bank or anywhere else. I was with Roger and you know it. And I'm not here to buy pottery or paintings for a client. I'm not even an art dealer. Like I said this afternoon, I help my aunt and uncle take care of your parents' home on Whidbey."

She stared at me and her voice faltered. "I—I don't understand."

"And I don't have time to explain. All you really need to know is that Duncan and Roger and I are here to help you! Caroline, your husband is a dangerous man. Philip Delaney found that out too late, and so did Marius's ex-mistress." I paused a moment to let this sink in, and saw the frightened look that came into her eyes.

"A few minutes ago, Marius made a date with me for noon tomorrow. If you don't believe me, try asking him to do something with you and see what kind of story he comes up with."

She drew a tense breath. "And you agreed to meet him?"

"Yes, but not for the reason you might think. I'm just a diversion so—"

A light tap sounded on the bathroom door and we both jumped. In true Victorian fashion, I jerked the towel up to cover myself as Marius opened the door and poked his dark head inside.

"Sorry to intrude, ladies. I just thought I'd check to see if everything's all right."

In spite of the towel, I felt naked and vulnerable in the dark heat of his gaze.

Caroline moved to the door, neatly blocking his view. "Everything's fine," she said smoothly. "Please reassure Señor Rodriguez that we managed to get the stain out."

"I'll tell him."

Marius shut the door and Caroline leaned against it with a shaky sigh. Her eyes met mine and neither of us spoke for a long moment. She looked as shaken as I felt.

"Do you think he heard?" she mouthed, more than whispered.

I shook my head, then moved to the sink and turned the tap on full force to help mask the sound of my voice. "Tomorrow morning, there'll be a ship waiting in the harbor—one of Duncan's ships."

Caroline sank down on the toilet seat, her face pale. "Why are you doing this? Why should you want to help me?"

"Because I love your brother, and I know how much he loves his sister." She looked up at me, lips parted, but said nothing.

"Twelve noon tomorrow," I said in an urgent whisper. "In front of the hotel. Duncan will be waiting for you. That's why I agreed to meet Marius. We needed a diversion to get him out of the way."

Her lips trembled. "What about Rafferty? He'll know I'm leaving and he'll tell Marius—"

"You don't need to worry about Rafferty. Roger has a wild goose chase planned for him. All you need to do is take your passport and walk out the door. That's all. Just walk out the door."

Tears filled her eyes and spilled down her cheeks. "I've been afraid for so long."

"I know." I hesitated, my heart twisting as she swiped at the tears. "You can do it, Caroline. You have to. And not just for yourself—do it for your baby."

"How do you know about—?" She broke off, and her eyes widened as she stared at me. "You were the server at our cocktail party! That's where I've seen you!"

"Yes, and believe me, I'm praying that Marius doesn't make the same connection. I have to keep Bronwyn's persona intact for one more day. Just long enough to get you onboard that ship."

She stood up with a shaky sigh and dried her tear-stained face on a towel. When she turned to face me, the expression in her eyes was no longer that of a frightened animal.

I turned off the tap and asked in normal tones, "Do you have a tee shirt or something I could borrow? I'd rather not go out like this."

She smiled and nodded. "I'll be right back."

After she'd gone, it was my turn to sink down on the toilet seat, my legs suddenly so shaky they refused to hold me up.

Caroline returned moments later and handed me a silky black top. "This should do for now." While I pulled it over my head, she took my blouse out of the sink, wrung it out, then put it in a plastic sack.

I took the sack and met her eyes. "Thank you for believing me."

"Thank *you*," she said softly and put her arms about me in a quick hug. "And Lucy . . . tell Duncan I'll be ready. Twelve o'clock."

CHAPTER TWENTY-TWO

Ruby Earrings

I left El Cid and walked unseeing past the small shops and stores that were squeezed between the two mammoth hotels. The night air was soft and far from cold, yet I couldn't prevent the nervous shivers that ran through me. My time at the party had accomplished far more than I'd dared hope for, and the accident with Señor Rodriguez and the wine couldn't have gone better if I'd planned it. So why this worrisome sense of unease?

I reached the Inn and crossing the lobby, headed for the double doors leading to the courtyard. I wanted to forget it all—the conversation with Marius on the balcony, the feel of his hands on my skin, and the sheer terror that flooded through me every time I thought about being alone with him. I shivered again as I hurried along the courtyard path, wishing I could somehow block the images from my mind. Especially the look on Marius' face when Señor Rodriguez and I were making our apologies. There was something about his expression . . . almost as if the incident had happened before.

I stopped short as memory suddenly made everything frighteningly clear. It had happened before. The cocktail party at Marius' home.

Instead of a wine glass, it had been a tray of strawberries and éclairs. Marius had reached out to steady me, and my words to him—*I'm so sorry . . . this is totally my fault*—were the same words spoken to Señor Rodriguez. No wonder Marius had looked at me with that expression of puzzled déjà vu. What if he were remembering that incident as clearly as I was now? Bronwyn McBride the art dealer would hardly be the sort to have a part-time catering job on the side.

I paused outside the door to our room, unable to still the trembling inside me, even as I tried to rationalize away my fears. There was always the chance that Marius would dismiss the incident as nothing more than a trivial coincidence. He had other things on his mind. Hopefully, that moment with Señor Rodriguez and the wine was long forgotten. What I needed to do was focus on the evening's successes. Caroline knew. She had witnessed Marius' lies first hand. And tomorrow she would meet Duncan. That was all that mattered.

I gave a light tap on the door and seconds later had the comfort of seeing Duncan's face and hearing his warm, but worried, "Lucy, thank God you're back. How did it go?"

His arms came around me, strong and sure, then he ushered me into the living room where Roger was sitting at the table, cards in hand.

"How did it go?" he asked again, and Roger, though silent, had the same question in his eyes.

"Everything's fine. It—it went fine." I got out with a quavering smile. "Caroline will meet you at noon tomorrow."

The relief and gratitude that flooded Duncan's face was all the thanks I'd ever need and made the entire hellish evening worthwhile. He pulled me close then asked, "What's this?" looking at the sack with my damp blouse.

My shrug turned into another shudder as I dropped the sack on the table. "N—nothing. Just a little accident with Señor Rodriguez' wine glass—which turned out to be a blessing in disguise, be—because I got to talk privately with Caroline."

Duncan gave me a close look. "Lucy, darling, what's wrong?"

When I didn't answer, he demanded roughly, "Was it Marius? Did he hurt you? If he did—"

"No . . . n—no," I got out through chattering teeth. "He didn't hurt me. It's just n—nerves . . . or r—reaction, that's all." I tried to smile away the worry in his eyes, and failed miserably.

"You look exhausted," he said, touching a hand to my cheek. "I think you should forget about meeting Marius tomorrow. It's not worth it."

"It is worth it!" I shot back. "Caroline's worth it—and—and I won't let you change everything, just be—because I'm having a small melt down."

His mouth softened. Without a word he pulled me close, pressing my head against the solid warmth of his chest. I clung to him, trembling, willing myself not to cry.

"Rog, make some tea, will you, while I get Lucy into bed."

"I told you—I'm f—fine."

"I know you are," he said, and picking me up in his arms, carried me into the bedroom. "You're also completely worn out, and the best place to have a meltdown is in bed with a hot cup of tea."

He plopped me down on the bed, and I watched wide-eyed while he fumbled his way through the contents of the dresser until he found my cotton night shirt.

I took it from him, thinking he would go, but instead, he sat beside me and began removing my shoes.

"Duncan, please . . . you don't need to—"

"No arguing," he said. "Doctor's orders."

I was trembling too much to offer any serious resistance as he took my sandals off and set them aside. Holding my bare foot in one hand, he gave it a gentle squeeze and ordered softly, "Now get undressed and get in bed."

"Yes, sir."

He smiled at the meekness of my answer, leaned over and kissed my foot, then left. The gesture prompted another shiver deep inside, but this time, the sensation was far from unpleasant.

By the time Duncan returned bearing a steaming mug of herbal tea, I was sitting up in bed, with the blankets tucked around me and pillows at my back.

"How's the meltdown? Feeling any better?" he asked, his blue-green eyes clouded with concern despite the smile.

"Much better, thank you," I assured him, taking the mug.

Duncan sat beside me on the bed, saying nothing, watching me like the male version of an old mother hen while I sipped the tea.

I set the half empty mug on the bedside table, then reached for his hand. "I really am all right," I told him. "You don't need to worry about me."

"I can't help worrying about you," he answered softly. "It's part of loving you. Don't you know that?"

I slowly shook my head. Knowing that I loved him beyond anything I could express was a given. Somehow, I hadn't really stopped to consider that he might feel the same. In that quiet moment, something passed between us, a depth of caring and commitment that went beyond words. I drew his hand to my face and kissed the toughened skin of his palm.

"I meant what I said, Lucy. You don't need to go through with meeting Marius tomorrow. You've already done more than enough, and I'm more grateful than I can say." There was a huskiness in his voice that I'd never heard before, and a suspicious brightness in his eyes.

Taking his face in my hands, I kissed his eyes, his cheeks and his mouth. "Duncan, I need to finish this. You know I do," I said softly, then hurried on, seeing the taut resistance in his face. "All I have to do is show up at a restaurant for a few lousy minutes. That's all. Besides, Caroline's counting on meeting you at noon, minus Marius and Rafferty. We can't change that now."

His silence confirmed my words.

I leaned back against the pillows and smiled at him. "There's so much I need to tell you. I was able to have a very plain talk with your sister tonight. She knows the truth about Marius, and she's—"

Duncan put a finger to my lips. "That can wait until morning."

"It can?"

He nodded. "There's a lot I need to tell you, too. How incredibly wonderful you are . . . and how much I love you." Leaning closer, he asked with a low laugh, "Do you usually wear earrings to bed?"

I put a hand to my ear, fingering the red stones. "I forgot all about them."

"Let me," he said, and gently removed the earring from my left ear.

I closed my eyes, seeing a moment's vision of the Frenchman as he removed Lady Dona's ruby earrings. Then Duncan began kissing me and du Maurier's imaginary characters simply faded away.

THE MORNING SKY was slightly overcast, with a gauzy scarf of white clouds softening the blue. High above the courtyard palms, a feathered squadron of pelicans flew past the hotel on their way to a day's excursion at sea. In the courtyard itself, three gardeners had just finished watering. The paths were neatly groomed and still slightly damp. Water droplets nestled like liquid pearls in the fronds of ferns and hibiscus blossoms.

I leaned against the patio wall, taking in the scene with a small sigh, trying to memorize all this tropical loveliness for some future day of drizzle and cold rain.

"Good morning. You're looking thoughtful, my love."

I turned to see Duncan standing in the doorway, and my heart, not to mention my breathing, reacted strongly to the sight of his tall, tanned body clad in khaki shorts, his black hair still damp from a shower.

"I guess I was feeling a little reluctance that we're leaving so soon."

"We'll be back," he said, coming to stand behind me and wrapping both arms around my middle. I leaned against his chest, holding the arms that held me, loving the feel of his skin.

"And next time, we won't have a built-in chaperone," he added, planting a kiss in my hair.

I smiled. "Poor Roger. He really has tried to disappear at the right moments."

"Or the wrong ones," he said with a laugh.

I laughed, too, then fell silent, needing nothing more than the quiet of the morning and his nearness.

After a moment, I felt a familiar tension enter his body and turned to face him. "You're worrying again."

Duncan's tight-lipped smile acknowledged this. "I was just thinking about your meeting with Marius. I'd feel a lot better if I knew exactly where you were and how things were going. I want you to take my cell phone with you. I'll have Roger's, so if you have any concerns—anything at all—I want you to call me."

"But what will Marius think? We don't want him to find out that you're here, or that I'm in touch with you."

"He won't. Not if you were to get a call from one of your clients, wanting to know if you're having any luck finding what he needs—which happens to be you, my darling."

He drew me close for a long kiss, then pressed my head against the warmth of his chest. "I love you, Lucy, and I want to keep you safe. If all goes well, we'll have Caroline onboard my ship by twelve-twenty . . . twelve-thirty at the latest. I'll call you as soon as we're there. You can give Marius whatever excuse or explanation you want, but make sure you let me know exactly where you are and when you're leaving."

"I will."

"And Lucy?"

"Yes?"

"If he touches you, Caroline will be a widow a lot sooner than she ever thought."

The thin clouds of morning had dissipated and the hot Mexican sun was high overhead as my taxi left the Inn and headed for Mazatlan's Old Town. The taxi was nothing like I had expected, but one of the city's many *pulmoneas,* a jeep-like affair with open sides and a canvas top. My driver was a short slender fellow with unfailing courtesy and a mouth wreathed in a perpetual smile. In addition to driving me to my destination, Sergio seemed to feel that it was his sworn duty to point out every site of interest along the way.

For the first mile or so, the road followed the curve of the coastline. We passed a string of hotels, shops and restaurants and were nearing a rocky outcropping where a white, Moorish-type palace was perched above the sea.

"Valentino's," Sergio informed me over his shoulder, with raised brows and a raised inflection in his voice. "Disco *bueno*."

A few blocks later he was gesturing toward a building with a large bronze fountain and a sculpture of two boys feeding a dolphin.

"*Aquario*," he said. "Very good *aquario*." Then, giving me a knowing wink and a nod, he pointed to the area's main landmark—an enormous statue of a voluptuous nude woman reclining on an anchor, her hand reaching toward a nude fisherman dragging his nets.

"*Monumento al Pesador*," he announced with pride.

"It's monumental all right," I agreed.

Not long after, the taxi left the beachfront and headed inland to what was considered Old Town. In a matter of a few blocks, we were in the heart of Mazatlan's business district, the narrow streets filled with people, cars and buses.

Sergio slowed the *pulmonea* and gestured toward a huge open-air market with tent-like stalls and booths, where Indian women sat behind buckets of shrimp and squid, and boxes of fresh produce were piled high.

"Inside, you find *beuno* gifts and pictures," he informed me. "Elvis on velvet. Very cheap."

I laughed, then caught my breath as the distinctive spires of a cathedral loomed not far ahead.

Mazatlan's cathedral, with its twin towers and intricate carvings, sat to one side of a large plaza filled with vendors promoting their wares. The lucky ones had set up their carts and tables under the sparse shade of the few trees that graced the area, but most were in full sun.

Getting out of the cab, I was tempted to ask Sergio if he'd be willing to wait and come back for me. But where? As yet, I had no idea where Marius and I would be going to lunch.

"*Gracias.*" Sergio's voice was as warm as his smile as I paid him the prearranged amount. Then he was gone, giving me a friendly wave.

In spite of Sergio's mini-tour, I was still several minutes early. I found myself wandering over to the arched doorway of the cathedral, and stepped inside. As my eyes adjusted to the dimness, I saw small clusters of tourists wandering about in respectful silence. My gaze, like theirs, took in the vaulted ceilings, the tall columns with their gilded plaster work, and the life-size statues of Jesus and his mother Mary. I breathed in the peaceful stillness of the place and glanced around the shadowy pews. Only a few feet away, kneeling in rapt prayer, was an old Mexican woman, her gnarled hands clasped tightly, her scarfed head bowed. Watching her intent devotion, I said a silent prayer of my own, then left the quiet sanctuary.

After the cathedral's shadowy coolness, the noonday heat outside had the fierce dry breath of a furnace. I put on my sunglasses to cut the glare and glanced at my watch. Eleven fifty-eight. Only moments from now, Duncan would be meeting Caroline and Roger would have a car ready and waiting for them outside the hotel. Rafferty should be on his way even now to pick up the "important papers" that Marius had left at a law office across town. I smiled, remembering Roger's official legal-sounding voice when he'd phoned the penthouse to give Rafferty the fictitious message. The man had taken the bait without question, and the plan was in motion.

Now, all that remained was for me to walk into a restaurant with Marius, politely excuse myself moments later, and take a cab to the harbor. I could almost believe there was nothing to worry about. Almost.

I was headed over to one of the stalls that had an assortment of tee-shirts and brightly painted animals, when a black Lexus pulled up alongside me, and a masculine voice called out, "*Buenas dias, señorita.* I hope I haven't kept you waiting."

I turned, heart pounding in my throat, to see Marius behind the wheel. Without question, he was an incredibly handsome man. Sunglasses resting on that head of smooth black hair, his mouth curved in a warm smile of greeting, one would never suspect what lay behind the smile.

Marius leaned across the seat to open the car door for me and as I stepped toward him, I felt assaulted by a sudden wave of warning. The feeling of danger was so acute I could almost taste it. I stopped short, trying to resist the compulsion to turn and run—run anywhere, any place, as long as it was away from this man.

Marius must have thought I was waiting for him, because he got quickly out of the car, leaving the motor running, and came around to where I stood. Dressed in casual slacks and an open-necked shirt, he still managed to look more distinguished than most men would in formal dress. Taking my arm, he gave me a kiss on the cheek and said, "Shall we go, dear?" then helped me into the car.

"That early night must have been just what you needed," he commented, giving me an admiring glance as we drove away from the busy plaza. "You look especially lovely today. Glowing, in fact."

Warm color rushed to my cheeks. "Thank you, but the glow is probably due more to the heat than anything else. Thank goodness for air conditioning." I leaned back against the car's soft leather seat and gave my watch a surreptitious glance. Twelve o' three. Caroline should be safe with Duncan and Roger this very moment. I blew out a thankful breath and turned to Marius.

"How did the signing go? Are you now the proud owner of a Mexican hacienda?"

"I am. It's taken months of meetings and negotiation, but the hacienda Delgado is all mine."

"Then a celebration is definitely called for," I said, adding, "Where are we going to lunch, by the way? I've heard the Shrimp Bucket is very good, and I think it's fairly close by."

"Yes, it is, but I had something else in mind. Something more worthy of a celebration."

"Oh?"

He glanced at me with an enigmatic smile. "It's a surprise."

I had no response to this. Especially when it dawned on me that we had left the busy streets of downtown Mazatlan behind, and were driving through a rough housing area similar to the *barrios* that I had seen on the day of our arrival. I glanced out the car window at stark cement houses with graffiti-painted walls and small yards of dusty earth and straggly shrubs.

"How far away is this surprise?" I asked, wishing my voice didn't sound so breathless.

Marius reached for my hand. "Not far. Only a half-hour or so. I'll take you to the Shrimp Bucket another time."

I moistened my lips, grateful for the dark glasses that hid my eyes from his gaze.

"I never was very good at keeping secrets," he went on. "How would you like to see my hacienda?"

"The hacienda?" I caught my breath and stared at him. "That's where we're going?"

He nodded and laughed, certain that my thunderstruck expression stemmed from delight rather than the cold stab of fear that shot through me. "I had the hotel pack us a picnic lunch. It's in the back. How does that sound?"

"I—I'm speechless. This is a surprise."

"And a very selfish one on my part," he said with a certain tone I was coming to know. "We could have gone to any number of places, but this afternoon I want you all to myself."

CHAPTER TWENTY-THREE

The Hacienda

I stared unseeing out the car window, my mouth dry and my heart pounding in fear's heavy, choking rhythm. What a naïve little idiot I was, believing that my plans would coincide with those made by Marius' devious mind. Duncan was right. Marius couldn't be trusted. And now, instead of going to a comfortably crowded restaurant, I was on my way to a remote hacienda with a man who considered murder a viable solution for anyone who stood in his way. Miles away from the nearest town. Miles away from Duncan.

Fear heightened into near panic, as my mind searched frantically for a means of escape. Jumping out of a fast-moving car into the wilds of the Mexican desert wasn't exactly a pleasant option, but even that sounded better than what Marius might have in mind once we reached the hacienda. In spite of my fears, the rational part of me knew it would be a serious mistake to let him know how terrified I was. Bronwyn would never allow it. Neither would Lucy.

Forcing my mouth into a stiff smile, I glanced over at him. "Tell me more about the hacienda. Its history and how you discovered the place."

He was only too happy to do so, launching into an abbreviated version of how he and Caroline had bought some of the hacienda's original furnishings at an estate sale, but without any mention of Bouguereau or the lost painting, *The Fairy Thorn*.

When "Scotland the Brave," suddenly burst forth from my handbag, I nearly jumped off the seat. Marius glanced at me with an amused smile as I quickly fumbled in my purse for the cell phone. In my panicky state, I'd completely forgotten about Duncan's promise to call.

"Hello. . . ?"

"Lucy, where are you? Is everything all right?"

I hesitated and drew a shaky breath, all too aware of Marius' interested gaze. "Mr. Phillips . . . hello . . . . Yes, I know I said I'd call, but I had to make an unexpected trip to Mexico."

"Are you with Marius?" Duncan asked. "Is he listening to this?"

"Yes. Absolutely," I answered, adding, "I understand your frustration with the situation, but I shouldn't be gone too long."

"Dear God, Lucy, where are you? Can you tell me?"

I drew a tense breath and gave Marius a little smile before answering. "I'm sorry, but I'm busy right now. I'm with another art dealer and he's taking me to see an old hacienda. . . . That's right. Could I call you later?"

Silence.

"Mr. Phillips? Hello—?" I stared at the cell phone, feeling as if I'd suddenly lost my lifeline, and not knowing how much, if anything, Duncan had heard.

"I—I guess I've lost him," I said, putting the cell phone into the pocket of my Capris rather than my handbag. If Duncan should call back, I'd be wise to keep the phone close at hand.

"I'm surprised you were able to get any reception at all," Marius commented. "Especially now that we're away from the city." He glanced my way with a slight lift of his dark brows. "So I'm a fellow art dealer," he chuckled.

"Well, in a way you are," I said, sensing that this pleased him.

He laughed again and took my hand. "Yes, I suppose I am."

The Lexus purred along the narrow highway as miles of rough desert landscape passed by, the vegetation mostly greasewood, cactus and chaparral. We had left the flat lands behind and the road was taking us north into the foothills of the Sierra Madres. Comparing this harsh land with the seaside luxury of Mazatlan's Gold Zone, I could understand why Philip Delaney had objected to Marius' headstrong plans. How many idle rich would choose a remote hacienda over the urban comforts of the city? Somehow, I doubted there would be many.

"Is anyone still living at the hacienda?" I asked, hoping the question wouldn't betray my concerns.

"After the guest ranch closed down, the Delgados hired a caretaker of sorts who lives on the property. There's not a lot for him to do now, except feed the stock."

"There are animals?" I asked in surprise.

Marius nodded. "The horses have been sold, but there are still a couple of donkeys and some guinea fowl—oh yes, and white peacocks." He peered ahead, then slowed the Lexus as we neared a gravel side road marked by two stone pillars. "We're nearly there," he said. "The main house is only a few miles down the road."

The road was little more than a dusty track, forcing Marius to slow the car's speed to barely 20 mph. Even so, clouds of dust marked our passage and soon covered the car in a reddish-brown film. Reason was still fighting with the desire to escape as we passed by a small house built of white-washed stucco. This, Marius informed me, was the "caretaker's residence." Caretaker's shanty would have been a better description. A battered gray pick-up truck was parked beside the house, but there was no one around other than a small spotted pig, whose dappled, brown and white markings provided the perfect camouflage against the thorny undergrowth where he was rooting.

A mile or so further, the road dipped down into a rocky, thorn-infested gulley, then climbed up a small rise onto a broad shelf of land. It was here the Delgados had built their hacienda nearly a century and a half before. The main house was very Spanish in appearance and much larger than I expected. Built of stone and thick stucco with a red-tile roof, it had two stories with wrought iron railings framing the upper balconies. Thick wooden pillars, blackened with age, supported a covered porch which ran the full width of the house. Amazingly, there were a few palm trees growing nearby, and masses of scarlet bougainvillea trailing from the balconies.

Marius parked the Lexus beside the house, then glanced at me, waiting for my reaction.

"It's lovely," I said. *And so remote.* Fear rose in my throat, but I forced it back with the hope that somehow Duncan would find me.

"What would you like to do first?" Marius asked, coming around to open the car door. "Eat lunch or take a quick tour of the place?"

"A tour is definitely in order," I answered, thinking I would do my level best to prolong that tour for as long as possible.

Marius was completely at ease and only too willing to answer my questions as he showed me around the grounds and outbuildings. Where did the hacienda get its water? What power source was available? How many guests would the place eventually accommodate? The large bunkhouse would be completely renovated and turned into a luxury spa, he explained, while individual *casitas* would be built for the guests. As we walked, he was so charming, so absolutely normal, that it wasn't difficult to understand how Caroline had first been attracted to the man.

"What do you have in mind for the hacienda itself?" I asked as we left the stables and headed for a circular stone patio located behind the main house, with a tiered fountain at its center.

"I haven't quite decided. I'll need rooms for an office of course, and a reception area—"

A shrill cry pierced the air, sounding exactly like a woman's scream of, "Help . . . help!"

I started visibly and glanced around as the harsh cry came again.

Marius chuckled at my reaction. "It's only the peacocks. Noisy devils, aren't they? See there . . . up on the roof."

I glanced in the direction he pointed and saw one of the elegant white birds strutting across the roof, its long, fan-like plumage snowy white against the dark red tiles.

Marius slipped an arm about my shoulders and turned his steps toward the house. "Shall we go in now?"

There was a certain silkiness in his voice, and when I looked up at him, the expression in his dark eyes awakened a new heartbeat of fear inside me.

I moistened my lips and fought to keep my voice light. "I hope the hotel packed some bottled water with our lunch. I'm—uh, not really used to this heat."

"I'm sure they did." He stroked my cheek with one finger. "Why don't you wait on the porch, dear, and I'll get our lunch from the car."

I gladly retreated to the shade of the porch, trying to think through my options with some measure of rationality. Every instinct told me to run. Hide. Escape from those dark eyes and that honeyed voice. But where could I go? My eyes searched the harsh landscape. Nothing but cactus and chaparral for miles. Other than the lonely sigh of the wind and the faint drone of insects, there was no sound at all—only the immense silence of the desert, which was almost a sound in itself.

I stared into the vast distance and silently prayed. *Please let Duncan come. Help him find me.*

Marius approached, carrying a large plastic cooler. He paused on the porch steps to give me an admiring smile.

"You have no idea what an enchanting picture you make. Bouguereau would have loved to paint you."

"In white Capris and a tee-shirt? I don't think so," I said with a shaky laugh. *Keep it light. Just keep it light.*

"He would have painted you in different attire, it's true," Marius agreed, coming onto the porch and setting the cooler down to take a set of keys from his pants pocket. "Take away the Capris and the tee-shirt, and you'd be a vision that even Bouguereau would find hard to resist."

I met his gaze, determined not to flinch as his eyes undressed me. "Then it's a good thing I wasn't born a century ago, because right now, the 'vision' is hungry and lunch sounds wonderful."

Marius laughed and unlocked the massive wooden door, then gave it a shove with his shoulder. Even so, it opened almost reluctantly, with a creaking whine.

"After you, mademoiselle."

I entered, just as reluctantly.

Once inside, it was as if we had passed through a magical portal and stepped back in time. A time of centuries long past, when Mexico was ruled by Spain and wealthy *haciendados.*

A stone entryway led us into the main room which had to be at least twenty by thirty feet in size. Thankfully, it was also a good ten degrees cooler than the blistering heat outside. I wandered about the huge room with real interest, taking in the beamed ceiling of dark wood and wrought iron chandeliers; the massive stone fireplace that looked big enough to roast an ox, and colorful woven rugs on the worn planks of a hardwood floor. The furnishings were of a much newer vintage, mostly leather and wood, but still maintained a strong Spanish flavor.

"Marius, it's wonderful," I said and meant it.

He smiled a smile of proud ownership and directed me through an arched doorway off the great room. "The dining room is through here."

Like the main living area, the walls of the dining room were white-washed stucco, and the furniture—a long table with six chairs to a side, and an ornately carved sideboard—was dark with age. Heavy drapes had been drawn across the windows, shutting out the day, and seen in this shadowy light, I had a sudden vision of the great dining hall at Navron House . . . and of the men sitting six to a side at the long table, with candles burning bright overhead. And the lovely hostess, with her ruby earrings and dark ringlets, who smiled and flirted outrageously with her guests, keeping them talking and drinking until midnight. . . .

Keep him talking. The thought planted itself firmly in my mind, as my thoughts returned to the present.

Marius set the cooler on one end of the table, then going to the windows, pulled a cord, parting the heavy drapes, and sunlight spilled into the room. A massive painting of the Sierra Madre mountains practically filled one wall, and I made a pretense of studying it.

"May I help with anything?" I asked.

"There's nothing to do really, except enjoy ourselves," he said, opening the cooler, where several plastic containers had been packed in ice.

I had to admit the man planned well and had impeccable taste. There was seafood salad stuffed in flaky, mini-croissants, a variety of sliced cheeses and fresh fruit. *Paté* with thin crackers. Even a shrimp marinade. Marius had his wine, of course, but there was bottled water and a slushy lemonade for me. From another sack, he took out plates, silverware, and snowy linen napkins.

"I hope everything meets with your approval," he said, pulling out one of the tall-backed chairs for me.

I sat down and picked up a napkin. "It's lovely. You've thought of everything." *The perfect setting for seduction*, I thought, my stomach churning.

"I make it my business to do so."

I managed to eat a few bites of a croissant and eagerly drank the bottled water, thinking that, at least wouldn't be drugged.

Marius looked at me from over his glass of wine, and the expression in his dark eyes strongly hinted that I was the next course on the menu.

"I'd give a lot to know what you're thinking about right now," he said. "I've never met a woman with such expressive eyes. A man could get lost in them."

The mouthful of croissant went down in a tasteless lump, but my mind moved into high gear. "It's interesting that you should use the word 'lost.' I was just thinking about a certain rumor I overheard at your party." His dark brows went up a notch and I went on with a demure little smile. "I'd love to know if the rumor's true."

"What exactly was this rumor?"

I picked a few grapes from their stem before meeting his gaze. "That you believe a lost painting by Bouguereau may be hidden somewhere on the hacienda."

Marius set his wine glass on the table. "And what if I were to tell you the rumor's true? What then?"

"Then I'd want to know how on earth you can sit here, calmly eating lunch, when we could be searching the place."

He burst out laughing. "Bronwyn, without a doubt, you are the most intriguing woman I have ever met."

I shrugged and smiled. "I don't know about intriguing, but I am definitely curious. A lost painting by Bouguereau! That's better than a pirate treasure. Have you given any thought at all to where the painting might be hidden?"

"Don't you mean, *if* the painting exists, and *if* it's hidden here on the hacienda?"

He was testing me and I knew it; wanting to know if I thought his theory had substance or was sheer foolishness.

"Obviously, you have a valid reason for believing the painting exists," I said. "And if it does, then you must have a good reason for believing that it's here." I paused and dared step a little further on the shaky path I was treading. "According to the rumor, the owners of the hacienda were also the owners of the painting. Am I right so far?"

He nodded, dark eyes gleaming. "Unerring."

"So, the next question would be—when did the painting disappear? Do you have any idea for a possible time frame?"

He gave another assenting nod. "It had to be sometime during Mexico's Revolution and Civil War—around 1912. That's when

Melville sent his wife and children to live with some relatives in the States."

"Melville?" I asked innocently, knowing full well who the man was.

"An American businessman who married Mercedes Delgado," he said. "He bought *The Fairy Thorn* as an anniversary gift for his wife."

"An American?" I questioned, toying with the grapes.

"Richard Melville was the son of a wealthy New York banker. He came to Mazatlan in the 1890s on business, married Enrique Delgado's daughter, and decided to stay."

"And you said that in 1912 he sent his wife and children to the States?"

"That's right. Like the rest of Mexico, the situation in Mazatlan was very unsettled, with bandits raiding even the big rancheros. The hacienda's remoteness, along with the Delgados' wealth made it a prime target. From what I could find out, Melville was alone on the hacienda with just a few servants when it was raided. Unfortunately, they were all shot and killed."

I set the grapes aside and thought a moment. "So Melville would have been the one to hide the painting."

"Yes, I believe so."

"Maybe this is a ridiculous question, but do you have any idea what size the painting was?"

Marius smiled. "It's not ridiculous at all—and it so happens I know the painting's exact size. It was written on the bill of sale when Melville purchased it in New York."

I hoped my expression was sufficiently surprised by this information. "You have the bill of sale?"

"It was with some papers in a desk we purchased at the estate sale. Bouguereau was known for doing life-size works, and *The Fairy Thorn* was quite large—60" by 48". Why do you ask?"

"I'm trying to create a scenario. Unless Melville had time to remove it from the frame, he'd have a hard time finding a good hiding place. Plus, a painting that large wouldn't be the kind of thing that bandits could easily carry off—not like money or jewelry."

"My dear, you are as brilliant as you are beautiful. I'm impressed."

I shrugged away the compliment and glanced around the dining room. "So what did Melville do with it?"

"Believe me, I've been asking myself that same question for months now, and so far, I haven't come up with any answers—other than the gut feeling that it's got to be here, somewhere."

"What year did you say the painting was purchased?"

"In 1902."

"And Melville was living here at the hacienda."

"That's right."

"But the hacienda belonged to his wife's family."

"Yes, why?"

Ignoring his question, I asked another of my own, excitement quickening in my voice. "How old is the hacienda? Do you have any idea?"

Marius shook his head. "I'm not really sure. I do know the Delgado family lived here for several generations before Melville married Mercedes. What does that have to do with the painting?"

I hesitated before answering, trying to come up with a logical reason why Bronwyn McBride would know anything about Mexican history, then decided it probably didn't matter. Marius wouldn't care what I knew, one way or another, unless it led him to the painting.

"All right. From what little I've read, the lawlessness and the raids by bandits weren't confined to the time of the Revolution. There were clashes between Spanish nobility and the natives ever since the Conquistadores first arrived in the country. And in remote areas like this, a safe or strong box for valuables wasn't always enough."

"What are you suggesting?" Marius asked, his dark eyes alight with interest.

"Well, it might sound a bit melodramatic, but I've read where some of the old haciendas had trap doors and secret rooms where valuables could be stored."

"A secret room?" he echoed.

"I know it sounds a bit far fetched—"

"No, no it doesn't," he interrupted, his voice breathless with excitement. "Tell me about these secret rooms."

"There isn't all that much to tell. Some were fairly small. Others could hide family members as well as valuables, and some even had a separate exit—a tunnel leading away from the house. The room might be hidden behind a false wall or in a wine cellar."

Marius caught his breath. "There's a wine cellar off the kitchen."

"Really? Have you seen it?"

He shook his head. "I know where it is, but I haven't been down there. The real estate agent who took us through the house said it hadn't been used for years and thought the stairs might not be safe."

Seeing the excited gleam in his dark eyes, I knew his interest in me had been replaced by something he wanted far more. And I was determined to keep it that way.

"I don't know about you, but I'd like to see what's down there," I told him.

"And if there's only dust and a few rats?"

"Then we look somewhere else, but at least you'll know."

Leaving our lunch on the table, I followed him out of the dining room and down a hallway to the kitchen. This room was on a scale equally as large as the others, with the same beamed ceiling and white-washed walls. In addition to cupboards and a wooden table, it also had the modern conveniences of running water, an electric range and refrigerator. On a far wall, I noticed a small door that looked as if it might be a pantry. Marius made straight for it and took out his key ring, trying one, then another in his eagerness. When the door finally opened, I could see little more than a flight of wooden steps leading down into musty darkness.

"Do you have a flashlight?" I asked, wrinkling my nose at the dank, musty smell.

"No need." Marius reached up and pulled a small cord hanging from the ceiling.

The weak light from a single bare bulb revealed a narrow staircase of some five or six steps, then a small wooden landing, followed by more stairs descending into blackness.

He took a few steps down, testing his weight. "They seem stable enough," he said, and reached out a hand to me.

I hesitated, curiosity warring with the desire to turn and run. But where could I run to? The caretaker's house was a good mile or more down the road. And despite my precarious circumstances, at the moment I was in no real danger. Marius' excitement over the treasure hunt for Bouguereau's lost painting superseded all else. Better keep it that way, I decided, and trust—trust that Duncan would find me.

Taking Marius' hand, I descended the stairs.

Chapter Twenty-Four

"The Fairy Thorn"

The wooden planks creaked underfoot as I descended the last few steps and glanced around. The bare bulb overhead lent a sallow glow to what had once been the Delgados' wine cellar. A place of mystery it definitely was not. The room was long and fairly narrow, no more than six feet wide and perhaps ten to twelve feet in length, with wine racks filling the far wall and wooden shelves running along the side opposite the stairs. The racks were empty, as were most of the shelves. I saw a few jars coated with dust and grime, a cast iron frying pan, and some empty bottles of dark green glass. Squatting in a far corner was a small wooden stool with an enamel pan leaning against its side. The floor was earth and hard-packed.

"There's not much here," Marius commented, frowning.

"Nothing at first glance, anyway," I said, hoping to keep the lure of the hunt alive. I moved closer to the shelves, my eyes searching for clues, yet not really knowing what to search for. The shelves on the side wall were made of sturdy planks about eight or nine inches deep, and free standing against the cold, white-washed stucco.

"What are you looking for?" Marius asked, a thread of impatience in his voice.

"I'm not sure." I moved to the far wall and stared at the rows of empty wine racks. "Well, here's something interesting."

"What?" Marius came to stand behind me.

"The backing of the shelves on this side is made of wood—not stucco."

"So?" The impatience was still there.

"So, what's behind those planks?"

Marius gave a little snort and shook his head. "You really are determined, aren't you?"

Determined and desperate, I thought. Aloud, I said, "I told you—I'm curious. Why would there be planks behind these shelves and stucco on the others? It doesn't make sense. I think they were put there for a reason. They had to be. When the wine racks were full, the planks wouldn't be noticeable—especially since they were white-washed like the stucco." I ran my fingers along the back and inside of the shelves.

"Now what are you doing?"

"Checking."

"Checking," he repeated with a short laugh, but the impatience was gone from his tone, replaced by tolerant amusement.

"For a knob or a handle . . . some way of opening—" I broke off as my fingers found a round knothole in one of the planks. Quite honestly, I wasn't expecting a thing, but I stuck two fingers inside and gave it a healthy yank.

"Careful there," Marius cautioned. "You're going to bring the whole thing down on us."

"No . . . no, I'm sure it moved!"

"Of course it moved! The thing's probably rotten as hell."

Ignoring him, I gave the planking another hard pull, and this time the shelves swung open with an unearthly groan. The suddenness sent me stumbling backwards into Marius, who quickly steadied me with both hands. His amused chuckle changed to a startled gasp and we both stared.

The wine rack was in fact, a cleverly camouflaged door, which opened to reveal another room, smaller than the wine cellar, but a room nonetheless.

Marius released me to peer into the room's shadowy depths, his breathing rapid with excitement.

The lone bulb above the stairs gave little light to the secret room behind the wine racks, but even in the dimness, I could make out several objects—a small table with a metal box and some books stacked on its top, a large camel-backed chest with brass hinges, and a pair of silver candelabras, black and tarnished with age, the beeswax candles still sitting in their holders.

There were a few stunned seconds when neither of us could speak, as the impossible suddenly became possible and legend was transformed into something tangible and real.

Then he was inside the room, grasping a tarnished metal box with shaking hands. Looking over his shoulder, I saw what appeared to be gold coins and a jeweled pendant.

He shook his head in dazed wonder, then glanced at me. "We need more light."

"There might be a flashlight upstairs in the kitchen," I said, backing away. "I'll go look."

He reached out and grabbed my arm. "No. No, wait. I've got something." Taking a slim lighter from his pants pocket, he lifted one of the heavy candelabras, and after shoving aside the books, set it on the table.

As he lit the candles, the musty shadows of the room changed to a mellow glow, and I blew out a sigh of sheer amazement. "It's like Aladdin's cave."

Marius was glancing about with a half-crazed expression. Then he gasped. "There! Behind that low chest! There's something large wrapped in cloth. . . ." Moving the chest aside, he flung off the dusty gray sheet, then stood, transfixed and speechless.

"*The Fairy Thorn,*" I breathed, as the painting's beauty pierced my heart.

Two lovers had found an idyllic place to rendezvous in a woodsy thicket and were resting against the gnarled trunk of an old hawthorn tree. The young man's dark curly head rested in the lap of his beloved, his eyes gazing into hers with the half-drugged adoration of sated love. Partially clothed, yet innocent as Eve before the apple, the young woman's beauty held both the sensual and ethereal, from the creaminess of her skin and unbound hair, to the warm passion lighting her eyes. Half-hidden among the hawthorn's leafy branches, a host of fairy folk peered down at the love struck mortals with secretive delight.

The unabashed emotion of the scene was surpassed only by the artist's masterful technique. His brush strokes gave new meaning to the matchless symmetry of the human form and the tranquil cadence of nature. How one man could use color and paint to create such a sublime blend of emotion and imagination I would never know. I could only stare, speechless, at the poetry and passion of young love seamlessly entwined with myth and magic. It was all there, captured on canvas by a true master.

A low sound brought me out of awe's silent reverie. Marius' laughter and half-mad mutterings.

"Philip thought I was crazy . . . they all did . . . but I was right. I was right! And it's worth millions . . . millions!"

I backed away as he rambled on, drunk with discovery and greed. I stumbled into the box filled with jewelry and coins and Marius never even glanced my way.

Grabbing the cell phone from my pocket, I ran toward the stairs. I paused on the landing to open the phone. My hands were shaking and so was my voice.

"Duncan . . . Duncan, you've got to be there. . . ."

There were no bars on the small lighted screen. *No service.* What was I thinking? Outside. I had to get outside.

Still staring at the phone, I ran up the remaining stairs and charged headlong into the solid bulk of Rafferty's body.

"Not so fast," he grunted, grabbing both my arms. "Where's Marius?"

"He—he's down there . . . in the cellar."

"And where were you headed in such a hurry?"

I swallowed and stammered, "Out—outside . . . to make a call."

The man's eyes narrowed and his grip on my arms tightened. "And why were you so eager to get hold of Alexander? What's going on between you two?"

"Nothing's going on! Let go of me!"

"Not until I get a few questions answered," he said and pulled me back down the stairs.

Rafferty's eyes widened as he took in the candle-lit scene in the secret room. Marius was on his knees, rifling through the contents of the metal box, a half-crazed smile twisting his mouth into a hideous caricature of his former self.

I willed myself not to struggle and fought to control my breathing, hoping Rafferty would ease his hold on my arms.

"Marius?" he grunted. "What's all this?"

Marius glanced up with a breathless laugh. "I found it! I found *The Fairy Thorn* and a treasure besides."

"All right, so you found the painting," Rafferty acknowledged, his thick lips curling in disgust. "Then I guess it doesn't matter if your wife's gone."

"What did you say?"

"Caroline's gone. When I got back from the lawyer's office—"

"What are you talking about?" Marius flung back, getting to his feet. "Why did you go to the lawyer's office?"

"I got a call from some guy saying you'd forgotten some important papers. When I got there, they didn't know what the hell I was talking about. I tried calling you, but couldn't get through. By the time I got back to the hotel, Caroline was gone—along with some of her things and her passport." Rafferty's grip tightened painfully as he yanked me in front of him and said, "I don't know what's going on, but your little friend here is mixed up in it somehow." He grabbed the cell phone out of my hand and shoved me toward Marius. "Maybe you ought to ask her why she was running away just now, trying to call Alexander."

Marius stared at me, his face a frozen mask. "Well, Bronwyn, don't you have anything to say?"

I fought to hide the fear pounding inside me with a rather pathetic display of anger. "I have no idea what the problem is, but I certainly don't appreciate such strong-arm treatment." I glared at Rafferty and rubbed my arm.

"Why were you trying to call Duncan?" Marius persisted. "You must have a reason. I'm curious to know what it is."

I stared at him, trying to come up with some reason or excuse, however weak.

Marius moved closer and his hands were like claws, clutching my shoulders. "Could it be that you and Duncan are working together?" he asked in a silky tone. "Plotting to take the painting and what's mine."

"What?" At first, I thought he meant Caroline, then he gestured to the contents of the secret room with a wild look that sent a chill crawling through me. I shook my head and mumbled, "No . . . that's crazy."

"Not so crazy. You know very well that painting's worth a fortune! Why else were you so eager to find it?"

"You're wrong. I—I had no idea the painting was even here."

"You're lying!" he ground out. "You knew it was here. Or why all that talk about Bouguereau and secret rooms. You know far too much, my dear." Anger and madness stripped his voice of its silkiness as he yanked me closer, his breath hot in my face. "You and Duncan—the two of you have been working together all along!" His dark eyes widened in sudden recognition as he stared at me. "I knew I'd seen you somewhere before, but I couldn't think where. You were the server at our cocktail party! I remember now . . . the way you were staring at Bouguereau's painting. Duncan sent you to spy on me, didn't he? Didn't he!"

I wrenched myself free from his grasp, only to have Rafferty seize my arms from behind. Gasping from the pain, my struggle was brief and useless.

"It's true, I was a server at the party. But I wasn't spying on you . . . for Duncan, or anyone else."

"Then why were you there?" Marius demanded. "And no more lies. Rafferty has a way of getting the truth out of people, but it's not at all pleasant. It would be much better if you told me now. It's entirely up to you, my dear. But I promise you this—" His mouth twisted in an ugly smile as he grabbed my chin and jerked my face close to his. "Once Rafferty's done with you, I fully intend to get what I want."

Sick dread clutched at my insides and my breath came out in choking gasps.

Marius smiled, enjoying my fear and said, "So what is it to be, Bronwyn? Lies or the truth?"

Anger suddenly fought its way past the fear and I met his eyes with icy fury. "The truth is, I'm not Bronwyn McBride, any more than you're Marius Charbot. And no matter what you do to me, you'll be found out. The lies have finally caught up with you, Mr. Mark Cabot!"

He gave a derisive snort and half turned away, then struck me across the face with a force that sent me sprawling backwards onto the floor of the cellar. Stunned from the pain, I put a hand to my face and struggled to sit up just as a tall form leaped from the stairs, knocked Rafferty roughly aside, and charged headlong into Marius.

"Duncan. . . ." The name came out in a dry croak, even as Marius met him with an angry lunge.

The man was no match for Duncan's strength and fury. One of Duncan's fists connected with Marius' jaw and sent him staggering back into the secret room. Marius recovered with a growl of rage and struck out with a vicious kick to Duncan's groin. I winced as Duncan groaned and stumbled, but still managed to avoid another wild blow. Grabbing Marius' arm, he twisted it behind his back. Marius fought to free himself like a man possessed, and the two of them went down, grappling on the floor. The force of their struggle knocked one of the candelabras off the table and there was a moment of wild, flickering shadows, then semi-darkness as the candles gutted.

In the dim half-light, I became aware of sudden movement beside me. Rafferty was on his feet, a revolver in his right hand. My warning scream sounded strangely muffled, as if it were coming from a long way off. Then everything happened at once.

I saw Caroline standing near the top of the stairs, her face pale as death. And Roger, beside her, leaping off with a yell, to land squarely on Rafferty's back. There was a single shot, sounding like the boom of a cannon in the enclosed space, the report echoing off the cellar walls and ringing in my ears.

Then silence. In the secret room, two men lay motionless and still.

"Duncan . . . Duncan . . . oh please, God. . . ." I tried to stand, to go to him, but my knees buckled, and I couldn't get past the grappling bodies of Rafferty and Roger.

The next moment, Rafferty thrust Roger aside, then pinned and straddled him, with both hands around his neck.

From above, I heard a pitiful cry, as Caroline stumbled down the stairs, only to slump on the landing in a dead faint.

I was helpless to reach her. Helpless to do anything.

Straining and choking, Roger fought to free himself from Rafferty's huge hands, but he was no match against the bigger man's stranglehold.

I glanced around wildly, and grabbed one of the empty wine bottles from a shelf. Crawling over to the two men, I brought the bottle down on Rafferty's head with a splintering crash. The blow did little more than faze him, but at least he released his hold on Roger's neck. Shaking off the broken glass like an enraged bull, Rafferty lunged toward me on all fours, his anger blinding him to everything else. I tried to back away, but my body was clumsy and helpless, and there was nowhere to go.

Then behind him, I saw movement and a face, grimly determined. Rafferty turned, but not in time, as Duncan slammed one of the candelabras onto the man's skull. Metal met bone with sickening force and Rafferty went down without a groan.

Dropping the candelabra, Duncan reached for me and I flung myself into his arms. We clung to one another, too shaken to speak, dazed and grateful to be alive. Our kiss was fierce with the realization of what we had come close to losing. Then he buried his face against my neck, his breathing ragged.

"Lucy . . . Lucy, I thought I'd lost you."

"I kept praying you'd come . . . that you'd find me."

"We never would have found the place if it hadn't been for Caroline. When she heard where Marius was taking you, she insisted on coming."

I raised my head and met his eyes. "Marius . . . is he?"

Duncan nodded. "Rafferty's bullet got him square in the chest."

From the stairs we heard a low moan, then Roger's worried cry. "Duncan—Lucy—I need help with Caroline."

We scrambled up the narrow stairs to the landing where Roger was supporting Caroline in his arms. As I bent down beside her, she turned pleading blue eyes up to me and reached for my hand.

"The baby," was all she said.

Roger smoothed her hair and mumbled broken assurances. "Don't worry . . . we'll get you to a hospital. . . ."

"There's a doctor onboard the *Isabel*," Duncan said. "That'll be faster and a helluva lot better." Leaning over, he kissed Caroline's pale cheek and said with gentle firmness, "Hang in there, little sister. You're going to be fine." Then, to Roger, "Let's get her to the car."

"What about those two?" Roger asked, glancing over his shoulder.

Duncan shook his head and gave Caroline's hand a little squeeze. "There's nothing we can do for Marius. And Rafferty won't be going anywhere for a long while." Turning to Roger, he said with quiet urgency, "You get Caroline to the car and I'll take care of things here."

Roger nodded and picked Caroline up in his arms as if she were a precious doll, then made his way up the stairs.

I stayed on the landing, leaning against the cold stucco for support, while Duncan dragged Marius' body out of the secret room and left him lying near Rafferty. He pushed the false shelves back in place and glanced around the shadowy cellar, then bent down for his cell phone that Rafferty had dropped.

"Lucy . . . we need to go, love."

My mind and legs couldn't seem to connect. I couldn't move, nor could I force my eyes away from Marius body, the once handsome mouth parted in a grim look of surprise and horror.

"What about the police?" I got out. "Shouldn't we call them?"

"The authorities will have to be notified," he agreed, "but right now, my first priority is Caroline. You can tell me what all this was about on the way." Putting an arm around my waist, he helped me up the stairs and into the kitchen.

"Did you bring anything with you?" he asked tersely. "When the police arrive, it would be better if they found nothing except—" He broke off, but I didn't need further explanation.

"My purse . . . it's in the dining room. Duncan, don't let go of me."

"I won't, darling. I've got you."

Leaning heavily on his arm, we made our way through the silent house. I glanced around the sunlit dining room with its long table and our half-eaten lunch. Was it only a few minutes ago I had sat here with Marius or another lifetime?

"Here it is." Duncan picked up my handbag from one of the chairs and gave it to me. "Anything else?"

"I don't think so . . . just the food."

Duncan's keen-eyed glance took in the cooler and cartons of food. He picked up my water bottle with its telltale lipstick stains on the lip. "Here. You'd better take this."

"What will the police think?"

"It doesn't matter what they think," he said. "As long as there's nothing to connect you with the place. Let's go."

Roger ran across the dusty yard to meet us as we left the hacienda.

"How's Caroline?" Duncan asked quickly.

"Cramping and miserable," Roger said, "but calm." He tossed a worried glance in the direction of the Lexus and a tan Chevy parked beside it. "What do we do about the cars?"

Duncan was already striding toward the Lexus. "The keys are in the car," he called back to Roger. "Check the Chevy and see if Rafferty was as careless as Marius."

Roger tried the car door and found it locked. "No go on this one."

Duncan gave the keys to the Lexus a good toss into some mesquite some twenty yards away, then approached the Chevy. "No problem. I don't think Rafferty'll be going anywhere, but in case he does—" Duncan glanced around the rough ground, then broke off a small, sharp twig from some low-growing sage. Removing the cap from the front tire's valve stem, he shoved the twig into the valve and listened with satisfaction to the hiss of escaping air. After doing the same to one of the back tires, he ran over to where Roger and I were waiting.

"All right. Let's get out of here."

As we drove away, I found myself glancing back for one last look at the hacienda. Strangely, my thoughts were not of Marius and all that had happened, but of the painting that had lain hidden in a secret room for over a hundred years.

Chapter Twenty-Five

The Adventure of a Lifetime

I leaned against a smooth wooden rail on the yacht *Isabel,* watching the Mexican coastline gently fade into the distance. Soon it was only a blurred line on the watery horizon. Above me, the yacht's white sails sang in a freshening breeze, and below, the calm swells of the sea were liquid jade.

I saw Duncan come out of the ship's cabin, stop for a moment to speak with one of the crew, then glance around. When he saw me, he smiled and raised an arm. I smiled and waved in return, feeling a quickening of joy inside. A few long strides brought him across the deck to stand beside me. Held close against his side, we watched that blurry strip of land disappear as if it were only a wisp of cloud.

I gave a little sigh and rested my head against his shoulder. "How's Caroline?"

"Resting. Roger's with her. The doctor said she'll be fine in a few days. No complications, thank God." He shook his head, and the expression in his blue-green eyes was somber. "For someone who's had everything handed to her practically all her life, she's taking things pretty well. It's easy to say that what happened was all for the best, but still—it's pretty tough to lose a husband and a baby all in the same day."

"Yes," I agreed softly. "It is." My mind went back to that moment in the cellar when Rafferty had fired and both Marius and Duncan had gone down. I shuddered and moved closer in Duncan's arms, knowing it could have been him and not Marius who lay dead on the cellar floor.

"You okay?" he asked.

I nodded against his chest. "Just feeling grateful."

His arms tightened around me. "Me, too."

"Can I ask a big favor?" he said after a moment.

"Of course."

"When we get to San Diego, I'm going to put Caroline on the next available flight to Seattle. I know Roger wants to be with her, but I think she needs the help of another woman right now. I've already called my folks and they'll meet you at the airport. Will you do this for me, Lucy?"

"You know I will, but where will you be?"

He hesitated. "I'll probably have to go back to Mazatlan. There are several loose ends to tie up, and some unpleasant details that I don't want Caroline to worry about right now—like getting Marius' body back to the States."

"Do you think there'll be any trouble with the authorities?"

"I don't think so. My main concern was getting clear of the harbor and out to sea, before calling the police. Everything I told them was essentially the truth—that my sister hadn't heard from her husband since he left the hotel to go to the hacienda, and she was worried that he might be in some kind of trouble. When I told them about the miscarriage, they didn't question the necessity of getting her back to the States for medical care. I've given them my number in case they need to reach me—" He glanced at his watch with a slight frown. "Which they'll probably be doing any time now."

I shivered as my mind replayed the bloody scene in the wine cellar. "I suppose there'll be an investigation."

"Yes, and it'll be Rafferty's fingerprints they'll find on the gun. As for the rest, well, the whole scene looks like a drug bust gone bad, and that type of thing happens in Mexico all the time."

"But what if Rafferty tells them that I was there?"

He drew me closer. "Rafferty's not going to get much sympathy with Mexican authorities, no matter what he says. Besides, as far as he knows, your name is Bronwyn, not Lucy. Try not to worry, love."

"How long do you think you'll be gone?" I asked, feeling an aching sort of disquiet at the thought of being parted from him.

"Not long. A few days at most. And then—" He broke off to give me a searching look and a little smile.

"And then?" I prompted.

"I was—uh, wondering when you'd like to get married. Please tell me you don't believe in long engagements."

I smiled up at him. "We probably ought to wait until Aunt Ivy and Uncle Milt get back."

"And when will that be?"

"Wednesday afternoon. Five days from now."

"Next Wednesday," he said and kissed me. "I think I can survive that long. Although, if it weren't for Caroline, I'd be tempted to ask the captain of the *Isabel* to marry us right now."

"Mmm, that is tempting," I agreed and kissed the warm pulse beating at the base of his tanned throat. "But Peggy would never forgive me. I promised her that she could be my matron of honor."

"Well then, we certainly can't disappoint Peggy," he said with a chuckle. "Any other critical reasons for delay?"

I shook my head. "Nothing critical, but it might be nice if we gave my aunt and uncle time to unpack. How does next Saturday sound—one week from tomorrow?"

"One week from tomorrow it is," he said, ruffling my hair.

I wrapped my arms around his brawny waist. "Do you realize that when we get married, I will have known you eighteen entire days?"

Duncan looked down at me, a thoughtful frown replacing the smile. "Eighteen days. Are you sure, Lucy? I want you to be sure."

"Very sure," I said with a kiss for added emphasis. "I remember reading somewhere that when you love someone, the length of time doesn't really matter—only the depths of time."

"The depths of time," he echoed softly. "I like that."

We stood for a long while, arms about each other, content to watch the emerald swells of the sea and the sunlight dancing on the water. The sun was warm on our backs, the breeze fresh and clean on our faces. When anything as commonplace as mere words could be introduced into the moment, I glanced up to see a certain sparkle lighting his eyes and a smile teasing his mouth.

"What's making you smile?"

"I was just thinking that after all the adventures Bronwyn McBride has had this past week, you might find being Mrs. Duncan Alexander isn't very exciting."

"On the contrary," I said, reaching up to kiss him. "Being your wife will be the adventure of a lifetime."

SKIES WERE GRAY and a soft April rain was falling, soaking the fields and forests of Whidbey Island, when I heard a car pull into the driveway of my aunt and uncle's home. Moments later, a door slammed and my aunt's voice rang out from the kitchen.

"Lucy, we're home!"

I left the living room to meet them and barely had time to offer a warm, "Welcome back," before I was enfolded in Aunt Ivy's soft embrace. Uncle Milt set the suitcases down he was carrying to give me a hearty hug and kiss on the cheek.

"Oh, Lucy, it's so good to see you! It feels like we've been gone a month, doesn't it Milton?" Before he could answer she went on excitedly, "We had such a wonderful time, and those ginger pills Ethel Sainsbury told me to take worked wonders. I wasn't seasick once. And Mexico was so lovely. I really quite enjoyed it. We'll have to take you there sometime, won't we Milton? We brought you back the prettiest silver bracelet—" My aunt suddenly stopped short and stared at me.

"Lucy, you cut your hair! Milton, she's cut her hair!"

"I can see that," my uncle put in with his slow smile. "It looks real spring like."

"But—but, your lovely hair," Aunt Ivy said, her voice stricken. "What on earth possessed you to do such a thing?"

"Peggy suggested it. She thought I might like a change. Don't you like it?"

"Well, I—I suppose I do," she said with enough doubt in her voice to make me laugh.

"Aunt Ivy, there's a lot I need to tell you. Why don't we go in the living room and—"

"Oh, before I forget," she put in, still a flutter. "I noticed a strange car parked by the side of the house. Do you know who it belongs to?"

"Yes, that's Duncan's car."

"Who's Duncan?"

"Duncan Alexander, my fiancé." I held out my left hand where a lovely diamond solitaire had recently taken up residence. "He's in the living room right now, waiting to meet you and Uncle Milt."

Aunt Ivy's mouth opened in a stunned sort of 'o' but no words came out. She just blinked at me and stared.

"Do you mean John and Evelyn's boy?" Uncle Milt asked, looking fairly thunderstruck himself.

"That's right," I told them. "I'm going to marry Captain Alexander's great-grandson."

"But—but—I don't understand," Aunt Ivy sputtered. "How? When did all this happen?"

I smiled at her and said with a little shrug, "I suppose it all started because I didn't do what I always do."

THE SEVEN DAYS that followed passed in a flurry of plans and preparation. Within the first twenty-four hours, all Coupeville and half of Langley were agog with the news that Lucy Norris, the librarian, was getting married. And the man in question was not Norman Phillips. Rumors were flying like kites in the wind, and in my happiness, I let them fly. Duncan's mother was in a state of nerves because the country club wasn't available at such short notice, and Aunt Ivy was distraught when old Ruby Farnsworth finally passed away at the age of ninety-six, and her funeral made the church unavailable. Duncan and I managed to appease both of them by announcing we would be married in the parlor of the Alexander home.

My two cousins called to offer their congratulations, along with their excuses, as they'd scheduled a fishing trip to Alaska, and wouldn't be able to attend. Surely I would understand why they couldn't make any changes at this late date. I did, only too well, and smilingly accepted their apologies, not minding in the least that they wouldn't be present.

How does one find words to describe images of love? The proud, tear-filled eyes of my uncle as he held out his arm and guided me down the stairs to the parlor, where those we loved best were waiting . . . dear Aunt Ivy and Duncan's parents, looking happy, but still a trifle confused how all this had come about . . . a beaming Peggy with her husband and little boys, all dressed up in their Sunday best and scrubbed within an inch of their lives. And Roger, a handsome best man with eyes only for Caroline, who insisted on coming despite her mother's concerns.

Duncan had asked an old friend and mentor, Captain Ian MacDonald, to perform the ceremony, and as we made our vows, I like to think there were others there as well—my parents, and perhaps the sea captain and his bride. I couldn't prevent my hand from trembling as I slid a simple gold ring on Duncan's finger and repeated the words that would bind our lives and our love. When I glanced up, I saw forever shining in his eyes.

Captain MacDonald's deep voice grew husky as he finished the ceremony, then my husband took my face in his strong hands for our first kiss as man and wife.

The old home rang with laughter that evening. The walls fairly ached with it. And I could swear the faces of Duncan's grandparents and great-grandparents were smiling down at us from their framed places over the mantle. Peggy and Aunt Ivy had combined forces to produce a lovely wedding dinner, complete with a three-tiered wedding cake.

The only shadow on the occasion was the sight of Caroline's pale face. Her smile, while lovely, was a bit too determined, almost forced at times. I had no doubt that she was happy for Duncan and me, but the timing of a wedding coming so soon after her husband's death and a miscarriage, had to be difficult. I couldn't help worrying about her, and when Duncan took me aside to say that Caroline wanted to speak with me a moment before leaving, my worry sharpened into concern.

"Is she all right?" I asked quickly. "I know this can't be easy for her."

"She's a little tired, but fine," he assured me. "She and Roger are waiting for us in the parlor."

Putting an arm about my waist, he ushered me out of the dining room and through the entry hall. He hesitated outside the parlor to give me a long kiss and a significant look. "I hope the festivities don't go on too much longer."

"I'm afraid your father and Uncle Milt are just getting started, trying to out do Captain MacDonald with their tall tales."

He groaned. "That's what I was afraid of."

I laughed and put a hand to his cheek. "Don't worry, Mr. Alexander. We've got all night."

"Only all night, Mrs. Alexander?"

"Forever," I whispered.

Inside the flower bedecked parlor, Caroline was resting on the settee with Roger beside her. Looking at the two of them, I had the warmest feeling that the Alexanders would be planning another wedding sometime in the near future.

"I wanted to have a chance to give you a wedding gift before Roger takes me home," she said, getting up and coming to meet us.

"Caroline, you didn't need to—"

"I do need to," she said, giving me a warm hug. "And I want to. I owe you so much, Lucy. Consider this a small thank you."

She glanced over at Roger who was lifting a large object from behind a high-backed chair.

My hand flew to my mouth as he carried *The Fairy Thorn* and leaned it carefully against one of the pillars of the fireplace.

I stared, unbelieving, at the resplendent woodland scene, the two lovers and the winsome fairy folk peering out of the old hawthorn's leafy branches. I'd never expected to see it again, let alone own such beauty.

My stunned glance moved from Bouguereau's masterpiece to my husband's smiling face, then to Caroline.

"I—I can't accept this. The gesture means more than I can say, but . . . I just can't. Caroline, the painting's yours."

Duncan gave his sister a knowing look. "I told you that's what she'd say."

Caroline reached out to take one of my hands. "You found it, Lucy. Who deserves it more than you? The painting would still be lost and forgotten if it weren't for you. I want you to have it, along with my love and thanks."

I put my arms about her, blinking back the tears.

After she and Roger had gone, I stood, staring at the painting with a mixture of awe and dread.

"Duncan, we can't keep this. It terrifies me to think of a million dollar painting lying around the house."

"More like five or six million, my love," he said, putting an arm about my waist. "She needed to do this, Lucy."

"I understand, and I love her for it, but—"

"But?" he prompted.

I gave the painting another amazed glance. "All this loveliness has been hidden away for so long. It just doesn't seem right that others shouldn't be able to see and enjoy it."

"We could always put it on loan to a museum or an art gallery."

"And you wouldn't mind?"

He smiled and shook his head. "I feel the same way you do. And I'm sure Caroline will, too, in time."

When everyone had bid us goodnight and given parting hugs and good wishes, Duncan and I climbed the stairs to the dormer bedroom where Captain Alexander had brought his young bride over a century before. The past ceased to be and thoughts of the imminent present set my pulse pounding as we entered the room.

The single light burning was an old-fashioned cranberry lamp which cast its rosy glow on the bed. Bronwyn probably wouldn't have admitted it for the world, but Lucy Alexander was experiencing a severe moment of nerves.

I looked at the tall figure of my husband as he shut the door behind us. "I love you, Mrs. Alexander," he said softly, and took me in his arms.

In the midst of his kisses, my nervousness disappeared, along with my wedding finery. Eagerness and passion took its place as he carried me to the bed.

There, lying open on one of the pillows was a small, clothbound book. I picked it up as he lay down beside me. Written in a firm masculine hand across the page of my last entry were the words:

Dear Bronwyn,

I love your cousin Lucy.

Duncan

AUTHOR'S NOTE

While the characters and events in *The Fairy Thorn* are entirely fictional, the French artist Adolph William Bouguereau is not. Bouguereau (1925–1905) was a popular, vital presence in the art world of the nineteenth century, whose work won many awards. As an artist he was extremely prolific, his finished works totaling well over 800, but to the best of my knowledge he never painted one titled *The Fairy Thorn*. Several years ago I saw the original painting of Bouguereau's *The Broken Pitcher*, in San Francisco's Legion of Honor Museum and I will never forget the stunning emotional impact it had on me. *Merci beaucoup*, Monsieur Bouguereau, for your magnificent and inspiring talent.

Also, it is no coincidence that my character Lucy Norris' favorite novel, Daphne du Maurier's *Frenchman's Creek*, happens to be one of my favorites as well. References in my book to du Maurier's work are a small but heartfelt way to saying thank you to a wonderful author.

About the Author

Dorothy McDonald Keddington is the author of seven romantic-suspense novels and the gripping true story, *A Square Sky*, with co-author Ahmad Sharifi. A native of Salt Lake City, now residing in Sandy, Utah, Mrs. Keddington has diverse interests and accomplishments, from writing, musical theatre and the arts, to her work as a professional genealogist. She is currently at work on another novel, Hearth Fires.